SOME PEOPLE
DESERVE TO DIE

COLIN KNIGHT

*For my wife, children, family and friends:
Thanks.*

Author

Colin Knight was born in Manchester, England in 1962 and immigrated to Canada in 1987. He holds a BA Honours in Political Science and an MA in International Relations. He has worked in the public and private sectors for thirty years, most recently as a National Security and Intelligence Analyst within the Security and Intelligence Secretariat of the Privy Council of the Government of Canada, and as a Strategic Advisor with Canada's Royal Canadian Mounted Police. He has traveled extensively, met many people, and enjoys writing.

About the Book

Some People Deserve to Die is the story of Alan Davies, a naive and nerdy high school boy who commits a horrible crime and runs away from home. Vulnerable and impressionable, Alan succumbs to the depravities of alcohol and drugs and enters the underworld of drug smuggling, which in turn draws him into international plots, guerrilla conflict and mercenary activities.

After twenty years Alan returns home to face his past and confront the men who tricked him into committing his crime. Confrontation leads to death and the truth. A truth that redefines everything he had believed and questions everything he has done.

CHAPTER 1

New Year's Eve 2011
Toronto, Canada

The weight and vileness of his despicable and disgusting crime had mangled his mind and corrupted his morality until, devoid of hope and empty of emotion, he existed without reason, and drew breath without pleasure.

Now, hidden inside ill-fitting, mismatched clothes, with eyes open, mind closed, feet numb, and stomach empty, he shuffled with instinct on Yonge Street.

One thousand eight hundred and ninety-six kilometres of street: two point six million people at one end, eight hundred and forty-two at the other. Toronto, the capital of Ontario at the big end, Rainy River, a provincial backwater, at the small end. The man had learned these facts two ways. First, the easy way at school. Then the hard way, when the street bore him away from his crime.

Limited by habit and mobility to a three kilometre stretch between Harbour Street in the south, and Queen Street in the north, his ugly fingers searched newspaper boxes and telephone slots for discarded coins. Only poor people without iPads or cell phones used newspaper boxes and phone booths, and they didn't forget their change: a fruitless forage in an indifferent city.

Coinless, the man stopped in front of an over-stocked electronics store. Through the window, a "thirty percent off" sticker for a seventy-inch plasma TV boasted vivid colour and a crisp picture. Beside the sticker, the TV, silent through the glass, flickered. A weatherman pointed to a map with symmetrical white snowflakes, blue and grey arrows, and a minus fifteen sign.

He stared at the weatherman, amused by the image of a man in a suit under hot lights gaily describing the bitter cold, and howling wind, that assaulted his body one blood vessel at a time. Through a taut smile, he mumbled, "At least I can't smell myself in this weather." On the bottom of the TV screen a ticker tape streamed right to left, cautioning towns and communities north of the city to expect extreme weather on New Year's Day. The warning repeated. One name caught the man's attention, forcing unwanted memories.

Vile, immoral memories which, after twenty years of running, still circumvented his efforts to forget and avoid. First, he hid on the South Pacific island paradise of Vanuatu, until betrayal and death forced him to run. Then to Scotland, where bad habits, and competition between drug gangs, threatened his life and forced him to seek safety and obscurity on a desolate North Sea oil rig. After tragedy destroyed his oil rig "family," he fled to the hinterlands of Nigeria, hoping wealth, warmth, and anonymity would keep his memories away. Instead, more death and horror stalked him. This compounded his guilt and gnawed away at the last remnants of his morality and compassion, until he was hollowed out and dysfunctional. Then the mercenaries he had somehow ended up with took pity on him and sent him home.

Now, faceless among the homeless who stalked Toronto's indifferent streets in search of calories to prolong their futile existence, the proximity to his crime fed his memories, an un-exorcised demon hounding him with guilt.

Who would have thought losing one's mind would be so difficult?

He left the weatherman to the warmth and safety of the studio lights. Habit directed his tired legs to St. Andrew's Church of the Apostles: a temporary refuge that discriminated against none, and provided hot meals to anyone who could enter, and exit, the church hall without assistance.

Nourished but not full, heated but not warm, he returned to the cold streets. Drunken youths staggered by. They threw coins at him and shouted, "Happy New Year, you fucker." The money bounced harmlessly off his multiple layers of clothing. He stooped quickly to secure the coins before others made a claim on them. *Toonies and loonies. Times must be good for some*, he thought bitterly.

With a cautious check for hostile or envious eyes, he scurried to Pizza Joe's on Queen Street. Not much nourishment but plenty of fill, and if he was lucky, a nice long wait while the pizza was baking.

Perched on a stool facing the window, he slurped a caffeine-and-sugar-laden drink between methodical bites of a double pepperoni and cheese slice. His breath fogged the window intermittently. The street was crowded. He craned his neck. A grime covered clock, a well-worn piece of tinsel draped lovelessly around it from Christmas past, blinked 11:45 p.m. Time he was going, time to get out of sight. Best to get out of harm's way, in case New Year's Eve revellry turned into a different kind of fun.

~ ~ ~ ~

The quickest route to his hovel, which was sandwiched between a back-up generator for an uninspiring provincial government building and the wall of an adjacent multi-story car park, was south on Yonge Street, past the Royal York Hotel and right on to Front Street. Not much of a place to live, but a castle by homeless standards because it was safe and dry.

Back in November, while relieving himself in the shadows of an alley, he'd noticed a padlocked, steel gate with signs warning of electricity, diesel fuel, hazardous materials, and danger. A lead-sealed tag, like the ones used on sea containers, wound through the lock. The tag indicated whatever was up there had been inspected a few weeks earlier and the next inspection was scheduled for May, 2012: a six-month inspection cycle.

Days later, after using begged-for money to purchase a padlock and hacksaw blade, he returned to the gate and replaced the lock with his own. Through the gate he discovered a sheltered area next to a generator. Using discarded cardboard and plastic, the staples of homeless homebuilding, he fashioned a refuge: At least until May and the next inspection.

Back on the street, warmed by Pizza Joe's ovens and food, he dodged through a thickening crowd of New Year's Eve revellers. He kept his eyes downward to avoid confrontation. Outside the Royal York Hotel, where a lifetime ago he had walked the grand foyer with his parents on a rare family visit to Toronto, the "Big Smoke", nameless street people fought over the discarded butt end of a fat, New Year's Eve celebratory cigar.

Caught in the scuffle, he became pinned against the thick, double glazed window of the hotel's street view bar: face pressed flat to the glass, hands spread wide for balance. His impact on the window startled the well-dressed patrons inside. Heads turned. Slim-figured women wearing strapless black dresses and designer high-heeled shoes raised ring-laden hands to their mouths, as if fearful the window might break and allow the unwashed to flood in and contaminate their beautiful world. Equally well-dressed, well-groomed men, on whom many of these women hung, frowned and gesticulated at him; their lips formed foul words he could not hear.

The press of people behind him swelled. The cigar butt was forgotten as tempers combusted. Despite writhing and struggling, he remained trapped.

Four tuxedo-clad men detached themselves from the merrymakers inside the bar and walked toward him. Their eyes, absent any New Year's Eve alcohol-induced friendship, conveyed malevolent mischief.

Each of these men blew smoke at the glass and held cigars to his lips in mockery. They tipped red wine toward the vagrant's mouth, and laughed as the wine ran down the inside of the window: the wine, too rich, looked like blood on the pane. The shorter of the men placed his middle finger against the glass and simulated nose picking while giving him the finger. Encouraged by the laughter of some of the other, drunker patrons, and their calls for more, the tallest and most handsome of the four pressed his own body against the window and spread his arms wide in tasteless mimicry of the vagrant's unfortunate plight. Then, at the urging of the other three, he puckered his mouth and "kissed" him through the glass in one last act of insensitive humiliation.

With lips locked through glass, one pair of eyes saw only the blurred eyeballs of another fucking free-loading loser who cluttered the streets like garbage. The other saw the cause of his crime and his life-long torment. The four men, character and morals loosened by drink and revealed through actions, swaggered back to the bar oblivious to the discomfort of the other revellers who, after being caught in the moment, swallowed hard to mask their shame.

A camera flash jarred the vagrant from the horror of recognition and remembrance. Repulsed, the man summoned untapped strength and recoiled from the window. He parted from the crowd with brutal blows and fled into the city.

CHAPTER 2

Oblivion

Dirt encrusted, blood stained fingers turned another bottle cap. Calmed by the familiar snap of the seal, and comforted by the scrape of metal on glass, the man prepared for oblivion.

Unneeded, the cap fell to the ground. Odourless vapour escaped as the bottle arched upward toward an eager mouth. Within minutes, forty ounces of Russia's finest vodka had flowed from glass vessel to human vessel. Temporary transformation began.

Oblivion soon came: Oblivion of bodily functions, sanitation, nutrition, and time, but not the oblivion of memory. Vodka played with his mind and memory, allowing moments of hope and illusions of escape, only to bludgeon and hammer until despair and reality returned.

The duplicitous spirit took him to the precipice. Forced him to look over, and then pulled him back to show glimpses of his torment in still monochrome pictures: pictures suppressed for twenty years by numbing his body and mind with alcohol, drugs, and violence. Two decades of running from his crime and guilt; from his home in Canada to the South Pacific paradise of Vanuatu to the desperate streets of Glasgow, Scotland. From a desolate North Sea oil rig to the ravaged Nigerian Delta region, until he reached this final, anonymous existence in Toronto.

Now vodka, a two-timing, two-faced, false friend, sped up the still black-and-white pictures, adding colour and texture, scenery and dialog. Like an old movie reel, they flickered faster and faster until they became a clear, brutal, unedited Blue Ray DVD.

Alan trudged home after an uneventful day at Powassan High School. Another day in a "nothing ever happens" small town north of Toronto, Canada. An early summer had made June, 1999, the hottest month since the near drought conditions forty-two years ago, in 1957. Heat and dust made the trek along the Deer Run side road arduous. Julie, his younger sister, hadn't joined him again. Alan was supposed to walk her home. "Probably at one of her after-school activities," thought Alan. How come she was popular? These days it seemed Julie deliberately did things right after school to avoid the walk home together.

"Or more charitably," thought Alan, "perhaps the death of our father two months earlier made Julie keep to herself." In April, his dad's car had skidded on River Road bend. The car had careened hood first into the massive hundred-year-old Maple tree everyone had said for years should be cut down before it killed someone. Well, they were right; the tree had killed his father. Instantly. The Maple remained standing, thanks to a bunch of conservationists who pleaded its case for existence, as if preserving some kind of sacred talisman for the town.

Behind Alan, the noise of a car engine entered his ears. Heavy bass music and testosterone laden voices grunting to the music's rhythm and lyrics mixed with the engine's whine. Alan turned to the sounds. An open top jeep with four school jocks roared past him. Dust and gravel punched into his nose, mouth, and eyes.

Mixed emotions tugged Alan as the jeep sped by. On one hand, he hated guys like them who teased and bullied him and others the most. On the other, they were the kind of guys he most wanted to be like: popular, small-town hockey team stars whom everyone seemed to like and who had everything anyone could want.

Alan peered through the dust at the departing jeep. Red brake lights illuminated. "Shit," thought Alan, "they're coming back." The jeep turned on squealing tires. Alan realised he had nowhere to run or hide. He stood there and waited for the inevitable humiliation he had no doubt they intended to inflict on him for their amusement.

The jeep stopped inches from Alan's knees. Alex, the undisputed leader of the group, jumped out. He clasped Alan on his back and declared in an unexpected friendly tone, "Hey, Alan, dude, why the fuck are you walking on such a hot day? Climb in and come for a ride." Between disbelief and indecision, Alan watched his backpack land in the back of the jeep. Steered by Alex, Alan followed his backpack.

Brett and Corey flanked Alan. They peppered him with questions. "Where are you going, Alan? What have you got planned for tonight, eh? Where's that cute sister of yours?"

Bewildered, Alan mumbled about homework and a new book he planned to read. Dale, the smallest of the group, cut Alan off and said, "Want to come with us? We're going to party and have some fun."

A beer was thrust into Alan's hand. He was afraid to admit he had never drunk alcohol before. Besides, the first sip tasted pretty good. Egged on by Alex and his friends, he swallowed, and the cold amber liquid went down like a soft drink. Alan experienced a novice's first buzz. Excited, he realised he was cruising in an open top jeep, drinking beer with four of the most popular guys in his school. Thank God his sister Julie had not shown up to walk home with him!

Later, Alan stood beside a recently used fire pit deep in the woods. He clutched and sipped another beer, and watched Alex roll a cigarette. The act reminded him of his father. His father had rolled his own cigarettes when he stood over a dead deer, *rabbit, or bird during one of their hunting trips. Alan hadn't enjoyed the killing part, but he'd been good at creeping up on animals, and was an excellent shot. More importantly, hunting had been the only opportunity Alan had to spend any real "alone-time" with his dad.*

Dale thrust one of the cigarettes into Alan's hand and urged him to take a drag. Startled out of his thoughts, Alan shook his head and said he didn't smoke.

"What kind of pussy are you, man?" said Corey. "These aren't ordinary smokes. We don't share them with just anyone. You want to hang with us, then you better not be saying our stuff isn't good enough for you."

"Come on, Alan," said Alex, "a spliff will do you good."

Even with three or four beers inside him, Alan hesitated before he took the cigarette. Nervous, he inhaled, coughed, and spluttered. Everyone laughed. The laughter made Alan determined. "I'm no pussy," thought Alan, and he inhaled more deeply each time. Despite being unsure how long he had been in the forest, or how many beers he had drunk, or "special cigarettes" he had smoked, Alan was euphoric; this was the most fun he had ever had. These guys were not so bad. Happy with his new-found friends, Alan didn't notice the quiet, calculated exchanges between the four other guys. Neither did he notice the sun touch the horizon.

Intoxicated, Alan swayed in the forest twilight. Alex said, "Come on, Alan. It's time for some real fun." Together, the five, four plus one, followed a rough path farther into the woods. A neglected building stood at the path's end.

"What's this place?" slurred Alan.

"Our 'love shack,'" said Corey, to the howls and laughter of the others. "We have a surprise for you inside."

Alex led Alan up rotten steps. A door hung askew on one hinge. Brett and Corey squeezed onto the top step and eased the door open. Motioned forward by Alex, Alan stepped through the doorway. An odour of dirt and decay entered Alan's nostrils. A moist dampness touched his skin. Darkness triggered his nerves. "Where are we? What's here?" said Alan.

In response, a flashlight provided jerky illumination. The beam arched across the walls and floor until it rested on the pale whiteness of a girl lying motionless on the worn floorboards of the shack. Naked, except for a rough sack over her head, tied at the neck. Alan stifled a cry as he stared at the firm bumps on her chest and the light mat of hair between her legs.

"Do you like her?" said Alex. "I told you we would have some fun. We all had her earlier. Now it's your turn, Alan. You can do whatever you want."

Alan couldn't look away. "Is she dead?" he asked.

"Of course not, you jerk," said Alex. "What do you think we are? We gave her some knockout stuff Corey's dad uses in his dentist office. She's asleep and won't remember anything. Go on, Alan, fuck her before she wakes up."

"This isn't right. I don't want to," said Alan.

"I told you he was a fag," said Dale. "Is that it, Alan, you'd rather fuck one of us than this bitch? We thought you were one of the cool guys, like us. Guess not, eh? We'll have to tell everyone you're a fag."

"Yeah, not a pussy, just don't like pussy," said Corey.

"I'm not a fag!" cried Alan.

"Prove it," they all said together.

Alan trembled as he lowered his shorts, shocked to see his erection.

"Hey dude, now that's better," someone said. "Guess you do like pussy. Well, it isn't going to reach from there, man. Get down and stick it in."

Blinded by the thought of humiliation and clouded by the alcohol and "cigarettes," Alan knelt down and inserted himself roughly into the motionless body. To the sounds of cheering and whooping, and another voice which sounded momentarily familiar, but which he couldn't quite identify, Alan thrust away until his hormone-driven, sixteen-year-old body expelled his seed and released him from the uncontrollable grip of late adolescent lust.

~ ~ ~ ~

Empty, the bottle slipped from his sweat soaked hand. The ring of glass on concrete distracted his mind and ended his personal horror movie. Frantic, he rummaged in his garbage strewn hovel for another bottle. Only empties remained, mocking his need with distorted reflections as he peered with desperate hope into each for an overlooked drop.

His feet crunched the broken glass of countless other bottles, smashed against the wall in punishment for being empty. He lurched and staggered to the gate, and exited into the steady stream of humanity heading with purpose in all directions.

Memory guided him to the underground maintenance and sewer tunnels that honeycombed the ground beneath the city, to prey on the unwanted and forgotten. Instinct and experience provided him with the ruthless brutality to beat, kick, abuse and harass the helpless and destitute human shells until he had bled them dry of anything that could be drank, smoked, eaten or sold. Recklessness made him break car windows and take anything that appeared valuable. Experience took him to the dishonest pawn brokers and the black-market traders, where goods were exchanged for thirty cents on the dollar with no questions asked.

Comforted by the familiar weight and feel of full bottles tucked and hidden securely into the recesses of his multi-layered clothing, he hurried back to his hovel. Through the gate, and into the bed of garbage he called home, he fell exhausted to his knees and unloaded and arranged his precious cargo.

Lying back, he stared at the Prussian soldier that adorned the label on the bottle. With a resigned salute, he unscrewed the cap and drank. Caught in the irrational subconscious hope of an alcoholic, he pleaded for the two-faced liquid to deliver him real oblivion this time. Duplicitous as ever, the liquid bypassed oblivion and delivered him straight to hell.

November, 2011. Five months since the incident in the forest with the girl. Alan couldn't think of it as rape because he didn't want to believe he was capable of doing such a thing. Sometimes he would remember it as though he had been the victim. Hadn't he been the one brought into the woods, made to take alcohol and drugs, and then forced to do it?

Other times he would tell himself the girl must have been a prostitute, and she had been paid to do it. Alex and the others certainly had the money. Most desperately, he told himself that it was the girl's fantasy. He was doing it for her and she had wanted him to do it. How else had she gotten there if she hadn't been willing?

These deflection and diversion tactics might have worked. Alan may have been able to move on with a life in which he would occasionally stare into nothingness for short periods, or at times seek solitude, or perhaps be sporadically absent from conversations. But three things kept Alan from this imperfect escape: the nightmares, the taunting, and the truth.

*Two nightmares tormented him. Both relived in vivid detail the event, but each depicted Alan in different roles. In one, like his daytime rationalization, Alan was the victim. He had been manipulated and coerced. Practically kidnapped and forced to commit some horrible act on another while being blamed for some never revealed outcome. The other nightmare was opposite and more terrifying: he was a **willing** participant, god-like, possessed with power and lust, benevolently injecting his majestic seed into an unworthy disciple.*

Both were frightening on their own, but they shared a more terrifying common theme. In both nightmares, during sex with the girl, he heard a voice. Not just the voices of Alex and the others, as accusers and condemners of a reluctant sinner, or as encouraging supporters of their benevolent god. There was another voice. A voice intermingled with the others, its tenor alternating between pity, hope, rage and sadness.

True to the nature of nightmares, Alan always woke on the cusp of revelation. Never able to discern the words, or the owner of the other voice. But he was certain the words were important and held a meaning crucial to the event. Sometimes he thought it was as though he wanted to know, and did not want to know, at the same time.

Alan knew all about taunting. He had never been popular. But the nature of the taunts, by Alex and particularly Dale, was excruciating in its subtlety. They all knew they could not tell or "out" one another without self-incrimination, thus the barbs and remarks were more meaningful for what they didn't say. Knowing smiles and vulgar gestures. Allusions to certain girls at the school being the "one." The worst was their threat that, once clear of school, they had a secret to tell him. Added to this was a nagging sense the elusive voice in his nightmares, and the secret they kept from him, were connected.

The truth had come in the words of his now dead sister, Julie. During the six months since the event in the forest, Alan had been dysfunctional. Consumed by guilt, harried by nightmares, and constantly tormented by Alex and the others, Alan had withdrawn from everything and everyone around him. He went to school, ate, and kept himself clean on autopilot. He didn't remember anything the teachers said, or even going to and from class. He responded to inquiries about himself with monosyllabic grunts. Alan's self-pity blinded him to the lives and problems of other people, including his own family.

Unsurprisingly he did not realise his sister was also having a difficult time and had, like Alan, withdrawn into herself. Unlike

Alan, and unknown to Alan, Julie's withdrawal had begun in January. Since then, she had spent long periods crying and sobbing in her room, and was absent from school more than she was there. Even stranger, and what Alan would normally have noticed, was their mother didn't seem to object to Julie missing school. In fact, his mother was herself often absent from work to spend time with Julie.

But when Alan returned home from school on November 15, 1992, just six days before his seventeenth birthday, even his self-absorbed pity could not prevent the reality of the scene outside his house entering his consciousness. A crowd of people huddled behind crinkled crime scene tape. Police cars and ambulances stood askew in front of his house. Alan ran. Arms and hands of people he did not recognise reached out and held him at the driveway. Stunned by alternating blue, yellow, and red emergency vehicle lights, and bombarded by garbled voices competing for his attention, Alan stared at his home.

Paramedics rushed through the front door. A stretcher strained their arms. Julie lay strapped to the stretcher, her vacant eyes unresponsive to the frantic activity and noise. His mother followed. Leaden footsteps compensated for by the support of uniformed people who steered her toward the ambulance doors. The door swallowed them both. A cloud of exhaust drifted into Alan's face as the ambulance sped away, its lights and siren fading.

Tricked by the distorted time of alcohol induced nightmares, Alan was back in front of his house. He and his mother had been brought home by the same ambulance that had taken Julie. No frantic activity awaited them. Only the soft rustle of falls' last leaves floating down from the birch tree, mingling with the flowers, wreaths, and cards placed sympathetically on the steps. Wordlessly, his mother stepped through the tributes and into the house. She hadn't spoken since the doctor told them Julie was gone.

Alan followed his mother, barely registering the disarray caused by the paramedics, police, and others when they had tried to save Julie. Exhausted and confused, Alan went upstairs and threw himself on his bed. Instinctively, he flipped his pillow. Underneath, a folded sheet of paper lay in wait. Julie's neat handwriting unmistakably proclaimed the note was for him.

Afraid, Alan unfolded the paper.

Why, Alan? Why? How could you do that? I tried to tell you; to get you to make it stop. Why didn't you want to listen? Why did you ignore me? Why didn't you help me? Did you hate me so much? Mom doesn't understand either. Why? Why? WHY? I can't go on anymore. Goodbye, Alan.

Like a rolling fog, with a microscopic needle in each of its wet molecules, the nightmares, the taunting and Julie's words coalesced into a suffocating blanket of vile comprehension and searing pain.

The voice of his nightmares, the voice he had been unable, or unwilling, to understand, the voice he knew was crucial, that was linked to the subtle knowing taunts, was Julie's voice. He had raped his own sister.

The pillow clutched tightly to his face did little to muffle Alan's screams.

The truth had not set him free.

CHAPTER 3

Reality

The spring sun had transformed his hovel into a steaming workshop. Diamonds littered the floor in a tantalizing display of opulence. He grasped the diamonds in rapture, only to feel the sharp prick of broken glass cut his swollen hand. He threw the glass down. Bewildered, his body and mind began to reset.

Rattle, scrape. Gate and chain. Raised voices arguing about who brought the wrong key floated into his mind. He battled with reason as he patted his pocket, thinking, "I have the key." More sounds and voices reached into him. Then silence. He lay back relieved. A loud crack, and the familiar squeak of the gate, pierced his mind. Agitated, upright, he squinted in the sunlight.

Out of the light stepped an alien. Its over-sized yellow head sandwiched between two enormous black ears, connected by some kind of silver blood vessel that curled over and outside the yellow head from one ear to the next. "Jesus fucking Christ. Who the fuck are you?" said the alien.

In response, he hurled his army of Prussian soldiers. He smiled as they crashed against the wall, transformed into deadly glass shards. The alien invader retreated. He stumbled wildly after, screaming obscenities and threats.

The invader passed through the gate and pulled it closed. He reached the gate, intent on pursuing the invaders to the death. But the gate wouldn't open. He fumbled for his key and tried to open the lock. Something was wrong. The key didn't fit. He shook and kicked the gate without result. The invaders counter-attacked and his fingers were crushed beneath the blow of the alien's hammer-like hand. He backed away from the gate. The invaders came in and out of focus.

Two men. Brown pants, beige jackets, and yellow hard hats with black ear protectors, stared in frightened disbelief at the human-like figure cradling its bloodied fingers. Its wild eyes bored into them with malice and hatred.

"No fucking way anyone will believe this shit," said the first man/alien. "Take a picture with your phone," said the second.

Backing away from the gate, the taller one spoke nervous words into a radio pinned to his shoulder.

Soon the invaders returned. Only this time, it was an army. His Prussian soldiers were no match for the water hose, batons, smoke, and finally the electric shock of the police Taser.

He didn't really understand the ambulance, the screams, the arguments, the handcuffs or the restraints. All he could sense was an endless stream of blurred faces hovering over him, reflecting human-like expressions of disgust, pity, and perhaps compassion. Finally, a soft rubber mask descended on his mouth and nose, and provided the oblivion he had so desperately sought.

CHAPTER 4

Rehabilitation

"Alan. Alan. Wake up, Alan. It's time for your lunch." Reluctant eyelids lifted. A nurse placed a tray of food before him. Beside the plate, bowl, and cup, several different coloured pills were lined up in perfect formation.

"What are those pills?"

"Antibiotics, painkillers, and vitamins."

"Where am I?"

"Serenity Rehab Centre."

"Are you always this friendly?"

"Yes, but only on good days."

Assured by the nurse's brisk hallway footfalls, Alan picked up the sandwich with a surprisingly clean hand. He sniffed the ham and cheese stacked between multi-grain bread. With the index finger of his other hand, he pushed the neatly ordered pills out of formation.

Satisfied the lunch posed no threat, Alan took a generous bite of the sandwich. Pills were inserted between bites. Orange juice washed it all down. Letting loose an unrestricted belch, Alan pushed the wheel mounted table to the bottom of the bed. He surveyed his room by sections. A technique used by experienced soldiers to search a room for booby traps or hidden compartments.

A large flat screen TV dominated the far wall. Sculptured bodies silently promised viewers how a simple daily workout would guarantee firm buttocks and rippled abdominals. A thorough search for a remote control yielded negative results. Inquiries concerning viewing options were met with the terse response, "The channel will be changed four times a day."

The anticipated channel change was a disappointment. The entire viewing options were limited to either exercise, Do It Yourself (DIY), or religious programming. All on mute! Un-entertaining options, curiously reflected in the choice of magazines available on the small table marooned between two vinyl covered, wingbacked chairs under the TV. Perhaps, thought Alan, a deal had been made among TV companies and magazine publishers to provide free magazines with certain TV packages. Or maybe it was the other way around.

In addition to the main door, the right hand wall held four mass produced abstract prints. Their vivid colours clashed with the subdued paleness of the wall. Alan wondered if the print purchaser and the interior decorator had ever spoken, or viewed the results of their work.

A large window, framed by heavy, blackout curtains, occupied the centre of the left side wall. More abstract prints framed the curtains. Turning left, then right, Alan considered the hospital-like equipment attached to the wall behind his head: blood pressure monitor, defibrillator, ear and eye light holders, oxygen mask with hoses anchored in the wall behind regulators, and a large, red emergency button on each side of the bed. A phone jack, but no phone.

A high, flat, white ceiling was interrupted by two cage covered strip lights. Between the lights, a white fan blew down on a shiny blue, grey floor. The edges of the floor crept six inches up the wall. A miniature wading pool.

On the far side of the room, a three-quarter length stall door shielded a shower, sink, and toilet. All arranged around a central drain to allow the entire bath and toilet area to be hosed down if needed. On the wall, another large, red emergency button hung like an angry full stop.

Reassured, and fatigued by his observations, Alan lay back and closed his eyes.

~ ~ ~ ~

"Alan. Alan. Wake up, Alan. It's time for your lunch."

"How long have I been here?"

"Six weeks."

"How did I get here?"

"Don't know."

"Is this a prison?"

"Some people think so."

"When can I get out of here?"

"When you are well."

"I feel well. Can I go?"

"Harrumph!"

It had been the same conversation for the last three weeks. Harrumph! *Fucking Harrumph,* thought Alan. Six weeks and always the same lunch: ham and cheese on multi-grain bread, orange juice, and something in a bowl. He didn't know what was in the bowl because he had not tried its contents even once. He didn't like the look of the bowl or the contents. Two things had changed, though; fewer pills and more TV. Not just fewer pills, but no more antibiotics or painkillers, only "Good for you vitamins," the nurse had said.

Last week he had been given the remote control and access to sports, gardening, and National Geographic channels. Harrumph!

~ ~ ~ ~

"Wake up, Alan. You have a visitor."

Alan opened one eye. A brown haired head with light brown eyes, fair complexion, and nice teeth sitting atop a well pressed brown suit, which in turn stood on well shined brown shoes, waited respectfully at the foot of the bed. He opened his other eye. The full lips that held the teeth moved and said, "Hello, Alan. My name is John Gardener. I'm your lawyer."

With the benefit of both eyes, Alan estimated his lawyer to be in his late thirties. About five foot seven, he was slim, but showing signs of the two pound a year weight gain that begins at thirty, keeping ahead of whatever exercise regimen the lawyer followed. He even looked like a lawyer. Not flashy, except for the black and silver designer glasses that clashed with the rest of his "shades of brown" self. His lawyer later explained his wife worked for an optometrist. She had selected the glasses for him.

"Why do I need a lawyer? Am I going to prison?"

"No, not at all. This rehab centre has helped you get better."

"How did I get here? Who's paying for all this?"

"I brought you here, Alan, and you're paying for it yourself."

"How?"

"Two months ago you were arrested for trespassing, assault, property damage, resisting arrest and a bunch of other offences. I don't know how much of it you remember, Alan, but according to the statements and videos from the police vehicles and head mounted cameras, you were out of control, tanked up on alcohol and drugs. You attacked and threatened to kill two maintenance workers, whom you accused of being aliens trying to steal your dilithium crystals for their warp engines.

Fortunately for you, one of the responding officers was a veteran who recognised you from the streets, and he said your behaviour was out of character. Instead of hauling you to the cells, they took you to hospital for treatment to multiple cuts and bruises and two broken fingers. After you were stabilised, you were put in detox and remanded in custody to await your hearing."

Alan was beginning to remember. Not at first, or in a flood, but slowly. Over the past few weeks, it had come back to him in larger and larger fragments, until he had a pretty good idea of what had happened. More importantly, he remembered with absolute clarity the night of New Year's Eve. But he wouldn't be sharing that with his new lawyer.

"Of course," said the lawyer, "your fingerprints were taken. When the police checked, they found a missing persons' report had been filled on you almost twenty years ago. The contacts on file for the missing persons' report were your mother and Harold Gardener, your mother's lawyer. Harold was my father. He died five years ago. I took over his practice and inherited your file. That's how I came to be your lawyer."

"My mother?"

"She died seven years ago, two years before my own father. Your mother left everything to you."

"Everything?"

"Mm, yes. Your mother was quite well off. She had significant savings, and her house. After her death, my father liquidated the estate assets, and placed the money in a trust linked with a modest investment strategy."

"How did she die?"

"I don't know exactly."

"What do you know inexactly?"

"Perhaps we could discuss that another time, after…"

"Look. You work for me now. Tell me how the fuck she died."

"The death certificate says natural causes."

"But?"

"Alan, I'm not sure this is a good time, or that you want to know the details."

"Tell me. Tell me the truth."

"Okay, Alan. My father told me your mother lost a lot of her energy after your dad's accidental death, as though some unspoken knowledge weighed on her conscience. Then, when Julie died and you disappeared, your mother suffered erratic highs and lows between frantic activities, as she searched for you, and depressed inertia, as she mourned Julie. Her initial confident search for you gave way to solitary rambles across the province, and she began to sit for long periods beside Julie's grave. Unable to find you, and inconsolable about Julie, the lows outstripped the highs and your mother grew reclusive and depressed. She rebuffed offers of help, and eventually people drifted away and left her alone. My father was concerned and arranged for a doctor to visit, but your mother refused to see the doctor and instead insisted she only wanted to settle her affairs.

My father found your mother, Alan. When he returned to the house to give your mother a copy of the estate documents, he could not get an answer at the door and forced his way in. He found your mother upstairs. She was in your bedroom, Alan. Your mother had wrapped herself in Julie's rainbow quilt and lay on your bed as though taking a nap. The room was full of Julie's baby toys and her collection of Beanie Babies. Photographs of you and Julie covered the bed and floor. Later, when paramedics removed Julie's quilt, they found a photograph of you helping Julie blow out the candles on her eighth birthday clutched in your mother's hands. My father said your mother's heart had broken."

Alan didn't hear anything else his lawyer said, and was only vaguely aware of him pointing to his watch and leaving. Alan hadn't seen his mother since the day he read Julie's suicide letter almost twenty years ago. He had run away that day and never returned. Since then, he had been too ashamed to consciously think of her. But unconsciously his mother had often visited in dreams and nightmares, to accuse him and blame him for Julie's death. He tried unsuccessfully to bring up an image of his mother. He drifted into a fitful sleep; broken hearts burst out of chests and fell in heaps at his feet as he tried in vain to put them back together.

~ ~ ~ ~

"You said I was arrested and charged with trespassing, assault, property damage, resisting arrest and other things. How come I'm not in prison?"

"Luckily, you didn't harm anyone when you were arrested. Although you scared two maintenance workers half to death. Also, thanks to your financial resources, I was able to pay compensation to the workers, pay for the cleanup and repair of the damaged property, and cover all medical costs. That, and a commitment to six weeks in rehab, enabled the judge to release you into my custody. Subject to a favourable psychiatric evaluation, you will be placed on probation for two years."

"If it's unfavourable?"

"Mm, let's cross that bridge if we need to."

"What financial resources are you talking about anyway?"

"Well, after the compensation, clean up, medical costs, rehab costs and of course my fees - all of which are itemised for you - you have a net worth of about eight hundred thousand dollars."

"Eight hundred thousand dollars! Where the fuck did that come from?"

"A large amount came from the life insurance payout for your father's death. Your mother's house was sold and your mother had significant pension investments. Plus the money has accrued interest with no principal deductions for seven years."

Alan rubbed his eyes. His head fell into his hands.

"Julie was my friend," said John quietly, unsure about broaching the subject.

At the mention of Julie's name, Alan looked slowly up and said, "I know. I have been thinking about you since your first visit. I remember a kid hanging around a lot. Julie always said she was going out somewhere with a boy who was her friend. She never said boyfriend, always a boy who was her friend. Was that you, John?"

Somewhat hurt John nodded and said, "We used to hang out together. We would meet at lunch time and talk about life and people. Julie was a lot of fun. Always interesting and positive about things. At least that's how it used to be, until mid-January of the year she died. She suddenly changed. One day she was herself, then, without explanation, she would just sit there not eating or talking or anything. I tried asking her lots of times what was wrong, but she never told me. By the end of March, I hardly saw her at all. She wasn't coming to school much. Do you know what happened?"

When John described Julie, Alan's brain stopped processing any more of John's words. Instead, Alan's thoughts turned to Julie and what he had done to her.

Observing Alan's face darken with pain, John chided himself for being insensitive. He made to leave, but Alan said, "Tell me about my mom, John. What happened after I left?"

"What I remember, and what my dad told me, was your mother thought you had run off to be alone after Julie's death. She believed you would be back in a few days. When you didn't come home, your mom thought maybe you had an accident, and were hurt somewhere. Search parties were organised every day for a week, but nothing was found. People stopped helping and began to believe you had run away for good. Some suggested you had something to do with Julie's death, and that's why you ran away.

"Your mom never gave up, though. Every Saturday she would search for you, walking and driving all over the county asking if anyone had seen you. Every year she would run advertisements in all the local papers seeking information about you. I guess now it would all be done on the Internet with web pages."

Alan couldn't handle any more. First he had raped his sister and caused her to kill herself. Then he ran away and left his mom to years of grief and worry. Tears, long overdue tears, streamed down Alan's face as twenty years of suppressed emotions tore out of his soul and coalesced into an immense despair. This time, his lawyer did leave.

~ ~ ~ ~

John returned three days later. All business. He brought stacks of legal and financial documents for Alan to read and sign. Then he explained what Alan should expect during the fast approaching psychiatric evaluation.

"They will ask you about your family, Alan; about your father's and Julie's death; about your mom and how you feel about learning of her death; and why you ran away. Mostly, they will want to understand who you are angry at and if you are going to hurt yourself or someone else. I can't tell you what to say, Alan, but you will need to answer the questions."

"What do I tell them if they ask about the last twenty years?"

"You tell them everything," said John. "Unless of course you did something illegal which, as your lawyer, I would advise against admitting. Even though whatever you say can't be used in a court against you, it might prejudice their conclusions."

"I haven't been a saint," said Alan.

John smiled as he responded, "Who has? It's not as though you killed anyone or anything like that, eh, Alan?"

Alan looked away. Discomforted by Alan's lack of response John pressed, "Is it, Alan?"

CHAPTER 5

Confession

His lawyer's nervous question about him not having killed anyone thrust Alan's consciousness back three weeks to the day he met a broken man in the common room. No lawyer had yet turned up and Alan had been unaware he had money and a future. If Alan had known a lawyer, even one who worked for him, or frequented the rehabilitation centre, he might not have been so forthcoming with the man.

Alan shuffled into the Serenity Rehab common room: chairs, tables, TV, nothing special. In the centre of the room on an uncomfortable vinyl covered chair a man, his skin grey and drawn, like an overused and under washed sheet, regarded Alan through milky eyes. Not wanting contact, Alan veered to the right. The man, with unexpected joviality, called out.

"Why are you here? Drink, drugs, or avoiding the press?"

Alan stared disdainfully in the direction of the voice. He had been confined to his room for three weeks, and now, the first time he had been allowed out, some scruffy old booze hound was subjecting him to a fucking inquisition.

"Fuck off!" spat Alan.

Ignoring the rebuke, the man continued. "Me, I've done it all. If it could be drunk, injected, inhaled, absorbed through skin, inserted, or implanted, I've done it. Didn't matter, though. I never escaped. Still haven't. But I will soon."

Unimpressed Alan mocked the man.

"Yeah, big man, were you? What - a drug lord, king pimp, or just a bad ass who beat on people?"

"Yeah, once upon a time, I was something like that. You?"

"Fuck off!"

Irritated and annoyed, Alan retreated to his room.

The next day, desperate to escape the confines of his room, Alan ventured back to the common room. The grey man was waiting.

"Want to tell me?"

"Tell you what?"

"What you're running from?"

"Fuck off, will you? I don't want to tell you any-thing."

"Sure, sure. I used to say the same thing. Well, I'll tell you something. I'll be gone in a few weeks, and I won't be coming back or telling anyone anything you tell me. So, as we both have fuck all to do here, why don't you tell me what's eating you up inside?"

Alan studied the man more closely. His grey skin struggled to contain purple veins on his neck, arms and lower legs, receded off-white hair, and dull teeth behind pale lips: a thin, weak body. *Used up,* thought Alan, like his friend Fred had been in Vanuatu. Softening his initial hostility, Alan responded, "You don't look as though you're going anywhere fast."

"I have a one-way ticket to hell. The Big C. Liver on its way out. It's funny. I get as much dope in here as I used to on the outside. Don't know why my family doesn't let me out to OD somewhere. No fuss. Save them a lot of money."

"Perhaps they want you to linger and suffer," said Alan.

"Well, if they do, it isn't happening. When I'm awake, which isn't so often these days, I can relax with a constant, low-level buzz. Like right now. My wife says I'm far more agreeable than I ever was. Although I don't like having my arse wiped and eating everything through a straw. Is that the plan for you? You don't look half as bad as you did when they brought you in here."

Despite, or perhaps because of, the man's persistence, Alan felt drawn to him. Alan sensed they had things in common. Maybe it was the spectre of death that hung over the grey man. Perhaps it was the loneliness. "What do you mean, you never escaped?"

Encouraged by Alan's question, the man replied, "From myself. From what I had done to colleagues, and friends, and finally to my own family. Oh, I didn't plan to hurt anyone or destroy lives. That's what happened, though. I was a real bastard. Still am to most people, I suppose."

Hooked, as the man no doubt intended, Alan asked, "What did you do?"

With a satisfied smile, the man stared through Alan and said "I asked you first. I'm not too strong at this time of day. How about you tell me yours, and I'll tell you mine? I'll give you a hint, though. What I did involved money. A shitload of money."

Alan didn't consciously know it, but his mind had been in need of a confessor for a long time. Who better than a dying man, signalled Alan's subconscious. Then, without any real intention, Alan told the grey man his story.

CHAPTER 6

Running Away

Alan started safe. He talked about his home town. Powassan was founded in the 1880s on the bend of the South River on the site of a saw mill. Powassan was an Indian word meaning bend, hence the name. After more than a hundred and thirty years, Powassan's population stood at about three and a half thousand people. One dentist, one Ford dealership, two lawyers, four gas stations, eight churches and a marina serviced the inhabitants. More than three hundred kilometres north of Toronto, Powassan remained a small town with small people. Stalling for time, uncertain as to how much he would, or could, say, Alan rambled about small town life until Mr. Grey, as Alan now thought of the pale man, interrupted and said, "What happened?"

Alan sensed a decisive moment. He needed a confidant, a confessor. He needed to trust someone. Mr. Grey waited. Silent. Assured by Mr. Grey's calmness, Alan described the day he had been offered a ride by the four high school jocks. The alcohol. The drugs. How it all made him feel important and "cool." How the jocks had taken him to a shack with an unconscious, naked girl. What he had done. He explained his guilt and fear: how he couldn't look at anyone or concentrate on anything. He told Mr. Grey about the taunting, the nightmares, and the voice.

Struggling to keep his composure, Alan recounted the day his sister Julie died. How he discovered Julie's suicide note and the brutal truth her note revealed: he had raped his own sister, and she killed herself. Taking a quick breath before he lost his nerve, Alan continued.

~ ~ ~ ~

It just sort of hit me. Dad was dead. Julie was dead. Mom knew what I had done to Julie and hated me. I was alone, destroyed. I had to leave. Go away, disappear. Run from what I had done in the forest. Get away from those four jerks, away from everything and everybody.

I wasn't thinking straight. I had no plan except to get away from the house, the town, from everybody. I stuffed my backpack with clothes, a sleeping bag, a radio, a rope, and a knife, like I was going hunting with Dad. I had about three hundred dollars, and for some reason, I took my passport. I had only had the passport for four months. I only got it because my dad was going to take me to the United States to hunt. We never did go to the States to hunt. He died in that car accident a couple of weeks after I got my passport.

I packed my bag and walked out. I didn't know where I was going. I walked up one street and down another until I reached Highway 11. I stood on the soft shoulder, sensing rather than seeing cars and trucks flash by. There had been a heavy snowfall the night before, and the trucks pelted me with salt grit and slush left by the snowplows. Instead of running away, I thought I should step in front of a truck and get it over with. Then a truck stopped. I climbed in. Without either of us speaking, the driver put the truck in gear and drove. I didn't know until later why the truck stopped, but when I did, I realised how naive and vulnerable I was. How lucky I had been.

~ ~ ~ ~

Bright light woke me. The truck slowed to pull into a truck stop. The driver, who somehow knew my name, said he would get us something to eat. He said I could get comfortable in the back. I had never been in a rig before, but I knew drivers slept in their rigs so I figured that he was offering me a place to sleep. I opened up the panel behind the seats and saw a narrow bed. The rear wall had shelves with a TV, a radio, and other stuff on them. I thought it was a pretty small space. No room for two. I wondered why he would give me the bed. A pull string for a light hung down from the cab's roof. I pulled the string. Then I understood why the driver had stopped, why he was getting us some food, and why he had told me to get in the back. Pictures of naked men and boys in various stages of embrace and intimacy covered the ceiling and walls.

Freaked out, I reached for my backpack. I could see the driver approaching the truck. He opened the door and climbed in. He had two McDonald bags and two bottles of water. He looked at his sleeping area; his eyes caressed the homosexual pictures that surrounded his bed. He knew I had seen them. Our eyes met. I shook my head. Disappointment and loneliness stared back at me, and I grasped my pack and reached for the door handle. Before I got out he held out one of the bags to me and said he couldn't eat two. The food would only go to waste. I accepted the bag and backed out of the cab. I ran for the light and safety of McDonald's. Inside I tossed the bag in the garbage and bought my own food.

Later, I met more people, especially young people like myself, who said I had been lucky not to have been drugged, raped, and dumped off at the side of the road. Some told stories of other kids. Kids who had accepted a ride with a trucker going in one direction and had woken up with another trucker going in the opposite direction. At least they said the stories were about others, although their eyes said it was more personal.

~ ~ ~ ~

Relieved and feeling safe, I sat in McDonald's until morning, defying the restaurant designers' achievement of making the seats uncomfortable after twenty minutes. I was surprised I hadn't been asked to leave, or that the police hadn't been called. I guessed I wasn't asked to leave because I wasn't sleeping, or drunk, or on drugs or doing anything except sitting and looking out the window: probably not the first kid they had seen.

Around 7:30 a.m., fighting to keep awake and up-right, and figure out what to do next, a Greyhound bus pulled into the parking lot. I watched passengers get off and head into McDonald's to buy breakfast and use the washrooms. The uniformed driver got off last and closed the door behind him. The sign on the front of the bus proclaimed it was headed for Winnipeg, Mani-toba. In fact, the bus was heading for Vancouver, British Colombia; the driver changed the sign at each major city for the next one.

There was no Greyhound ticket office at the truck stop. But I knew you could pay the driver cash for a ride to the next stop with an official ticket office and then buy a proper ticket. The driver finished his break-fast and went outside with the last of his coffee and a cigarette. I followed him out. I intended to buy a ticket, but before I reached the driver he turned and said, "Ten minutes before we leave, kid." My confused expression gave me away because he went on to say, "Sorry, kid, I thought you were one of the passengers come to nag me about getting going." Seizing the opportunity, I explained I had fallen out with my girlfriend and she had driven off and left me, and I wanted to buy a temporary ticket to the next Greyhound ticket office. I don't think he believed my story, but he shrugged and said mildly, "Still ten minutes, kid," and carried on with his nicotine and caffeine.

Ten minutes, fourteen dollars and twenty-two cents later, I clutched a temporary but official Greyhound receipt in my hand, and collapsed into the seat directly behind the driver. Then I slept. I woke to the sound of air brakes and bustle of impatient human movement as the bus lumbered into a large parking lot. Passengers stretched and yawned. Some, at journey's end, gathered bags and assorted packages, eager to leave the stale air and cramped seats. Others, still en route, stifled their anxiousness to escape the bus.

A black, rectangle clock jutted down from the ceiling at the front of the bus. Yellowy green, digital numbers declared it was 11 p.m. I had slept fifteen hours. Through the window, faded white letters on a blue sign welcomed visitors to Thunder Bay. We had come almost one thousand two hundred kilometres. The driver looked at me and smiled.

"I've heard that 'girlfriend left me at the road stop' story maybe a hundred times over the last ten years. Don't worry, though. I've gotten pretty good at sensing what people are like, and you seem like a good kid to me. A new driver takes over from here and I can't take you any farther. If you want to continue, you'll have to buy a ticket at the counter. If you do, I will come with you and get you a discount."

After the incident with the truck driver, I was apprehensive about accepting help from another driver. Uniform or not. But, with no other plan, and no obvious option, I nodded and followed the driver to the Greyhound ticket office.

"Where to?" asked the ticket agent.

A map of Canada hung on the wall behind the clerk. I followed the green line of the Trans-Canada Highway from east to west, reading the major cities in my head. The green line ended at Vancouver.

"One way?"

"Yes."

"That'll be one hundred and thirty-six dollars and fifty-eight cents, kid."

I clutched my ticket and followed the driver outside. With sympathetic eyes, and a slight shrug, he wished me luck and told me to be careful. Then he turned and walked to an old pickup truck where a middle-aged woman sat waiting. I felt abandoned. Irrationally I begrudged the abrupt departure of this kind stranger. I resumed my seat behind a different uniformed driver and fretted about what I would do when I reached Vancouver. I needn't have worried, though. I didn't arrive in Vancouver until six months later in May. By then I had a plan.

~ ~ ~ ~

On the bus I met two guys. Mark and Steve. They were going to the Banff Springs Hotel in Alberta. I had learned about the hotel at school when my class did a research and presentation project on UNESCO. The Banff Springs Hotel was a World Heritage Site located in the heart of Banff National Park. The guys told me they had jobs washing dishes and laundry during the winter ski season. They had done the same job for the last two winters, making, they said, enough money to allow them to travel the world during the summer.

Six months in Australia and New Zealand had taken up the bulk of their summer and fall. The year before they had travelled throughout South America. I said I was surprised anyone could make enough money to travel the world by washing dishes and doing laundry. Easy, they said, when you work twelve hours a day, seven days a week for five months for cash and paid no taxes. Also accommodation was cheap. The hotel provided subsidised staff quarters for only fifty dollars a week. Plus, there was plenty of free food if you didn't mind uneaten food from the hotel's breakfast, lunch, or dinner buffets. There was another reason they liked to work in a large hotel, but I wasn't told about it until, as they later informed me, "we could trust you."

Mark and Steve were veterans. Easy going, relaxed, confident. Even cocky. I liked them. They asked me what my story was. I told them I had sort of up and left home with no real plans or anything. They didn't ask why. Instead they suggested I take a chance on getting a job at the hotel, as there were always people who had agreed to work for the season, but didn't show up.

They were right. The hotel was short of busboys for their three restaurants. A busboy occupies the bottom of the restaurant industry totem pole, along with the "dish pig." No experience or training required. I used the last of my money to buy appropriate black shoes, pants, and waist coat, along with a white shirt and an elasticised bow tie. Then I bussed tables for one hundred hours or more a week for cash in a luxury hotel in the middle of Canada's Rocky Mountains.

Independence, freedom, income, friends. I had never had it so good.

~ ~ ~ ~

Like a crash course in human nature for the sheltered, small town hick, the service industry underworld taught me a great deal about people, money, privilege, power and envy. Lessons about compassion, selflessness, luck, and honesty were also available, but I didn't seem to absorb these to the same degree. My new friends were quick to introduce me to the pleasures and excesses of alcohol and marijuana. Both became good friends. As did many of the female staff, whom, after a lot of denial, anxiety, and suppression of my guilt, together with alcohol and dope, I allowed to repeatedly relieve me of my "virginity."

I also learned how to obtain, record, and hold credit card information for later use. This was the "other" reason Mark and Steve liked to work in a large hotel, and how they really made the money needed for their global travels. Mark or Steve, when opportunity came, would obtain a brief look at a credit card and record the card number, the three digit number on the back, and the card holder's name.

They didn't use the information immediately, but waited for several months until far away from the hotel. Then they would sell the information for cash to people who knew how to exploit it. About a hundred credit card details for the five months at the hotel was their target. Each set of credit card information brought them between one hundred and fifty dollars and three hundred dollars depending on when, where, and to whom the information was sold. This provided them up to thirty thousand dollars for their summer travels and lifestyle.

Bussing tables was hard work but fun, and I enjoyed my new-found knowledge and independence. Most of all, I had escaped my nightmares, my guilt, and the fear of facing my mother. At least I thought I had. Not until later did I realise that working one hundred plus hours a week, drinking, smoking, fucking and sleeping the rest of the time had distracted me from, rather than erased, my demons.

~ ~ ~ ~

I left Banff in early May: more street wise, more world wise, and more confident. I was also more cynical, more consumptive, and more dishonest than I had ever been. I had thirty-two hundred dollars in my pocket, marketable skills, and thirty-three credit card details. But most surprising, considering my situation and limited experience, I had an exotic and dreamlike destination.

Working at a five star hotel provided me with an abundance of things to read. With access to complimentary newspapers and magazines for the guests, books and magazines left in rooms, and lots of promotional travel material constantly on display, only time limited my opportunity to read. This abundance of reading material, which I had never been interested in, or exposed to, became the catalyst for my planned destination.

Mark and Steve gave me lots of suggestions. One key piece of advice was to decide on my next destination well before the hotel job ended. They were going to Scandinavia. They didn't invite me. Lesson learned. My nightmares had begun to resurface as the stress of leaving Banff mounted. I searched my ever changing library for an obscure place to hide and forget. Mostly I searched for warm, sunny places where I could sit on a beach, drink cold beer, smoke pot and seek opportunities for carnal pleasure. I didn't realise it, but I was desperate for distraction.

A major travel magazine profiled a place called Vanuatu:

"An island archipelago one thousand miles northeast of Australia, and one of the last places in the South Pacific untouched by any significant development. An island paradise secured by a stable government based on former British and French colonial experience and perfect for anyone seeking to get away from it all."

Vanuatu was also about as far away from Canada as my desire and need could hope for.

In addition, and from a tongue in cheek perspective for the vacation traveller, the magazine noted Vanuatu's lax immigration controls, and suggested, "If a visitor became seduced by the climate and its friendly people and forgot to leave, chances were they might never be bothered by law enforcement or immigration officials."

Striving to meet readers' needs, the same magazine conveniently provided details on how to get to Vanuatu, and as they had implied, forget to leave.

On May 22, 1993, I boarded US Air flight 301. The first of six flights that took me from Vancouver via LA, the Cook Islands, Auckland, Fiji, and finally to Port Villa, Vanuatu. It was the first time I had used my passport. Using my passport should have ended my running away, but in the early 1990s Canadian police agencies were still implementing multi-jurisdictional police databases such as the Canadian Police Information Centre, and my mom's missing persons' report only resided in the Ontario police database. Vanuatu was also a hell of a lot farther than the original reason I had gotten a passport, which was for a cross border hunting trip with my dad. It was also my first flight."

~ ~ ~ ~

Alan felt exhausted but gratified to have unloaded a portion of his story on this stranger. Serenity Rehab Centre was hot. Sweat sheened on Alan's forehead, pooled in his armpits and collected between the toes of his feet. He hadn't spoken this many words at one time for several years. There had been no one to talk to, and no one to listen. Tired but relieved, Alan looked expectantly for a reaction from Mr. Grey. A sage smile stretched the man's dry lips as half-closed eyes fought the dulling side effects of his hourly dope allocation.

CHAPTER 7

Vanuatu

Unconcerned by Mr. Grey's fluttering eyelids, and a little relieved that maybe not all would be remembered, Alan transported Mr. Grey from the sticky heat of Serenity Rehab Centre to the refreshing warmth of Vanuatu.

Six flights and seventy-two hours later, I arrived at Vanuatu International Airport. Cramped in coach seats for twenty-five hours I had watched movies, eaten artificially preserved food, and drank naturally preserved beverages. Fifty-three hours' ground time punctuated the flying. I waited in terminals, browsed malls, and for one beautiful day, lounged on the pristine beaches of the Cook Islands.

Tired, excited, and distracted, I stepped off the plane into the promised tropical paradise of the under-developed South Pacific Island of Vanuatu. Located west of Fiji, south of the Solomon Islands, and about one thousand miles east of Northern Australia, the island made me believe I had left my problems behind.

Customs, passport control, and baggage claim blurred by. A taxi stopped. I climbed in. I gawked through the open window of the taxi at the lush road-side vegetation. Warm, mid-seventy Fahrenheit, salty ocean air wafted over my airline stale body. What a beautiful place. Vanuatu's warm air wasn't numerically much more than the mid-sixties Fahrenheit of Vancouver, but the air carried with it a calm, relaxed quality that soothed and caressed my senses. I was filled with optimism and hope. I thought a small thank-you to the author of the magazine article that had been the catalyst for my arrival, in what seemed to me, a promised land. Vanuatu was indeed a tropical paradise, but Vanuatu had a dark side, and we soon found each other.

~ ~ ~ ~

"Where to?" asked the taxi driver for the fifth time as I struggled to break free of my wide-eyed, head turning review of paradise. I hadn't thought that far ahead. My blank stare and non-response prompted the driver to consider me more closely, and establish an experienced conclusion about my worth, stature, and needs.

"How long you staying for?"

"I don't know yet. I'm in no hurry. Depends if I can get a job."

The car slowed. The driver pulled over and stopped. I thought he was going to ask for proof I could pay. Instead, a wide, teeth-filled smile split his face as he explained my accommodation options.

"Eight dollars per day sharing a room in the Bluepango Motel, seventeen dollars for a private room. Seventy-five dollars per day for a room at the Holiday Motel."

I was about to say I didn't want to share a room when he said there was another option.

"Local families sometimes rent room for thirty dollars a week."

I did some mental math. The one thousand six hundred dollars in my pocket, at thirty dollars a week for a room, and thirty dollars a week for food, would last me almost six months, whether I found a job or not.

The driver mistook my mental math for poverty because he immediately reduced the room price to twenty-five dollars a week. I agreed to take a look. The driver introduced himself as Max, and with an even wider smile than I thought possible, took me to a rough looking, wood and metal, four room shack. Similar structures lined the dirt road at irregular intervals. Dense tropical jungle surrounded everything. The shack became my home for the next two years.

I had shed a lot of my naiveté at the Banff Springs Hotel, but I was still surprised to discover Max lived in the shack. I had also agreed to pay about thirty per cent more than I would have at the next shack over. But life's mix & match seemed to work out, and Max and I became close friends. At least that's what I thought.

~ ~ ~ ~

Max said the first thing I needed was an education in all things Vanuatu. A task for which Max had a seemingly endless amount of time and enthusiasm. Max explained how taxi work almost entirely depended on the arrival and departure schedules of the three daily flights, or the weekly cruise ship. Most people, meaning natives, walked, biked, hitched, or rode one of the two island buses that erratically and unreliably serviced the island. Hence Max had plenty of time.

Like a well-trained but irreverent tour guide, Max gave me an overview of Vanuatu beginning, as guides often do, with his own simplistic interpretation of history:

"My people were happy and content until the Spanish came about four hundred years ago. People fished, grew yams, watermelon, spices, and eggplants. They lived a natural life. Families shared, cared for each other, and drank Kava."

I learned Kava was a local drink made from the roots of indigenous plants. Intoxicating, but more like a sedative than alcohol. It tasted awful, but that didn't stop me from drinking far more than was good for me.

"No one bothered about who was in charge. We didn't need other ideas about who created the world, or who, or what, a king was. Of course, the Spanish told everyone about our beautiful island. Soon after the French, then the British, showed up with their own gods, kings, and ideas of what was best for us. They cut down the forests, and made us grow cotton, coffee, bananas and coconuts to satisfy the 'exotic needs' of pasty faced people in faraway places.

"In the 1940s, the Americans came and really fucked things up when they built a military base to protect themselves from the Japanese. When they left, in the 1950s, they dumped everything into the ocean. Millions of dollars-worth of tanks, guns, jeeps, and boats, all left to rot.

"In 1980, we kicked out the French and British and became independent. We believed we had gotten our island back. We thought we would control things and decide what happened and everything. We would raise cattle, grow our own food again, and drink lots of Kava. And only let people come for vacations, not people who want to take things out of our island. But in the past few years, Australians, Chinese, and Indians have brought their cocaine and heroin here, and with it corruption and lies. One day we will get our island back."

Max's history lesson had poured out of him in a mixture of regret, resentment, and hostility, finally ending with a sense of pride and ownership. Seeing a hint of challenge in his eyes, I held back what I had read in a *National Geographic* publication of 1991. The article acknowledged the inevitable European colonial period and the overbearing American WWII presence, but provided an alternative view:

European presence fostered economic diversity, social, educational and health reforms, and established a parliamentary political structure supported by a long-term commitment to financial and economic investment. Not altruistic, but with enough to tally more on the positive than negative side.

The brief American presence, contrary to Max's view, had been credited with sowing the seeds of nationalism. A nationalism which initiated the island's own independence movement of which Max was so proud. Even more unpalatable to my new friend would be how American dumping of military equipment in the ocean unintentionally created a magnificent reef. A reef now called Million Dollar Point and recognised as one of the top scuba destinations in the world. Drugs and corruption hadn't made the *National Geographic* publication, so I assumed Max had exaggerated.

Max's emotional and one-sided narrative continued for several days. My history lesson included many front-seat rides in his "taxi." We would cruise around the island while he would show me significant landmarks, and introduce me to his extended family and numerous friends.

An exception was the main city, Port Villa. Max mostly drove through without stopping. He did point out the few hotels, three bars, and restaurants that competed with more than fifteen banks for premium street or waterfront space. Max referred to Port Villa as a symbol of the exploitation of Vanuatu by foreign investors. He usually avoided Main Street if possible.

With knowledge, and the right words, I might have recognised Max for a committed historical revisionist. I might also have glimpsed the radical nationalist he was becoming. But I didn't. And while I sensed a tension between his need for my money and his resentment of foreigners, our shared poverty and youth kept the tension at bay. On this fragile foundation we established a mutually beneficial, if not warm and fuzzy, friendship. A kind of microcosm of the island itself.

~ ~ ~ ~

Max was versatile. When I told him I needed a job to pay the rent, he immediately refocused his priorities. Seamlessly Max switched from tour guide to employment counsellor. He explained various work options for unskilled labour, most of which involved the need to pick, pluck, or plant something. None of these appealed to me.

I feigned interest, and said I would think about it while I took a solo tour into town. I made for the swankiest hotels in Vanuatu to bestow my five star Banff Springs hotel experience on the highest bidder. It didn't turn out that way, though. All the hotels had the same structure: foreigners managed, natives did everything else. My five-star experience didn't include management. Bluntly forced into a more realistic evaluation of my service industry skills, I headed for the next logical place: Port Villa's three bars.

The first two occupied small lots on side streets off the main street. Similar one room establishments, except one, sold locally produced Tusker beer and Vanuatu Bitter, while the other offered a variety of imported bottled beer. The inevitable price differential was reflected in the clientele. Non-whites drank Tusker and Bitter. Shades of whites sucked down the imports. Due to the limited dining facilities, I didn't inquire about employment at either establishment. The third, the Waterfront Bar and Grill, was my last option.

Three things attracted me to the Waterfront Bar and Grill. First, somebody had commercial sense because both domestic and imported beers were available. Second, the lily British white to ebony Congo black variety in the complexions of the bar patrons suggested a more cosmopolitan and less divided clientele than the other two bars. Third, and most encouraging, was the dining facilities for about fifty people. Tables to be bussed. Wicker backed, swivel bar stools lined the bar and I claimed a seat. I asked for a beer and received a cold Vanuatu Bitter. Casual smiles and inquiring eyes tracked my progress and rested intermittently on my back.

My presence in the bar wasn't suspicious: annual tourism numbers were less than thirty thousand people per year. Twenty thousand came in batches of fifteen hundred once each week when a cruise ship dropped anchor for a twenty-four hour island tour. I had arrived in Vanuatu at the end of the rainy season. The first cruise ship was not due for another week. Consequently, I had been pegged as a non-cruise ship newbie, thus the curiosity. I also looked every one of my nineteen and a half years.

I tried to study the bar/restaurant through the mirror over the liquor cabinet behind the bar. I couldn't figure things out so I used the stool's swivel function and turned left and right to take a proper view.

The entire back of the restaurant opened on to the marina. Assorted brown and off-white wicker tables and chairs stood in a loose semicircle on a brown-beige tiled floor. They provided a soft barrier to the grass and shrubs that curved around the open dining area. Bamboo-like beams, thatched with some kind of broad leaf, arched from their perimeter supports to a central peak. Light streamed in. Between the dining tables and the bar, an open area provided mingling space for drinkers and bar patrons. Nautical flags, pictures of yachts, and a large "ship's bell" hanging on an inverted anchor near the entrance, underscored the nautical theme. I liked what I saw.

My empty bottle hit the bar. I nodded to the bartender for another. Busy with my reconnaissance, I hadn't paid much attention to the bartender. He placed the beer in front of me and said,

"I suppose you need a job? What can you do?"

The man's brisk, direct question, as well as his quick and accurate assessment of my needs, surprised me. His stocky build, tattooed forearms, and clichéd, grey-haired ponytail gave me the impression this barkeep possessed a well-developed bullshit radar. Instead of trotting out my embellished five star hotel experience, I said, "Honest, reliable, clean, polite, do as I am told, sir."

I immediately thought the "sir" had set off the bullshit radar, but he smiled and said, "Tomorrow, 7 a.m."

No name exchange, no employment history, no reference check. No nonsense. He placed the bill on the bar. The interview was over. Living up to my improvised, ten word resume was harder than I imagined. My success depends on your point of view.

~ ~ ~ ~

Max sat on the front step. A half coconut shell, the native way to drink Kava, rested in his hands. Unfocused eyes and limp body indicated he had consumed more than the half shell his hands so carefully held.

"Where you been, man? I had some Kava here for you, but I didn't want it to spoil so, you know, I drank it so it wouldn't be wasted."

Max's chuckle at his own joke about "wasted" was pretty consistent with what I would later learn resulted from about four half-shells, or three cups, of Kava: a relaxed, friendly demeanour ready to engage in everything at half-pace or less.

Unconcerned about missing the Kava, as I hadn't yet reached the point where its effects overcame its unpleasant taste, I told Max I had gotten a job at the Waterfront Bar and Grill.

Max's relaxed state precluded a gush of congratulations or enthusiasm, yet I felt disappointed when Max just nodded and said, "Yeah, that's where you belong." I was about to challenge him on what he had meant when he seemed to make some internal connection and said with contradictory enthusiasm, "Great. That will work out just fine for us."

Confused by his second comment, I again asked Max what he meant. But Max had already gotten to his taxi and started the engine. By the time I did understand how my job at the Waterfront Bar and Grill would "work out just fine," people were dead, and I was on the run.

~ ~ ~ ~

I woke at 5:40 a.m. No Max. No ride into town. Washed, dressed, and fed, I left at 6 a.m. A dirt road, rutted and erratic, wound for .5 Kilometers to a paved road that circumvented the island. The Waterfront Bar and Grill was an asphalt Kilometer farther. With no other option, I walked.

At 6:48 a.m. I arrived. The door stood open, ceiling fans pushed brewed coffee and sea salt laden air. At 11 p.m., I stopped work and walked back home. Undressed, fed, and rewashed, I lay on my cot at 12:10 a.m. So began my routine for the next two months. Sixteen hours a day, seven days a week, I cleared tables, washed dishes, stocked the bar, refilled salt, pepper, mustard and ketchup bottles and kept on being honest, reliable, clean, polite and doing as I was told. So much for paradise.

Bill had been the no-nonsense bartender. He owned the Waterfront Bar and Grill. Rough and pithy with his employees, smooth and affable with his customers. Three wait/bar staff provided front of the house service: Fred, Glen, and Howard. Two Aussies, one Kiwi. Natives did the cooking, cleaning, and dishwashing. Non-natives did everything connected with customers, money, or supplies. No women. Natives were not allowed on the premises unless Bill, Fred, Glen or Howard was present. Despite this strict and segregated environment, people appeared content. People knew their responsibilities, their jobs, and their place. The Waterfront Bar and Grill was efficient, and according to Fred, profitable. Yet, my limited experience at the Banff Springs Hotel suggested a degree of illegitimate furtiveness accompanied the usual restaurant business.

After two months of grunt work, paradise improved. Bill promoted me to waiter/bartender/inventory controller. Serving tables and tending bar improved my lot considerably. Really, I switched from dirty dishes with discarded food, to clean dishes with fresh food, but the increased interaction with customers was much more fun. More important, the extra pay and the generous tips increased my income threefold. My new duties and new hours were split between myself, Bill, and the other waiters, Fred, Glen, and Howard. This split reduced my work to six to eight hour shifts, depending on the number of customers, plus a half-hour a day for inventory control. Inventory control was a fancy way to say I had to make sure we didn't run short of basics. When stock got low, I told Bill. He did the rest. At the Banff Springs Hotel, inventory control had been serious business due to the scope for theft and corruption. Smaller scale opportunities existed at the Waterfront Bar and Grill, but Bill's aura curtailed any temptation. Later, I realised Bill had a reason for tempting me.

~ ~ ~ ~

Promotion opened doors. Specifically, the ex-pat service industry underworld. The small number of pubs and restaurants necessitated a broader underworld membership. Ex-pat employees, who worked at the island's dive shops, motorcycle rental outlet, fishing trip providers, catamaran cruise shop, and other tourist related business, were core members. Cruise ship wait staff, and airline cabin crew, also participated when schedules allowed. Foreigners monopolised the tourist service industry. They had capital, and as I later learned, paid the required bribes.

The Banff Springs Hotel service industry subculture had four mainstays: alcohol, drugs, sex and petty crime. Vanuatu had the same, and more. A well-developed exchange system between service industry members thrived alongside the mainstays. Members used each other's services, either for free, or for significant discount. In this way, I obtained an open water divers' certificate. I learned how to sail, climb, fish, parasail, drive power boats, navigate and read maps.

Less wholesome activities included plenty of gratuitous sex, and an increased desire and use of alcohol and marijuana.

A year later, as another rainy season ended, I was an enthusiastic member of the "ruling" expatriate community. Cheerful and ignorant, I displayed and engaged in the worst colonial-like excesses. Uncaring and insensitive to anything except my own physical and mental gratification, I consumed paradise - except for the nightmares, the memories, and the guilt.

The initial sixteen hour days, seven days a week, had been a blur. Two months of exhaustion had kept thoughts of Julie and my crime away. I missed my mother, but I was afraid to think of her. Despite my repressed thoughts, I suffered unbidden visits from my mother who slid wordlessly into my exhausted sleep, to accuse and berate through pained eyes and pointed fingers, tugging at my conscience.

Six to eight hour shifts, subject to customer flows, gave me a decent amount of free time. Especially during the rainy season when few tourists visited Vanuatu. Free time led to more alcohol, marijuana, or Kava. Consumption of more mind influencing sub-stances left me vulnerable. My torment returned. Unhurriedly it crept around the edges of my awareness, interrupting, pricking, yet unable to overcome my physical or mental high. Then, weakened by dope, booze, and Kava, my subconscious capitulated. My mind opened and my torment rushed in. Unopposed it established itself as my true master, compelling me into a unbreakable cycle of dream, drink, drugs, work, dream, drink, drugs, work until my torment controlled and determined my existence. Paradise became hell. Two years on I leaned more and more on a weak and deceitful crutch of dope and booze, unable to escape my demons or my dependencies.

Through this toxic lens, a neo-colonial expatriate view of Vanuatu natives materialised; the islanders were lazy, absent initiative, and responsible for their own situation, which was pretty much shafted by everyone. My increased myopia fed a perception that locals were resentful of all things non-native and all the things expats monopolised. Max was the exception. An exception who seemed to go both ways, but for different reasons.

Max provided a change from the ex-pat world. His shack had become a retreat from the excesses of the expatriate service industry subculture. Although, I didn't notice how my time at Max's had become a private and lonely indulgence of the same excesses, rather than a retreat from them. Max was also incredibly tolerant of my behaviour. Eager to help, fetch, and carry, and sit for hours of ignorant discussion. Always friendly and interested in my work, and workplace gossip. Even though I had money to live in town, I stayed with Max. I paid more rent, and shared the booze, drugs, and provisions I brought to my retreats. We were friends. Then, at the height of my low, Bill gave me another job. It was a long time, and too late, before I understood the connection.

~ ~ ~ ~

No recruitment poster announced an opening. No initiation ceremony accompanied my acceptance. No secret handshake, or compulsory tattoo. And no opportunity to decline. My new job was sort of added to my other Waterfront Bar and Grill duties. One afternoon, during a lull in bar business, Bill said, "Alan, go down to the dock and help Fred unload some packages from Barney's yacht." Barney was from Australia. He spent his entire life sailing between various South Pacific islands. He stopped by Vanuatu once or twice every month for a brief stay.

The next day Dutch arrived. Dutch, a South African, never drank in the bar if a local was present, and as far as I know, never stepped farther inland on Vanuatu than the men's washroom. Bill and Dutch exchanged words, and then Bill told me to load Barney's packages onto Dutch's yacht. Of course, I thought about it in some distracted way, but in line with my original resume, I did as I was told. The absence of questions or objections on my part was, I assume, taken as an agreement to participate. I soon became a regular "dock" worker, transshipping cargo from one yacht to another. Four or five weeks later, after I had transshipped almost a dozen cargoes, Bill formally introduced me to the South Pacific drug trade.

The drug trade, said Bill, was simple, profitable, and safe. Heroin from East Asia and cocaine from South America, destined for the U.S., Canadian, Australian and New Zealand markets, came to the South Pacific for transshipment. Larger quantities, on freighters, or large fishing boats, were transshipped at sea. Smaller quantities, on yachts or small cargo ships, landed at island ports to be split into smaller packages, and shipped onward by private yachts.

Bill had been in the business for ten years. When I asked him about police, customs, and all the usual stuff that goes along with shipping things he snorted and said,

"Everyone gets a cut. Law enforcement, customs, political leaders, even the paramilitary get a cut. Some get a monthly fee, some get paid per shipment. Some get cash, others in drugs. That's why it's so safe. Everyone's involved. A cut. The key is not to get greedy." Then he added ominously, "If anyone does, they get punished." Flattered at being taken into Bill's confidence, I gave no thought to how dangerous such knowledge could be.

I soon graduated from dock worker to storage, quality control, repackaging, and under Bill's direction, cutting and skimming. I didn't graduate to a customer, though. Marijuana and booze satisfied my needs: bad enough but not as destructive as heroin and cocaine. I also didn't like the thought of snorting anything through my nose, or sticking needles in myself.

Fred, a mellow Australian, became my mentor. He had worked for Bill for six years. He arrived in Vanuatu as a crew member on a private yacht from Australia. The yacht owner, said Fred, had been a real bastard. Fred abandoned him as soon as they dropped anchor. Luckily for Fred, the yacht owner pissed off Bill. With a common gripe, Bill and Fred met. Bill hired Fred as a waiter. Two years later Fred entered the drug trade: a similar career path to my own. Assigning Fred made sense. He had trained me as a waiter, and introduced me to the ex-pat community. At twenty-three, we spoke the common language of youth, had no pretensions, and had nothing to lose. Outside of work, we became friends. We dove, sailed, and climbed together. We partied, chased women, and drank together. The only thing we didn't share was drugs. Marijuana and heroin/coke don't mix. I didn't like Fred when he was high.

Drug work opened my eyes. Human smuggling, prostitution, offshore banking, its companion money laundering, flags of convenience, and passport selling and document forgery provided ample choice for the enterprising criminal. Taken together, these activities were mutually supportive, feeding into, and off, each other to create a dynamic black market economy. An economy that provided well for the participants, but did little for the native population: crime paid well for the few and compounded the misery of the majority.

~ ~ ~ ~

Drug traffic increased in the summer. More legitimate travellers to mask drug activity. My role increased. So did the level of trust, responsibility, and information. More money flowed. Less work in the restaurant. I buzzed along contentedly until I realised my increased involvement in the drug trade was gained at Fred's expense. The more I did, the less he did. And the less he did, the more he seemed to snort and inject. Fred, ignoring warnings and interjections from friends, became more of a drug customer than worker. His increased drug dependency brought unreliability, indiscretion, and erratic behaviour.

Fred gave me endless advice and tips on the drug trade and how to take care of yourself. One day, between cocaine snorts, Fred calmly said, "Alan, You need two more passports and a gun." Initially, I didn't see the need for the first, and was reluctant to do the second. When I asked Fred about needing two passports, in addition to my own Canadian passport, he provided additional advice:

"The first passport is the one you reluctantly 'let slip' to everyone, like Bill, or me, or others in the business, that you have. The second is the one you tell no one about. Not even me."

"And the gun?" I asked.

"The gun," said Fred, "just makes sense in this business. Everyone will assume you have one. It's better to work on the basis that if they think you have one, you better have. That way they might think twice before shooting at you."

Then again, I thought they might make sure they shot first and shot straight. I mulled Fred's advice over for a few days. Then I got a gun and two additional passports. One passport identified me as an Australian; the other said I was British. I hid the gun and passports at Max's shack. Fred's advice saved my life. I wish I could have saved his.

~ ~ ~ ~

Fred taught me something else. He didn't want to, but Bill insisted. I didn't grasp the significance of the lesson, or the profound effect it had on my life. I also didn't grasp how this lesson, and several others Fred had been involved in, had taken their toll on Fred. Perhaps that was why this lesson was reluctantly delivered.

Fred and I sat on the dock. We had loaded a small shipment onto Dutch's yacht and secured the hidden compartments in the bough. Bill, who had watched us from the end of the dock, waved for Fred to join him. After a brief discussion, Bill handed Fred a small canvas bag and called me over to join them.

When I reached them, Bill said, "Go with Fred and do as he tells you." To Fred he said, "Make sure he does them all." Bill walked away and Fred took my arm and said, "Come on, Alan, we have no choice."

We walked away from the dock toward Bill's warehouse. I heard the clink of metal from the canvas bag which, now that I was closer, appeared heavy. I assumed the bag held tools and guessed we had some kind of building work to do. The bag did contain tools, but we didn't build anything. We only destroyed.

Fred didn't speak. We walked to the warehouse. Bill had built the warehouse a year after he purchased the Harbour Front Bar and Grill. An unremarkable building, isolated at the end of the dock area more than three hundred feet from any other building. We repackaged, mixed, and cut drugs in the warehouse. I couldn't imagine what we would need a bag of tools for.

Fred paused at the small side door. We locked eyes. He said, "I'm sorry, Alan. I hoped you might have been spared this part of the job, but this was what Bill wanted."

Apprehensive, I asked Fred what the fuck was going on. He didn't answer. Instead he cut me off with an upturned hand and said, "Do what I tell you. Don't think about it. Don't speak unless I tell you to." Fred stepped into the warehouse. I followed, unaware I would soon lose whatever small sliver of innocence I might have still had.

~ ~ ~ ~

I moved from bright afternoon sunlight to the dust grey twilight of the warehouse. I blinked away blurred shadows inside my eyes. A wooden structure forced itself into focus. I hadn't seen the structure before, but I did recall a pile of lumber had been neatly stacked where the structure now stood.

The lumber had been erected to form a four walled room about ten feet by ten. Instead of wood, or drywall, the walls were made of thick, transparent plastic. The plastic seemed to be stained, as though some kind of brownish liquid had been haphazardly splashed all over it. Bewildered, I strained to see through the brown marks. A man sat motionless at a table, his head slumped forward on his chest.

Frightened, I turned to demand an explanation from Fred. He silenced me with a finger to his mouth. His determined expression left no room for misunderstanding. Fred placed a bundle in my hands and gestured instructions for me to put the bundle on. I unfurled the bundle. A head-to-toe, one piece plastic overall, complete with attached hands, and a rigid face mask that provided space to breathe hung from my hands.

I was afraid. My gut churned. I had a sudden urge to run. Fred must have sensed my fear and desire. He took hold of me and put his mouth to my ear and whispered, "Alan, you have to do this, or you might be the one in the chair. Now put the fucking suit on."

Reluctantly, and with some difficulty, I squeezed myself into the overall. I felt trapped and vulnerable: as though I had voluntarily stepped into my own plastic coffin.

Fred drew a sheet of plastic aside and stepped into the makeshift room. I followed. The room had a ceiling; it too was made of plastic. So was the floor. I felt like a specimen in a giant Petri dish waiting for the ceiling to descend and squish me into goo for study under a microscope.

The canvas bag hit the table with a thump. I jumped. Fred told me to take out the tools and lay them on the table in front of the man's hands. I had avoided the man. Tried to deny his existence, afraid of what, or who he might be. Now I was forced to acknowledge him.

The man was young. Perhaps not much older than me. He had natural muscles, the kind developed in perfect proportion to the body. Formed by hard physical work that taxed the entire body, rather than the mismatched muscles formed with unbalanced weight regimes at designer gyms. Strength flowed from his body. I was relieved by the straps binding his torso to the chair. Plastic ties bound his forearms and hands to the table top. Cuts and scraped skin told of his struggles to free himself. Bruised and swollen face spoke of the tactics used to subdue and secure him.

The bag held six tools. Claw hammer, hack saw, Stanley knife, small pipe cutter, welding torch & bottle, and a battery operated drill with drill-bit attached. I shuddered. I placed each one on the table. An unavoidable realisation the tools were not going to be used for their intended purpose drained moisture from my throat.

Fred stood behind the man. He pulled his unconscious head back and placed a small, brown bottle under the man's nostrils. Brown eyelids flickered open, dark pupils floated in bloodied, pink eyeballs straining to focus. The man found me. His eyes shifted from me to the table and back again; comprehension clear, fear real.

His mouth opened, but his intended scream came out as an incoherent muffle as Fred placed a wide band of duct tape over his open mouth. The man's body flexed and strained in violent, desperate writhing, until exhausted and resigned, he spasmed and stilled.

Fred came around the table, fixed on my eyes, and spoke words that sent bile to my throat. I shook my head from side to side in refusal. Fred grasped my chin and repeated the words: "One finger with each tool. You choose which fingers." Then Fred added, "Bill is here. Watching. This is a test. You have to do it. It's how he binds you to him. You have thirty minutes."

Fred stepped out of the room and stood unmoving. On the other side, through my peripheral vision, a figure leaned into the plastic. A blurred ghoul waited to feed: Bill.

My finger touched the claw hammer. A stifled scream somehow pushed its way out of the man's body. I stared at the man. Was it possible for vocal sound to travel through skin, or had the scream come through his nose or ears? This detached thought was the first of many that filled my head to insulate me from the fear and pain the sounds conveyed.

I brought the hammer down on the knuckle of his left hand index finger. Bone erupted through skin. I wondered if he used this finger to pick his nose, and if so, would it be a great inconvenience for him now that knuckle was crushed.

And on it went. Silly questions or thoughts about the loss of function of one finger or another. How awkward would it be for him to have mangled stumps for digits? How would he do his buttons up or zip his fly? What would his mom, his girlfriend, his whatever say when they found him? Would they care? Would they berate him for getting into trouble?

I was careless with the welding torch and melted a small spot of plastic on to my hand. The sensation of pain brought me back from wherever I was. I looked down on the chopped, hacked, and burned blobs that lay at odd angles on the table. My work. Nausea choked me.

Fred returned to prevent me from falling. He took the welding torch from my hand and led me out of the plastic room. He stood me on another sheet of plastic and told me to take off the overalls. I slithered out, careful to prevent the blood, or mushed fragments of flesh the drill had splattered everywhere, from touching me. Fred took my arm again and led me to the door. He pushed me out and into the light without a word.

Fred and I became closer. We only spoke of the plastic room on one occasion when Fred told me he hoped I would not suffer the same dreams he did. I didn't tell him I already had enough of my own.

I returned to the plastic room many times. Each detached finger taking with it another piece of the small town kid until, through practise and growing indifference, I needed only ten minutes, not thirty.

~ ~ ~ ~

Despite enough money and connections to rent a house of my own with a pool, maid, and any electronic gadget I wanted, I kept living, or at least "sleeping things off" at Max's shack. Harbour Front Bar and Grill work was infrequent and mostly a thin cover for my illicit drug trade employment. Bill had brought a new boy into his web. He did most of what I used to do.

Time, money, a degree of status, and light work respon-sibilities, allowed me to maintain a close and loving relationship with my twin crutches, marijuana and alcohol. In contrast to many others, I believed I controlled my dependencies. Sure, I had mind blanking episodes where whole, and sometime several, days would disappear, but I always managed to adhere to three rules. One, I always binged at Max's, and never took to excesses at work, or with anyone in the drug business. Two, I never missed a drug related work task. Three, I kept my mouth shut. I was wrong about rule number three.

I binged in style. My usual "hamper" contained chilled beer, vodka, ice blocks for the coolers I had purchased and left at the shack, cold meats, cheese, bread, and of course cigarette papers, tobacco, and weed. A taxi would accompany me to the various stores. I would load the taxi and head to Max's. I could always count on Max being home. He would help me unload my hoard. I had plenty to share and Max would fetch more if needed. In return, Max shared his never ending supply of Kava: symbiotic enablers.

In addition to the coolers, I had also purchased two leather arm chairs and a wooden table. I took them to Max's and placed them on the tiny front deck sheltered by a corrugated metal roof that overhung the deck. In one of these chairs I habitually pursued my R and R, rising only to replenish or expel. Max claimed the other chair. Comfortable and provisioned, we made existential journeys. We laughed, shared jokes and anecdotes, and marvelled at the simplicity of life, our good fortune, and the joy of paradise.

While I "lived the dream," or more accurately, lived **in** a dream, Max pursued his own agenda. An agenda that fed Max's own dream. A dream in which I played an unwitting but crucial part.

When I binged, Max gathered. Between jokes and anecdotes Max had pumped me for information on the South Pacific drug trade. How the drugs came in. How they went out. The boss, the workers, where it all happened. Who in government accepted payments. Judging by later events, Max squeezed just about everything out of me except, thanks to Fred, my second fake passport, and my gun. In fact, it was Fred's departure that brought me to my senses in time, and with just enough competencies to escape paradise alive.

~ ~ ~ ~

Fred had fallen. Hard. His smart, harbour front apartment had been replaced by a squalid room in an illegal brothel out of sight of the harbour and far away from the Waterfront Bar and Grill. No longer employed in any capacity by Bill, his money had run out.

He existed on handouts from former associates, who either through misplaced charity, or cold malice, provided just enough to keep Fred on a slow but steady decline.

I tried to help Fred. I sheltered him at Max's to keep him away from cocaine and heroin, but I couldn't watch him constantly. Unmonitored, Fred would stumble his way to town and the inevitable "score" would occur. Bill had cooled toward Fred and made it clear Fred was a liability. "Stay away from Fred," Bill told me. I did. I abandoned Fred and witnessed his decline into a full blown junkie.

Unexpectedly, one bright, fresh April afternoon, Bill brought Fred to the bar. Fred was clean shaven, dressed in new clothes, and sported a beaming ear to ear smile. He looked like a perfect mannequin. Surprised and pleased to see Fred, despite his wax-like appearance, I moved to greet and embrace him. Blank, incomprehension stared back. Bill steered Fred past me. Over his shoulder he shouted, "We have to hurry. Fred is sailing with Barney home to Australia. His family will fix him."

I followed Bill and Fred to the dock. Barney stood by his yacht. Sail covers off, latches closed, and the auxiliary 15 HP motor murmured in neutral. Ready to sail. Bill and Barney manoeuvred Fred into the yacht. They sat Fred in the stern, and propped him up with seat cushions. No one said goodbye, or good sailing, or fair winds or any kind of farewell salute. Bill tossed Barney the rope, the engine engaged, and Fred sailed into the bright afternoon sun. I called to Fred, but he didn't respond. Bill touched my arm and said, "It's for the best."

Australia is about one thousand miles from Vanuatu. A round trip by yacht should take between sixteen and twenty days. Within ten days, Barney returned. Bill's words of, "It's for the best" took on a whole new meaning for me as I realised Fred had never made it to Australia. Barney, the bastard, had dumped Fred overboard. Fred had been my mentor, my friend. My first real friend. I should have saved him.

~ ~ ~ ~

I wanted to make a hamper. A big one. Drink and smoke my shame away. Instead, I woke from my dream. With effort and pain I eased off the weed and the booze. Three or four days after Fred's departure, I had enough wits to check on my passport and gun which I had hidden months ago at Max's. I found the gun with ease. A long deceased truck sat rusted and neglected at the back of Max's shack. My gun, wrapped in plastic, rested unimaginatively under the rear wheel rim. Luckily, for me, my passport was more difficult to find.

I thought I had hidden the passport inside the shack to keep it dry. I had used a small metal box to keep insects away, but as I stood in the living room, I had no idea where the box could be. Exasperated and resigned I began a methodical search. I started in my bedroom and worked my way out to the main room. The shack was small, and hiding places were few. After half an hour I was certain my passport wasn't in my room, the main room, or the kitchen. That left Max's room.

I had never even thought about Max's room before, let alone been in it, but who knows? Maybe in some flash of drunken brilliance I had thought Max's room would be a good place to hide my stuff. I hadn't had any brilliant flashes, though. My passport wasn't in Max's room. Something else was. Something that scared the shit, and the booze, and the drugs right out of me. Something that snapped me into a sobriety I hadn't seen for a long time.

A slim, black, notebook, benign yet threatening, hung on the back of Max's headboard. Aware I was about to transgress, I looked over my shoulder. I eased the book off the headboard and sat on the bed. I held the book unopened, conflicted between loyalty to a friend, especially after abandoning Fred, and a growing apprehension the book contained things I needed to know.

The book contained old news. I already knew its contents: page after page of neat handwritten notes detailed everything I knew about the Vanuatu and South Pacific drug trade. All Bill had told me, all the things I had pieced together: names, dates, commodities, amounts, payments, ships and schedules. Even details of my Canadian and Australian passports.

A death sentence. If Bill found out about this, I would be the next one-way passenger on Barney's yacht. I put the book back. In shock, I stumbled to the deck and fell into my leather chair. Where the fuck was my third passport? Fear and desperation forced my memory to action. I gave a nervous chuckle as I lifted my arse off the leather chair. I reached under the cushion. With huge relief I withdrew a small metal box and my secret third passport.

~ ~ ~ ~

Tuesday, April 22, 1996. One month shy of my three year anniversary in paradise. Seven months before my twenty-second birthday. Fear and panic consumed me. Fred had sailed to a certain death. He had become a better drug customer than purveyor. I subsequently discovered Fred had offered information to law enforcement officers in exchange for money to buy drugs. Fred was so compromised by drugs, he didn't recognise the police officer. He was on Bill's payroll. Fred's indiscretion came straight to Bill, who immediately arranged Fred's last sail. What would be done to me for helping Max compile an A to Z of Bill's drug trade? Barney, the plastic room in the warehouse, alone time with Bill!

Max. Who the fuck was he? Who did he work for? He had enough information to arrest half of the police force and customs officers, as well as a large number of ex-pats, and elected and aspiring politicians. Max had also made careful notes on the banks, and how the money moved in and out. What was he going to do? Surely he wouldn't blackmail me? Or others? He would be dead within an hour. Oh, fuck me. Had I told him about the Empress?

In two days a massive drug shipment would arrive in Port Villa. Bill told me this would be the biggest shipment of his career. If all went well another would follow. Within a year he would be able to get out of the drug business. A lot depended on this shipment. Everyone would be watching. The shipment, said Bill, would be accompanied by "watchers" from the Chinese crime gang that organised it. I was fucked. Even if I removed the book, Max knew everything. Did he have a copy? I had one option. Run. Fast and far.

~ ~ ~ ~

Max approached. Engine splutter preceded the taxi's arrival. Max stopped inches from the deck. A swirl of dust overtook the car and added another layer to the shack. I waited in my chair. Sweat gathered in the usual places. Nothing out of the ordinary. Max greeted me with his friendly and disarming manner.

"Hey, Alan, you staying for the day, man? Need any help with anything?"

"Yes, I'm staying, but I don't need anything. I'm a bit rough today."

"Yeah, you look tired. Want me to fix you a little Kava? It'll help you relax, you know. I can make some before I go. I got a few fares today. I just stopped by to get something."

To be consistent, I replied Kava would be good.

"Maybe bring some booze on your way back?"

"No problem, man. Happy to."

Max entered the shack and returned a few minutes later with a cup of Kava for me. He gave me the beverage and our eyes met momentarily.

"You look different today, Alan. What you been doing?"

Madness seized me. I wanted to shove my gun in his face. Make him tell me what the fuck he was up to and who he worked for. Instead, I smiled weakly and said, "I don't know. Something I ate."

Max promised to come back in a few hours with some cold ones. Engine whined, wheels spun speed. More dust settled. When the sound of Max's car faded, I hurried to his room. No book. Shit. Shit. Shit.

Back on the deck I shook with fear and withdrawal. I tossed the Kava away. Time was short. I needed a plan. On Thursday morning, in just thirty-six hours, the Empress would weigh anchor at Port Villa's main harbour. Three hundred kilos of cocaine, worth fifty million on North American or Australian streets, would be unloaded and taken to Bill's warehouse. There Bill, me, and a few others would repackage the drugs into smaller quantities for shipment via the network of private yachts. I stepped off the deck and headed for town.

Sobriety startled me. I couldn't remember the last time I walked through Port Villa's downtown without being under the influence. I hesitated, afraid to enter the press of people coming and going until I remembered Max said he had some fares today. A cruise ship must be in port. The hustle and bustle was the twenty-four hour frenzy of tourists eager to spend money on "native" wares.

I searched for inspiration. Something to give me a plan. I didn't want to be around when the Empress arrived. Based on the abundance of information in Max's little book, I had likely blabbed about the Empress and her cargo. No matter who or what Max was, 50 million was a tempting target. I had an unpleasant sensation in my gut that had nothing to do with my withdrawal symptoms.

Caught in the tourist shopping binge, I was buffeted from one store front to another. I caught my breath outside one of Vanuatu's two "travel agents." Travel agents, meaning ninety-nine per cent of their service, provided tourists bookings for a catamaran cruise, deep sea fishing trip, scuba diving to Million Dollar Point, or an inland jungle hike. They also provided ticket service for the daily Air Vanuatu or Aircalin flights to Fiji.

I fingered my Canadian, Australian, and British passports in my pocket. A plan materialised. I would book two flights to Fiji. One as Sam Davis, Australian. The other as Karl Robinson, British. Once in Fiji I would book Sam a ticket to Australia and Karl a ticket to Europe. I had followed Fred's advice and ensured Bill knew about my Australian passport. If he, or others, wanted to find me they would probably, hopefully, follow Sam's trail.

Not a sophisticated plan, but the best I could come up with in my condition and with little time. Pleased by having made a decision, I entered the first travel agency and asked for a seat on the first flight out on Wednesday. Some author, or poet, wrote something about the best laid plans of mice and men, well quick, "only available" plans also get screwed. All the flights were booked!

I must have looked pathetic. The ticket agent asked if I had some special event, or reason, for my trip to Fiji. If I had, perhaps I would like a stand by ticket. I could wait at the airport for flights with no shows. "Of course," she assured me, "you can use the ticket Thursday, when several seats are available on the noon flight."

The thought of even the fragile comfort of a stand by ticket tempted me, but I would have to wait at the airport for several hours. Also, Wednesday was the day before the Empress arrived. I was expected to be on hand. No, I needed a reserved seat so I could show up at the last possible moment. In fact, the more I thought about it, the better a noon flight on Thursday sounded.

I assured the agent I had no special or urgent event and presented my Australian passport. I purchased a ticket for the noon flight on Thursday, not sure if I would make it, or be a no show. I left the store and took a circuitous route to the other travel agent. There, as British Karl, I purchased a second ticket.

I wasn't expected at the Bar and Grill today. Being in town frequenting travel agents was seriously out of character for me. The chance of a deliberate, or passing, remark about my activities in town reaching Bill was a definite possibility. With this in mind, I made a decent show of buying my usual binge supplies and taking a taxi back to Max's place.

~ ~ ~ ~

Late afternoon shadow clawed at the yard. I had returned to Max's, unloaded my stuff, and sank into my leather chair. Max had not returned as promised. Unusual. A sign something was amiss. My shakes and withdrawal had gotten worse. I needed to eat, but my lips refused to allow the food passage. I had to calm down, be normal. I drained a beer. Instant relief. I reached for a second. This one I drained slow. I maintained the same pace for several hours; enough to keep me steady. No vodka, no marijuana. Surprisingly, I fell asleep. I woke at 6 a.m. Wednesday.

Bill expected me at the warehouse at noon. He wanted to review the plan for Thursday morning. We had already discussed the plan once. My job would be to hump the bags from the shipping pallet, weigh them on a scale, and put them into the back of Bill's van. Then Bill would drive the van to the warehouse. I would unload, and conduct a quality check with Bill. Over the next two days, we would cut and repackage for the yachts.

I arrived early. So did Bill. We went over the plan again. Only one change. The cargo would be unloaded at 9 a.m., instead of eleven. The Chinese "watchers" wanted to go scuba diving in the afternoon! I nodded. No problem. I would see him tomorrow. Nine a.m. Scuba diving! Fuck! They had been on a ship for two weeks and wanted to go scuba diving. Why not the brothels like the rest of the fucking crew! More screwed plans.

My plan for a noon flight escape had been based on two possibilities: if everything went as planned, and there was no "Max factor," Bill would be too busy unloading the cargo at 11 a.m. to do much about my absence. Sure, he would send someone to find me, but it would be well past noon before he got around to really searching for me. By that time, I would be almost in Fiji.

Alternatively, if Max did turn up in some way or another, it wouldn't be until the cargo had been unloaded. Eleven a.m. Or later. Whatever happened would keep everyone busy until after the noon hour. Again I would be well on my way. But 9 a.m. fucked up both possibilities. If I wasn't there at 9, Bill would send someone. By 9:30 Bill would know I wasn't at the shack. Concern, suspicion, would be aroused. Bill would have ninety minutes to make calls, which would undoubtedly include inquires at the airport. Then again, being around to witness Max's intentions might lead to anything.

I walked home. Options, scenarios, and possibilities battered my brain. All evening and into the small hours, I searched for an alternative, but when 7 a.m. arrived I had no solution. I concluded the best of the worst options was to show up at the dock at 9 a.m. as planned. *Maybe,* I thought desperately, *Max had no designs on the shipment, at least not right away.* Once the drugs were safely in the warehouse, perhaps I could make a run for the airport. I was wrong. Again.

~ ~ ~ ~

Thursday morning. Slumped and knotted on my leather chair, I shivered in a half-wake. Overcast sky and chill breeze added to my dread. Because I could, I cursed the weather. Then I apologised. The brisk weather was the first thing to go my way. I could wear a jacket. The jacket would conceal my passports, money, and tucked in my rear waistband, my gun. I took it as a good omen.

Eight-fifty a.m. Ten minutes early. Bill already dock-side in his truck, engine idling. I approached the truck from the rear, exhaust fumes, suspended in moist air stilled by the bulk of the Empress, lay heavy at waist height. The drab, grey hull of the Empress loomed over me. Rust streaked from hull rivets and portholes to the blue green ocean; a ship weeping in embarrassment of appearance and guilt of purpose. How imaginative and hopeful the builder had been to bestow the name Empress on such an ugly freighter.

Through the side mirror, Bill followed my progress. He opened the passenger door. I climbed in and sat, silent. Sweat pooled behind my ears as I searched the dock for Max. Bill turned to me and said,

"You know, Alan, when you showed up in the bar three years ago and told me you were honest, reliable, clean, polite, and you could do as you were told, I thought to myself, *Oh yeah? What a crock.* I thought you might last a couple of weeks, maybe even a month, but you proved me wrong, Alan. Listen, when I said this was the big one, and after a few more like this I could retire, I meant it. I've been thinking you might be the one to take over from me. Do you see those two chinks up mid-ships? They are not only here to watch the cocaine, Alan. They are here to watch you, as well. They want to see how you handle things." Bill paused, held me with a definitive stare, and said, "So don't fuck up!"

A diesel engine coughed and the ship vibrated. Bill's attention shifted from me to the ship, missing the panic in my eyes that would have caused questions. Hook and cable descended into the ship's cargo hold. I got out of the van. I stood, still sweating despite the cold, and waited while Bill pulled the truck forward. I opened the back doors and took out a portable scale. From within the belly of the Empress, muffled voices called instructions. The crane's cable tightened. A pallet rose out of the hold, cleared the ship's rail, and descended to within six feet of the back of the van.

"Okay, Alan," commanded Bill, "get it weighed and loaded."

Thirty ten kilogram bags didn't take long. In ten minutes the last bag hit the truck's metal floor. The scale followed. I closed the doors and returned to the passenger seat. Focused on loading the thirty bags quickly, I hadn't time to worry more about Max. Nothing had happened. No police, nobody trying to steal it, no trigger happy chinks. At 9:20 a.m. I passed the dock gate, and drove the short distance to Bill's warehouse. Relieved, I breathed hard; I would have no problem catching my plane. Max still had his little book, and I wasn't waiting around for it to be published.

Bill whistled as we entered the warehouse yard. I got out, unlocked, and opened the warehouse doors. Bill drove past me into the gloom. I followed the van, closed the doors, and locked them from the inside.

All business, Bill had opened the van doors and hauled out the scale. Booted footfalls exited the gloom. Alerted, Bill hesitated mid-reach for one of the ten kilo bags, his left hand darting for his right arm pit. Three men stepped from the shadows, automatic assault rifles levelled at Bill's torso. Faded blue-grey uniforms, and scuffed boots indicted experience. Out gunned, Bill dropped his left arm. Left, right, and nowhere to run I mimicked Bill and stood still.

Max stepped from behind several crates, his wide, toothy grin a contradiction between the crisp collar and stiff hat of his "first-time worn" camouflage uniform. He too carried an automatic assault rifle, but without the ease and confidence of the three soldiers.

"Hello, Alan, my friend," said Max smiling as his teeth crowded out his lips.

Bill glared. Misinterpreting Max's familiar greeting, Bill turned and lunged at me. "You fucking traitor. I'll kill you." Bill didn't reach me. One of the soldiers delivered a nonchalant blow to the back of Bill's head with the butt end of a rifle. Felled, Bill's blood seeped from his head and pooled under his chest. Afraid, inert, my mouth hung open.

Max substituted his rifle for a pistol. He pointed his gun at me and told me to unlock and open the warehouse doors. Outside, with the engine running, Max's taxi waited. Another soldier backed the car in. Under Max's gun, I bundled Bill's blood soaked, but still breathing, body into the trunk.

I had seen a lot of gangster movies and expected I would be next in the trunk. I calculated the odds of using my gun to any useful effect, other than getting myself immediately shot. Before completing my math, Max motioned me into the driver's seat.

Max got in the back and told me to drive. "Follow the main road away from town," directed Max. Ten minutes later, Max had me turn onto a dirt track. Five more minutes of rough, boulder strewn driving, and the track dead-ended at a steep-sided ravine.

"Turn off the engine and give me the keys. Then put your hands on the steering wheel and keep them there."

I gave Max the keys, and gripped the wheel.

"Look, Max, we can work this out. There's plenty to share. If we keep this quiet, there will be more shipments. Lots for everyone."

The rear view mirror reflected Max's face. No toothy smile. Cold and distant, he said, "Shut up, Alan, and listen. When I picked you up at the airport and offered you a place to stay, I thought you might be different from the rest of the self-important white men that come to Vanuatu. You were young. You seemed innocent and honest. I believed you were looking for something fulfilling, a place to grow. I took you in, helped you understand Vanuatu, introduced you to my family and friends, and advised you on getting honest work. But you didn't listen, Alan. When you got a job at the Harbour Bar and Grill, I was going to throw you out. Then I thought it would be better to use you. The way you and your kind use all Vanuatuans.

"One person I didn't introduce you to was my uncle. He is a senior member of the Vanuatu Mobile Paramilitary Police Force. He had talked about the Harbour Front Bar and Grill many times. The police already suspected the bar was used for drug shipments, but they had no proof. No one would talk. When I told him about you and your job, he told me I must keep you close, become your friend, and learn everything I could about the bar and the drug business.

"I watched you jump into the filth and corruption that plagues our island. You joined them. Became one of them. I suppressed my desire to beat you as you began to loathe Vanuatuans, and treat us with indifference and contempt. I listened to your pathetic stories of how you had done something terrible to your family. That it hadn't been your fault. You had been tricked, forced, coerced. You always had someone or something to blame for your actions. Everything you have done you blamed on others: the drugs, the booze, the plastic room in the warehouse, Fred's murder. Every time you showed up with your little hamper of marijuana, vodka, beer and food, I sat and listened to you whine and complain about how unfair the world has been to *you*!

"I'll tell you what's unfair, Alan. Vanuatu's rape. That's what's unfair. First, the Spanish. Then the French, the British, and the Americans. Now it's all of them plus Australians, Chinese, and Indians. For four hundred years, it's been one rape after another. But no more, Alan. After today everything changes. Tomorrow, my uncle, and five other senior officers of the Vanuatu Mobile Paramilitary Police Force will arrest President Jean-Marie Leye and take him to another island to stand trial for treason."

Max had leaned forward and his face filled the rear view mirror. His eyes shone with pride, hope, and conviction. His expression a stronger, more determined, more certain version of the one he had three years ago when, as my tour guide, he had recounted his revisionist history of Vanuatu. As Max stared into some distant utopia of his own creation, I blurted, "How will stealing drugs and murdering people change things, Max? You are the same as everyone else."

Hate momentarily distorted Max's features. I thought he would shoot me. Confident about the conclusion of our discussion, Max calmed and continued.

"Sometimes, Alan, you have to get in the shit to get the pigs out of the sty. That's what we have done today. The money from the drugs will not go into the pockets of people like you and Bill. It will not be given to other foreigners who own everything on Vanuatu. Those who oppress and keep us in poverty while they sail beautiful yachts, build big houses, and drive new cars. The money will not pay bribes to the corrupt government officials, customs officers, and yes, even to some police officers.

"This time the money will provide a new beginning for Vanuatu. The Paramilitary Police Force will take over the government. We will throw out the criminals and drugs users, the prostitutes, the corrupt bankers and everyone who doesn't belong. Thanks to you, Alan, we have a list of everyone who has betrayed Vanuatu. When we take over they will all be gone, and Vanuatu will belong to the people of Vanuatu again. Then we will have elections and the people will decide!"

Then, with his face flushed with the certainty of rightness, Max said, "You should be proud, Alan. Without you, this plan might never have happened. Your death you will give Vanuatu a new start."

Shouts and bangs from the trunk ended the moment. Bill had regained consciousness and wanted out. Max told me to get out of the car and lie face down on the ground. Max opened the trunk. Bill rolled himself out of the trunk and fell heavily on the ground. Blood soaked his body.

"Get up, you pig," shouted Max.

"I can't walk," said Bill.

"Then crawl, dog."

Bill leveraged himself on the car. Max gesticulated with his gun, and Bill and I edged reluctantly to the ravine edge. I thought about telling Bill it wasn't my fault, but Max's words remained in my head and I said nothing.

Bill offered, threatened, and pleaded. Resolved, Max ignored Bill.

"Stop," said Max. We turned around. An updraft from the ravine caressed my back, birds sang, water gurgled close by, trees yielded to the breeze: paradise. Max pointed his gun at Bill.

Bill didn't have a chance, but I wasn't surprised when he lunged toward Max. Max's first bullet had entered Bill's chest, and the second was in flight, before Bill had completed one step. Bill's lunge did not save him, but it saved me.

Max dwelt too long on Bill's spasming torso; he savoured Bill's pain and death. While Max drooled, I fumbled my gun from my waistband under my jacket. I had only fired the gun once before. Fred had borrowed a boat and took me to a secluded inlet. I fired three eight shot clips into the water. The handgun had felt nothing like the rifle my dad and I used when we hunted together, but the basics were the same. Hold steady, squeeze slow, aim at what you want to hit. I did none of these. I shook, crushed the trigger, and fired in the general direction. Eight shots, ten feet. I hit both of them. Bill spun some more. Max arched up and backward; a bullet entered his cheek and continued on and into his skull. He lay monstrous and still in the dirt: white teeth stained red, no smile. Bill lived, distorted words pushed through a blood filled mouth.

"Good job, kid. I'm sorry I thought you betrayed me. I knew you were the one to take over from me. Wipe your prints off your gun and put it in my hand. It'll look like we shot each other."

I did what Bill told me, as I always had. Alone in the dirt, Bill died. Paradise continued, unmoved by the human drama. I angled my wrist. Eleven a.m. I had time to catch the noon flight. I took the car keys from Max's pocket and drove to Port Villa International Airport.

~ ~ ~ ~

I had a window seat. The Air Vanuatu DC 6 lifted off the worn asphalt runway and headed east to Fiji. I peered down on Vanuatu. I thought about the magazine I had read in the Banff Springs Hotel and the article that had described paradise. I wondered if the writer had actually visited Vanuatu, or made it all up. Three years ago Max had welcomed me to Vanuatu with his wide, teeth-filled smile. My bullet destroyed that smile. I had come to escape guilt and pain, and forget my sin. Instead, I had become an instrument of pain, piling up more sin. I betrayed those who trusted me, and abandoned those who called me friend. I had wallowed in self-pity, an eager victim, blameless and obedient. First a rapist, now a murderer. How could it not be my fault?

Three days later, I watched a BBC news story about Vanuatu:

On Friday, April 20, 1996, a group of Vanuatu Mobile Paramilitary Police Force officers abducted President Jean-Marie Leye and flew him to a neighbouring island in what was at first believed to be an attempted coup, but was later determined to be an industrial dispute about unpaid overtime. In the resulting fallout, one hundred and thirty-eight Police Force members were arrested and charged. Six senior officers resigned and left Vanuatu by private plane and have not been heard of since.

I thought about Max and his plans for a new Vanuatu. Cynically, I thought about the six senior officers of the Paramilitary Police Force and fifty million worth of cocaine. I also asked myself if one of those six officers was Max's uncle.

~ ~ ~ ~

Alan expected the mention of fifty million dollars to pique Mr. Grey's interest, considering Mr. Grey had suggested his own crime had involved a "shitload of money." Well, fifty million dollars was a shitload, and Alan was momentarily annoyed at the lack of response from Mr. Grey until Alan lifted his head. Opiates had overcome Mr. Grey. Alan wondered how long his confessor had been asleep, hopeful that perhaps he hadn't heard everything. Exhausted and depressed by the telling of his story, Alan left Mr. Grey and returned to his room.

CHAPTER 8

Glasgow, Scotland

Like sinner to priest, Alan returned to Mr. Grey's bedside. A firm voice greeted Alan.

"Good Morning, Alan. Sleep well?"

"No, not really."

"Hm, I'm not surprised. That was a hell of a time you had in Vanuatu."

"Oh, you remember, do you?"

"Of course, I'm not dead yet. So, what happened next? Where did British Karl end up?"

"Glasgow," replied Alan.

"Glasgow, Scotland?" said Mr. Grey in disbelief.

"Yeah."

"Why, how?"

"I didn't intend to go to Glasgow. When I landed in Fiji, the first flight out with available seats was to Amsterdam, Holland. When I landed in Amsterdam and there was a flight to Glasgow in two hours, I was scared. I wanted to get far away from Vanuatu as quickly as possible, so I thought what the fuck, Glasgow."

Mr. Grey smirked and asked, "How did you like Glasgow then? Glasgow is a shithole and no one can understand anything the Glaswegians say."

"You heard right. A shithole with hemorrhoids. Grey, wet, and cold. And, yes, I only understood them half the time."

"Go on then, tell how you fucked up in Glasgow."

"What do you mean? Who said I fucked up?"

"You're in here, aren't you? Only fuck-ups get into rehab."

Torn between telling the old man to fuck off, and the need to continue the catharsis he had begun, Alan kneaded his hands together.

"Okay, I'm sorry," said Mr. Grey. "Why don't you tell me what happened?"

Face saved, Alan continued:

I stepped out of the new Glasgow Airport, which had opened just four months earlier in January 1996, and wondered what the hell I had done. What the fuck could I do in Glasgow? I had exited departures and stood curbside. Rain, cold and voluminous, beat the sidewalk. Sheltered by an overhang, I stood, vacant, hoping for a sign. A scruffy man got in my face and asked me questions. I couldn't understand a fucking word he said.

He must have thought I was dumb, because after a couple of minutes, he walked away shaking his head and mumbling. Trapped by the rain, I fingered the four hundred pounds in my pocket. I had three thousand U.S. dollars when I left Vanuatu, but the plane tickets ate most of the money. An exchange rate of 1.62 U.S. dollars to the pound whittled away the rest.

Four hundred of any currency isn't much, and I decided not to spend money on a taxi. A sign indicated the #900 bus to downtown Glasgow departed every half hour for a fixed price of one pound, seventy-five pence. I took the bus. The ride took about twenty minutes; it depressed the shit out of me. Three types of building dominated Glasgow: original Victorian era houses, pre- and post-industrial terraces, WWII prefabricated homes, and brutal 1970s urban experiments. Indiscriminate dirt and grime covered them all. A nationalist, either ignorant of my origins, or hiding a racist bent, said Glasgow's buildings had been "turned into slums by foreigners." After meeting many native Glaswegians, few of whom radiated health, cleanliness, or pride of ownership, I doubted the nationalist claim.

The bus ride ended at Buchanan Street Bus Station. Another decrepit, dirty edifice. I got off the bus and followed some other passengers to a cafe. I asked for coffee, but the server told me a "wee cup o tee" would be better for the rain and the cold. Uncaring, I accepted the tea and made for a vinyl covered, metal chair tucked under a small, square table in front of an unwashed window. The chair legs, rubber covers long worn through, screeched on the tiled floor. My tea spilled on the wobbly table. I peered through the soiled glass, through the rain, and saw nothing. I thought of Max's wide, teeth-filled smile welcoming me to Vanuatu: no smiles in Glasgow. I threw the thought away.

I sipped the hot, sweet tea. The server had been right. I needed two things as soon as possible: a place to sleep and a job. I thought about my skill set and job options. Three categories came to mind: clear and wait tables, tend bar or wash dishes. Alternatively, test, weigh, cut, package and load/unload any manner of illegal drug. I could also torture people by detaching fingers from hands with a variety of everyday tools, or simply shoot them. Oh, I was also adept at drinking, smoking, and blabbing about secrets. I was also a lousy friend.

On the next table, a well-used copy of the *Glasgow Daily Times* lay discarded and folded open at the classified section. I wasn't the only person looking for a job. No drug trade, torturing, or murdering jobs leapt from the pages, but I found several bar/club/restaurant openings for waiters, line cooks, cleaners, doormen, and coat checkers, etc. Conveniently, or more probably the result of some marketing strategy, the page following the classified section listed accommodation options: bed, bed and breakfast, or bed and meals options. No ads for furnished apartments, houses, or condos. I decided to find a place to sleep first, and given my limited funds, opted for a bed-only place based on mid-range prices.

~ ~ ~ ~

"Clean bed in own room for five pounds a night," claimed the fifteen word ad. Two hundred and twelve Shuna Street, near Possil Park, North East Glasgow. A city area map, posted behind dirty, cracked plastic on the bus station wall, suggested a half-hour walk from the station would put me on Shuna Street. Glasgow hadn't grown in straight grid lines like Canadian towns. Meandering streets, dead ends, cul-de-sacs, crescents and drives conspired to disorient me. Several wrong turns, and an hour and twenty minutes later, I stood in front of one of those original Victorian era houses. Thick grime covered the house, as though not cleaned since first built. Worn steps led me to a peeling front door, which opened before I knocked. A toothless mouth, owned by a disheveled, greasy old man, greeted me with unintelligible words. I caught the words, "follow" and "me."

He shuffled a dim, musty corridor, over threadbare carpet, and halted at a brown door with a white number eight painted crudely off centre. He opened the door, pointed inside, and waited indifferently while I surveyed the Spartan contents: bed, chair, table, coat stand, lamp and a small rug placed over a scuffed and stained wooden floor. Faded beige curtains hung from the top of the window frame to the floor on either side of a once white radiator. I turned to ask a question, but met the departing back of the old man as he ambled deeper into his labyrinth. He stopped and pointed at another brown door - WC/MEN.

Satisfied with his tour duties, he brushed past me to the front door. He stood waiting. "Da ya want the room or nay?" When I nodded, a hand shot out from his side, open. I placed five pounds in the hand. The hand remained open, and he said, "Three day's is the rule." I gave him ten more pounds, and he produced a key from his pocket. He gave me the key and a curt, "Good day ta ya, laddie." I returned to the room, lay down, and slept until the following morning.

~ ~ ~ ~

For two days I criss-crossed Glasgow via foot and bus to fifteen or more bars and restaurants. Each had listed various service industry jobs in the classified section of Wednesday's *Daily Times*. No one wanted me.

The old man appeared early Friday evening to collect three more days' rent. His eyes lingered on my crumpled newspaper and circled ads and he said, "Try the garage." Two hours later I figured he meant The Garage: a huge student bar located underground in large, stone walled rooms with three separate bars and an enormous dance floor. The Garage was located on Buchanan Street, two blocks from the bus station! More familiar with the streets, I arrived in twenty-eight minutes.

Posted on the outside wall, a hand-written sign informed patrons of the cover charges: three pounds from 8 p.m. till 10 p.m., and five pounds from 10 p.m. to 1 a.m. I checked the time. 7:30 p.m. I went in.

I sipped beers, listened to the music, and observed: heavy drinking, marijuana smoking, pill popping, prostitution and a lot of young people having fun. Scuffles and fights were roughly dealt with by large, unattractive men wearing black tee shirts with the words Staff and Security written on them. Uncomfortable being sober, I left at midnight.

The Garage opened at 11 a.m. I returned the next morning and sought the bartender. I explained the old man at my rooming house suggested I ask for a job. The bartender raised an eyebrow, laughed, and said, "He tells everyone to come here." Despondent, I turned to leave. "Are you Australian?" he asked.

"No. I'm Canadian. My name is Alan." I forgot I had arrived in Scotland as British Karl Robinson, not Alan from Canada. So I became Alan Robinson!

"I'm Matt. I'm from New Zealand," he said.

"How long you been here?"

"Four days," I said.

"You okay with washing glasses, mopping the floor, and shit like that?"

"Yeah, whatever it takes," I said.

"Hold on."

A few minutes later he returned and told me to come back at 5 p.m.

At 5 o'clock I returned. Matt still tended bar. He showed me around, explained my job, and gave me my equipment and instructions:

"Mop, bucket, tray, a few cloths, and a black tee shirt with the letters STAFF on the back and front. Cruise the bar, collect dirty glasses, take them to the kitchen and run them through the washer. Dry them, take them to the bar, and stack them. Clean up any spills with the mop and empty the ash trays."

Uncomplicated grunt work. I started at 5 p.m. and finished at 4 a.m. Wednesday through Saturday, with Sunday through Tuesday off. I became eighty per cent nocturnal, only venturing out on Monday afternoons and Tuesday day. That was my life. Four nights a week, eleven hours per night, for one hundred and thirty pounds cash per week. I had no energy, no time, and no one to go anywhere, or do anything, with. I paid thirty-five pounds a week for my room and about fifteen pounds for food. By the end of two months I had saved several hundred pounds. This had become a problem because I had to keep the money in my pockets, as I didn't trust leaving anything valuable in my room. Later, echoing lessons learned from Fred, I opened two bank accounts. One as myself, and one as Karl Robinson.

Lemming-like, I gravitated to Glasgow's service industry sub-culture. Centred on alcohol, drugs, and sex I quickly fit in. But while allowed to drink, smoke, and fuck with the rest of them, it took much longer to gain people's trust: Glaswegians are a distrustful lot to begin with, even more so when it comes to their criminal activities. More than a year of glass collecting and cleaning up spilt beer and puke passed before Matt asked if I wanted to earn a little extra money. When I said yes, without asking what I had to do for it, Matt told me I would be a "shipment lookout."

Based on my Vanuatu drug experiences, and the activities in The Garage, I had a pretty fair idea what I would be "looking out" for, but I feigned ignorance. Matt provided clear instruction: "Stand where you're told, watch what and where you're told to watch. Squeeze this button three times if there is anything we should be worried about. Don't speak into the radio; only squeeze the button three times."

Easy. Money for nothing. Every week, sometimes twice, I had "lookout" duties for a drug transfer. Either in dark alleyways, where heroin on trucks from Amsterdam dropped off packages, or at the River Clyde docks where ships from Ireland brought Asian cocaine. Twice, I stood beside train tracks as cartons of Ecstasy pills flew from darkened freight cars. A variety of methods and places were used to collect drugs. I admired their coordination and discipline. Everyone knew what to do, and did it without question.

Lookout duties lasted for three or four months. I didn't fuck up, so I was given a position loading and unloading. Déjà vu! I handled that task without issue, and was gradually trusted with more knowledge and greater responsibility.

Mr. Grey raised an eyebrow.

Yeah, yeah, I know. I hadn't forgotten what happened in Vanuatu. But what could I do? I was good at drugs and I liked the money. I moved out of my one-room place into a three room flat with my own bathroom. I enjoyed living the good life again. One thing, though. I really did keep my mouth shut.

~ ~ ~ ~

Glasgow, dirty and shitty, had been good to me. I had a place to live, a job, and money. I drank and smoked modestly, most of the time, and got laid at will. More importantly, my nightmares about Julie, and the unbidden visits from my mother, while more intense, had become less frequent. Sometimes, a whole month passed before my subconscious reasserted its mastery and crushed me with memories and imaginations. Yet absent memories provided mixed blessings: I wanted to think about Julie and my mother. I had loved them. But within me a tide of shame and guilt swamped and choked the love with vile images of my actions and distorted imaginations of an unforgiving and pain-filled mother: consciously I could not think of them. Unconsciously, I had no choice.

"Don't tell me. Too good to last?" said Mr. Grey.

"Yeah. Two good years, then I was on the run again."

"I thought you kept your mouth shut?"

"I did. Remember back in Vanuatu? Bill's rule that greedy people get punished. The Glaswegians used the same rule book."

"Oh. Did you…?"

"No. Not me."

"So tell me."

Forty kilos of cannabis had to be unloaded from the trunk of a car wreck. Wrecked cars were another creative way to move drugs. A car from the destination city would be driven to the import city, in this case Liverpool. The car would be deliberately crashed into a wall to smash the front end. The trunk, intact, would be loaded with drugs. The car would be hitched to a tow truck and brought back to the destination city: a wrecked car on the back of a tow truck was an unlikely target for law enforcement attention.

A regular shipment, except my first as boss. Big Mac, a cruel, street-worn man, ran The Garage drug business. He said this shipment would be a chance for me to show him I was ready for more responsibility. "Don't fuck up," had been his parting words.

The tow truck arrived, and I positioned the look-outs, readied the money, and signalled Jumbo, my unloader, to get the drugs from the trunk of the wrecked car. Jumbo waddled toward the car. He didn't make it. Flame, sparks, black smoke and a boom ended Jumbo's waddle; I thought a firework had gone off. The firework travelled horizontally twenty feet, from point of origin, to Jumbo's midriff. Jumbo jumped up and back. An unnatural movement, impossible for a man his size.

Another firework flew into my car's rear window. The clutch let go and the car, driven by Specky, left me exposed in the road. My eyes tracked the trajectory of the firework to its origin. Two short, pipe-like objects, smoke drifting from their open ends, jutted from a shadow. A gloved hand reached from the shadow and grasped the pipes. Click, the pipes folded down and pointed at the ground. Pop, two cartridges ejected. The hand withdrew back into shadow. Rustle, tinkle. No more clues needed. I didn't wait to witness another discharge from the barrel of a sawed-off shotgun. I ran. Wildly, until I stopped a taxi and headed back to The Garage.

The car, its blown out rear window and pellet dented body, stood askew near the rear entrance to The Garage. Specky, the driver, smoke and drink in shaky hands, sat at the bar. The lookouts had run, and Jumbo, the unloader, was full of holes. I joined Specky at the bar, grabbed a drink, and sucked air. The lookouts arrived a few minutes later. We waited.

I thought being shot at, robbed, and scared shitless was bad enough. Sure, serious questions would be asked. What the fuck had the lookouts seen? What happened to the drugs, the money? Who talked? I expected to be grilled, but I wasn't prepared for what happened. I wasn't prepared for Big Mac.

I shouted at Specky for leaving me in the road, but before he could answer, Matt told us to go to the basement. The basement had a sub-basement. The sub-basement had a room; a quiet place to dole out punishment. I hadn't given the room much thought until I walked, sweating, toward the thick wooden door. Matt followed.

~ ~ ~ ~

"Don't fuck up," Big Mac said. Well, I fucked up. As "boss" of the drug transfer, I entered the room first. Alone. My breath misted in the cold air. Moss and mildew eked an existence between the cracks and gaps of the exposed brick and boulder walls. Viscous brown moisture slid into minute droplets, before dripping from brick to brick. Pervasive dampness smothered everything. A matched set of steel table and two chairs huddled together in the room's centre. Both scratched and dented. One of the chairs had been set into a square block of cement. Immovable. Make-shift wiring brought power to a single, un-shaded light bulb.

I sat on the immovable metal chair. Matt, voice cracking, said Lenny would be along shortly. The mention of Lenny scared the shit out of me. Lenny was the head doorman, or bouncer, at The Garage. Huge, lumbering, violent. Lenny stopped fights between drunk or doped-up university students; he broke arms and hands indiscriminately until calm had been restored. Visions of the plastic room in Vanuatu, and my role in its horrors swam in my head.

Lenny entered the room. His bulk smothered the other chair. Cold, indifferent eyes, like my eyes when I detached and mangled fingers in Vanuatu, studied me. Fear squeezed my intestines. Behind Lenny came Big Mac, number one in The Garage pecking order. He ran The Garage and associated "business" for Glasgow George, the undisputed drug king of East Glasgow.

The first time I met Big Mac, I thought thug. Every feature of his face had been rearranged in some way or another, and scarred hands, and swollen knuckles, spoke of his past. A squat, uncompromising man with a countenance that transmitted sadistic perversion. An intimidating, cruel man.

Lenny had no subtlety. He asked what had happened, and I told my story. After me, Specky and the lookouts had their turn in the room, and presumably told their version of events. After everyone had been questioned, I returned to the room to face Big Mac. He explained how things would be handled:

"Here's how I figure it. First, the good news. I believe your version of events, and accept you had nothing to do with the ambush, or who was responsible. Why would you go to such lengths and potential trouble for a mere forty kilos when you have information on much larger and more valuable shipments? Second, the bad news; you were in charge and you will have to sort it out."

I parted my lips to say thanks, but he cut me off with a flick of his hand.

"I doubt Jumbo was in on it because he wouldn't have gotten himself killed. That leaves you, the lookouts, and Specky. So, it is your job to ask them all again how this happened. Of course, if none of them knows who is responsible, I'll have to have Lenny talk some more with you."

So there it was. I either got the "truth" from Specky, or one of the lookouts, or the "truth" would be gotten from me.

I looked into Big Mac's eyes, and Lenny stared back: peas in a pod. I thought about Vanuatu, the plastic room, my talents for meting out punishment and obtaining the "truth." Resigned, I said, "I will need some tools." If Big Mac had been surprised, he didn't show it. I listed the tools I wanted, and he said Lenny would bring them in an hour.

~ ~ ~ ~

Ten minutes after Lenny delivered the tools, he returned with Dave, one of the lookouts. Dave was about nineteen, thin, spotty, and scared to death. I felt his fear. All I would have to do is show him the drill and the poor bastard would tell me anything. Anything not to be hurt, and anything but the truth. I told Lenny I wanted Specky first. Lenny shrugged and took whimpering Dave away.

Specky seemed scared all right but cocky too; something about his manner said he was scared but not worried. I soon discovered why. Like Vanuatu, I had Lenny secure Specky to the chair and fix his arms to the table. I set the bag on the table and took out the tools one at a time, making sure Specky had plenty of time to consider what might happen. All this time Specky stared at Lenny, expectantly. Lenny remained motionless and impassive in the corner.

While Specky silently called to Lenny, I whipped up the claw hammer and brought it down on Specky's left hand thumb. For a second, Specky did not react. Specky neither spoke nor moved. Then he screamed at Lenny, not me. He shouted, "What the fuck is going on?" Lenny smiled, inhuman, and said, "You had better tell him."

While Specky and Lenny had their moment, I slipped into autopilot, and without waiting for Specky to say anything else, I placed hacksaw to skin and sawed through his index finger. In response, Specky gushed words as fast as the blood gushed from his severed finger.

He barked that he, Jumbo, and that fucker Lenny, had done the job. He and Jumbo made the plan, but Lenny had arranged the shooter. One of the lookout kids would take the fall. Lenny would get a confession.

"What the fuck is going on, Lenny?" said Specky.

I turned to Lenny. He nodded and opened the door. Big Mac strode in and said to me, "Ya did good, laddie. Now run along and have yourself a drink. Lenny will tidy up in here."

~ ~ ~ ~

One drink later, Big Mac joined me at the bar. He explained what had happened.

"I suspected Specky and Jumbo of skimming product and money. In order to test my suspicions, I had Lenny pretend he was dissatisfied with his lot and approach Specky and Jumbo with an offer to score big by stealing a large shipment. Specky and Jumbo fell for Lenny's offer. I decided to use your first time as boss to expose Specky and Jumbo. I also thought it would be good to take your measure and watch how you handled yourself in such a situation.

"Specky and Jumbo asked Lenny to arrange for a shooter to show up, flash the gun, and make you hand over the money and the drugs. When you came back, Specky would suggest one of the new kids had acted a bit suspicious. Lenny would then use his talents to get the kid to 'confess' and blame the ambush on the Miller Brothers who run drugs on the south side. The kid would be disposed of, and Specky, Jumbo, and Lenny would split the goods and wait for another opportunity."

I sipped more booze. I wanted a joint.

"Lenny was supposed to shoot both of them, but Specky got away and well, I saw a chance to improvise.

I thought it would be a good chance to test you. And I was right, eh, lad? I don't want to know where you learned to chop fingers, but I think that from now on you would be more useful to me with your little bag of tools than running around with bags of dope."

With that explanation, and no choice, Big Mac laughed and called me his "Handy Man." The name stuck. The job became regular.

My return to severing people's digits at Big Mac's behest brought my nightmares back with a vengeance. There seemed to be a connection between the pain I inflicted, and the intensity and frequency of my own nightmares. The more I hurt people, the more vibrant and vivid my nightmares became. Each part of my sordid crime revealed itself in ever increasing details until I could see Julie either beneath me, or strapped to the stretcher in still monochrome photographs. Each one slowly revealing lines of pain, betrayal, and abandonment on Julie's face. Hell had found me again.

For twelve months I was Big Mac's Handy Man: dispassionately dispensing drug justice to those unfortunate enough to cross Big Mac. Then, in late 1999, I got a break. Big Mac, Lenny, and two hookers died in an apparent car accident. They had been driving back from a night in Edinburgh when their BMW 5 inexplicably left the road on the A 229 and careened down a gully, and like all good movie scenes, burst into flames. There wasn't much of a police investigation and rumour suggested Glasgow George had begun to suspect Big Mac and Lenny were getting too ambitious for their boots, and, well, the drug business didn't have a retirement plan.

Afraid I might be accused of something by association, I packed my bags and set off in the one direction I thought no one would think I would possibly go.

North. My reasoning was, who in their right mind would run away to the north of Scotland and allow themselves to be trapped? The other part of my reasoning was that I had been planning just such a run for several months, and had, in fact, a place to run to.

CHAPTER 9

The North Sea

Mr. Grey laughed at the name Handy Man. He mumbled something about life and how things turn out and said, "Okay, you got me. Where the fuck can you run to in Northern Scotland? You were already in Glasgow. That's probably the last civilised city north of England."

"Yeah, well, I'd gotten a bit smarter since I fucked up in Vanuatu. A Handy Man job for Big Mac had a limited shelf-life. A bad end awaited me. I mean, how long could I smash hands before someone came for me one night? That, or Big Mac would start to think I knew too much, and maybe Lenny would 'tidy me up,' like he did with Specky. Either way, I started planning six months before Big Mac and Lenny took early retirement."

"Don't tell me. You read another travel magazine?"

"Yes and no. The idea started with a couple of guys in the bar. They came to buy marijuana and told me they planned to resell it to oil rig workers for a fat profit. Rig workers, they said, paid a premium for weed because it was difficult to get the dope on the oil rig. Workers and their bags were subject to random searches. They got a lifetime ban if caught taking dope to a rig, as well as possible criminal charges. Although few received criminal charges because rig owners didn't want any negative publicity. I didn't learn until much later how dope got onto oil rigs, but our conversation got me interested in oil rigs, and so yes, I did buy a magazine. It was called *Offshore*."

"*Offshore*? Sounds like a money laundering magazine," said Mr Grey.

"*Offshore* provided information about the North Sea oil industry. How the industry had experienced growth, and how a shortage of workers needed to be addressed. Articles described life on a rig, and emphasised the isolation of rig life, and how disconnected from the world a worker would be, especially if he had a job as a roustabout."

"What's a roustabout then?"

"Ah, that's what got my attention too. On an oil rig, roustabouts are at the bottom of the totem pole. They do all the grunt work. Kinda like a labourer who does all the unskilled work on a building site. On a rig, the roustabout maintains things like oil lead lines, stock tanks, salt water disposal pumps, lease roads, lease mowing, dikes around tank batteries, and all sorts of other crap. Of course I didn't know anything about all this stuff, but the magazine had articles and advertisements about roustabout and offshore safety training courses."

Mr. Grey regarded Alan sceptically and said, "Are you trying to tell me you planned to go from being a drug trade enforcer to a 'dog's body' on an oil rig in the North Sea?"

"Yes. The way you are thinking is exactly how I thought anyone in the Glasgow drug trade, who might be looking for me, would think: no fucking way Handy Man would head out to a North Sea oil rig. Besides, I thought working on a rig would be an adventure. And that's where I went.

"First, I got trained. Sort of. I didn't exactly take all the courses, though. An ex-oil rig worker gave me a three-day crash course for 500 pounds. He also provided genuine certificates proving I had taken, and passed, all the required courses."

"'Don't worry, '" he told me, "'even though enforcement of training regulations has been tightened since the massive gas explosion on the Piper Alpha rig in 1988 when one hundred and sixty-seven people died, it is all bullshit. On the surface, the need for training has increased a lot, but 'certification' is more important. As long as you have a certificate proving you have been trained then everyone, meaning the oil rig owners and managers, is covered in the event of an accident.'

"He also told me if an accident happened on a rig, I probably wouldn't be around to worry about the quality of my training or the validity of my certificates. I thought he was being a bit dramatic to scare me. He wasn't, though. North Sea oil rigs are dangerous. To muddy the waters a little, I got the certificates in my own name. In Glasgow I had been Alan Robinson, Handy Man. Who would search for Alan Davies, roustabout?"

~ ~ ~ ~

In mid-November, 1999, I slipped out of Glasgow and headed to Peterhead, 51 Kilometers northeast of Aberdeen, on Scotland's east coast. Peterhead, according to *Offshore*, was the major hub town for the North Sea oil industry. Everything and everyone related to the oil industry went through this town at some point. *Offshore* also reported how a man, with the required certification, could find a rig job in Peterhead.

Offshore was right. I secured a job at the first place I applied. Aside from the shortage of workers, I found a job because of the time of year: November. I hadn't given much thought to the weather in the North Sea. Scotland has shit weather, even in summer. I had gotten used to grey clouds, cold winds, and constant dampness, but I hadn't thought about the difference between on-shore weather and off-shore weather. Many seasoned rig workers left the North Sea in November for extended leaves, or quit with the hope, or expectation, they would be hired back in the spring. With more roustabout openings than takers, my certificates were noted, and I was hired.

Jock, the man who interviewed and hired me, said I would leave at 5 a.m. on Thursday, November 23, weather permitting. He said I needed some kit. He gave me a typed list of essentials, and the name of supply stores in town where I should buy the stuff. Excited to have a job, and relieved I would be heading off into the anonymity of the North Sea, I didn't give much thought to the little phrase "weather permitting." A North Sea understatement, which after a few weeks on a rig, I began to fully appreciate.

~ ~ ~ ~

Five a.m., on a wet Thursday, November 23, 1999, I entered the Delta Oil and Gas company offices. Jock, red faced and stocky, told me to go through to the waiting room and make myself comfortable. Four other men arrived. Each carried a kit bag. Their bags, stained and crumpled, conveyed much more experience than the crisp, clean beige of my new kit bag. The men, less stained, but a little crumpled in the early morning, also radiated experience.

They exchanged familiar nods and quiet greetings, as though by some unspoken agreement they had decided 5 a.m. on a cold, waterlogged, morning did not merit the expenditure of any more energy. No one spoke to me, but they scrutinised, exchanging opinions and thoughts through facial and body language: opinions which appeared to range from indifference to resignation, but not hostility. Months later, I would sit, stained and crumpled, and silently evaluate wide-eyed newbies with clean kit bags as they awaited their first flight to an oil rig. Poor bastards.

Jock entered, nodded to the four veterans, introduced me, said I was their new roustabout, and reminded them to be gentle with me, as this was my first time. The men nodded, stated their names, and fixed me with more direct stares.

The whomp of helicopter blades saved us from the awkward silence that often follows such scenes. All eyes focused on the window, transfixed by the glare of the forward spotlight of a Super Puma helicopter illuminating the white and blue helipad before landing with a bump, and wave of spray.

I flinched as the rotor down draft hurled puddles from the overnight rain against the window. Jock, and the four men, hoisted their kit bags and walked into another room. I followed and watched them struggle into survival suits. My three day off-shore training with the ex oil rig worker had described these suits and explained no one could fly on a helicopter to a rig without wearing one. My crash course had not included trying one on. I waited, awkwardly trying to remember if Jock's equipment list had included a survival suit. I guess not because Jock pointed to a suit hanging on a hook and told me to get a move on before the weather changed.

Okay, I thought, *what's the hurry? Let's wait until the weather gets better.* Later, I realised, Jock was talking about the weather getting worse, not better, and he wasn't joking.

I struggled to walk and carry my kit bag in the survival suit, but I followed Jock and the others to the helicopter and climbed aboard. I had never been in a helicopter before. Had I known what a helicopter flight would be like, I wouldn't have stepped on the helipad, let alone climbed aboard. The first clue of imminent unpleasantness was when Jock told me to sit in the back on my own. The second was the three puke bags he pushed into my hand.

The noise of the rotors, the engine, the wind, and the crack of loud radio talk made me dizzy before we lifted off. Alone in the back, like a bag of dirty laundry, I felt the vibrations of accelerating rotors rattle my teeth and clamped my mouth shut. My stomach wobbled in and out, up and down, until it seemed to be everywhere at once. Through the tiny window, and before I shut my eyes, the coastline disappeared from view; my last conscious thought being, "If we crash in the ocean, I won't survive."

I didn't take a first step on the oil rig. I crawled. On hands and knees I followed the yellow floor markings to a door, patiently held open for me by Jock. I inched through and slumped down against the cold, hard metal of the rig. "Not bad for ya first time, laddie. Wait till we have a bad weather day, though. That's something else altogether." I looked at Jock in disbelief, thinking that wasn't very funny. He wasn't being funny, though. My first helicopter ride to the rig had been bland by North Sea standards, but as the winter wore on, the rides became much worse.

~ ~ ~ ~

Jock allowed me a half hour to put my stomach back in place. Then he came for me. First, we toured the living quarters and I was assigned a small room of my own. I tossed in my kit bag and Jock took me topside to the platform. He introduced me to other rig workers, Derek, Davey, Roger, Sven, Paddy and the captain, and showed me where I would spend most of my working time. I already had an idea from my "training" of what I would most likely be doing, but none of the descriptions prepared me for the noise, activity, and danger of the drill platform.

Back at the door of my room, Jock handed me a thick binder and said, "Read and remember. It might save your life." For five hours I studied and memorised the rig layout, emergency exits, safety equipment, staging points for evacuation, and practised putting on my cold water survival suit. Derek Miller, the three year veteran roustabout I had met topside, came by and introduced himself again. He would give me on-site training for the first few weeks until I got the hang of things.

Noise, vibration, claustrophobic rooms and passageways, stale inside air, and nervousness ate my mind. By lunch time of the second day, doubt engulfed me; I had made a terrible mistake. At 4:30 Jock, whom I learned was the Driller, and as such, the leader of the drill team to which I belonged, told me my first shift would start at midnight. I had better get some rest.

Sleep would not come. I worried I would fuck up badly and I was afraid something nasty would happen. Derek came to wake me at 11:30 p.m. I didn't want to get up. I wanted to stay warm and safe in my bed.

Derek gave me three seconds of sympathy. Then he yelled, "Get the fuck up and at it," which turned out to be one of his favourite expressions. Over and over all night, and for the next ten days or so, Derek shouted, "Get the fuck up and at it," until I began to do things right. Doing things right changed Derek's motivational technique to a more encouraging, 'Come on then, Alan. Up and at it, lad."

My main duties were to clean, maintain, paint, remove, move, fetch, carry and all other manner of menial tasks. When I was done with these, I kept the deck clean and clear of hazards, moved equipment around the rig, connected sections of pipe for the well, rigged and slung loads being moved by the rig's crane, and pretty much anything else anyone needed doing. Hard, uncomplicated work, but a lot better than working for Big Mac in Glasgow. After a few days I laughed to myself because, in a way, I was still a "Handy Man."

Two weeks after I crawled my way from the helicopter, I donned my survival suit for the flight shoreside and two weeks' rest. Eleven twelve hour, midnight to noon, shifts had exhausted me. I needed a rest. I didn't need puke bags for the return ride, and with my eyes open this time, I appreciated the bright afternoon sun, calm winds, and rolling sea. Through snatched and overheard conversations, I learned my team members all had plans for their two week leave:

Jock would be in Edinburgh with his wife, and Davey would be in Newcastle with his; Derek planned to consume his usual ration of sexual deprivation in London's Soho district while Sven would go home to Denmark for more wholesome "girls and adventure." The captain said he would be in Manchester visiting some "mates," and Roger would be with his mother in Blackpool, on the West Coast. Paddy evasively said he also had a wife to visit. A few months later Derek told me Paddy had two wives; one in Dublin and one in Belfast, and he visited each on alternate shore leaves!

I had no plans. I had been holding out for some kind of invite from one of the team, but I guess that while I had done okay I hadn't made the grade for that kind of friendship. As I got to know them more, I understood how, after two weeks of living on top of one another, everyone wanted to get away and have their own space. Yet, I also learned the reverse was true. After the two weeks' leave, everyone looked forward to returning "home" to the rig. After a few months, I began to understand the feelings and emotions rig life gave a person. Even though many psychiatrists described rig life as a dysfunctional family, it was a family nonetheless, and it had been a long time since I had any family.

~ ~ ~ ~

We landed. Goodbyes were quick. I remained alone outside the company hanger. The pilot, Nick Porter, after completing a visual walk around his helicopter, came over and said, "You must be the new roustabout. Derek said you did pretty well." I needed a positive word, and I guess my face showed relief because he continued, "Don't worry, kid; everyone's first time is hell. Listen, you're with one of the best teams in the field. Jock is the best drill team leader in the North Sea. Watch, listen, and learn and you'll do well. I guess you didn't make any plans for your two week leave, eh? Not to worry. You should head into town to O'Grady's. It's a decent pub, and the owner, Gregor McTavish, lets rooms for a reasonable price. Tell him you work with Jock, and he will fix you up."

With a wave and a smile, the pilot climbed back in the cockpit and started his pre-flight checks. I humped my kit bag over my shoulder and started to walk toward town. About halfway, a van stopped and gave me a ride to O'Grady's pub.

O'Grady's was old. Not run down but old. White plaster walls, dark beams, lead lined windows, thick wooden doors and a slate roof. Signs, inside and out, listed a wide variety of regional and international beers, lots of genuine single malt scotch, and basic home-cooked food.

I entered and met Gregor McTavish. Two hours before noon and business was slow. McTavish polished glasses behind the bar, and introduced himself as soon as I entered. An imposing bull, with a no-nonsense but friendly demeanour. He shook my hand with meaning, listened attentively when I explained how I worked with Jock on the rig, and how I needed a room for two weeks. Jock's name opened his face. He motioned me to sit down, telling me he would be back with some-thing for me to eat.

Half an hour later I had eaten, drank beer, and McTavish had shown me to a plain but clean room at the back of the pub. "The view," said McTavish, "is Peterhead Bay." The price included breakfast, dinner, and twenty-four hour access via a side door which allowed entry without having to go through the pub itself.

For the first forty-eight hours, I succumbed to my off-shore conditioning and slept by day and paced the deserted streets and my room by night. By day three, I had started to adjust and began venturing out during the day like a normal person.

Living above a pub brought temptation. On the rig, I had not drunk alcohol, or smoked anything more than a cigarette. Two weeks was the longest I had been without either since I had arrived at the Banff Springs Hotel in the winter of 1992.

With no plans and knowing no one, I played tourist. I became familiar with the town's buildings and surrounding area. Most buildings had been built with red granite stone, and boasted interesting and unusual architecture. Especially the Parish Kirk built in 1804, and the Town House built in 1788, which had a tall steeple and a four-faced clock. To the northwest of town, beside the River Ugie, I visited the remains of the Inverugie and Ravenscraig castles. I also took long walks on Peterhead's beautiful beaches and rugged cliffs. Like so many others, I was inspired and cleansed by the brisk North Sea air and the relentless, cold wind that blew perpetually landward from the sea.

Gregor McTavish remained unobtrusive, never asking much or offering much in return. Yet he was always friendly, willing to provide advice on how to get somewhere, or what I should look out for, or avoid.

My two weeks' shore leave ended sooner than I had wanted. I had reunited with drink and smoke, but in moderation. I felt real regret at leaving O'Grady's, and the stark town I had begun to think of as a home. I had, without intending to, found peace and security in Peterhead. I left, looking forward to my return.

Gregor called me a taxi and carried my kit bag out to the parking lot. He wished me a safe trip and with a chuckle, "Merry Christmas and a Happy New Year!" I was puzzled for a moment until I realised it was December 21st. I would spend Christmas and New Year's Eve off-shore. I couldn't imagine what Christmas and New Year's Eve would be like on an oil rig, but it didn't matter much, because I'm sure whatever I might have imagined would not have come close to what actually happened.

While the events of the festive season revealed the darker side of oil rig life and set the tone for the next three years of my off-shore/on-shore life, they also stimulated friendships and camaraderie that would forever change and influence my life.

~ ~ ~ ~

We departed the company hanger at 5 a.m. An uneventful flight, except for an air of expectation and mischievousness among my fellow drill team members. Nothing explicit; a vibe, a sense of expectancy. A twelve hour, midnight to noon shift, waited for me: a different expectancy.

Derek had worked and trained me for the first two weeks. Now he would work a 6 p.m. to 6 a.m. shift, which meant from 6 a.m. to noon, I would be on my own. Apart from my nervousness, I had no problems. I ended my shift tired but not exhausted as I had been during my first two weeks. I had found my "rig legs" and developed some muscle and stamina. At shift's end, my routine was to shower and eat before relaxing with either music, video games, or occasionally reading. With tension calmed, I would collapse into bed until woken by my alarm at 11 p.m.

On December 22, after my shower, I sat down in the mess to eat. Jock entered and sat next to me. He asked about my on-shore leave and his friend Gregor McTavish. He also wanted to know how I thought my first two weeks had gone. Did I have questions, or concerns, about rig work, or the team? Hesitant at first, worried I had done or said something, but detecting no deception in Jock's eyes, I told him the truth.

"The first two weeks were hell. I was scared and nervous for the first few days, and to be honest, I would have left the rig without a second thought. But after a week, and with Derek's help, I began, at least I thought so, to get the hang of things. I was still scared of being on the open platform in bad weather."

Jock nodded and agreed I had picked things up well. He told me Derek had confidence in me. "Being scared of the platform," said Jock, "is good. Respect for the danger can save your life."

I thought the discussion ended, but Jock went on to explain the importance of the drill team, and how everyone cared for each other.

"Rig life," said Jock, "is hard. People need distractions to help them cope with the on-shift risks, off-shift boredom, and the psychological effects of shift work and isolation."

I wasn't following.

"Look, Alan, it's Christmas in a couple of days and then New Year's Eve. The rig will be a bit different this week. Some things will be happen that you probably thought never would occur on a rig. A lot of these things go on all the time. You were too exhausted on your first off-shore rotation to notice. What I'm saying is, Alan, accept what happens at the least, and don't say anything about it, or if you prefer, join the rest of us, and you'll be welcome."

I still didn't understand. I started to ask Jock what he was talking about, but he held up his hand and said,

"On Christmas Eve you will start work at 8 p.m. instead of midnight. You will still work until noon the next day. Also, you will sit in my control office, and not be out on the drill platform. You will monitor the pressure and flow indicators. If anything appears wrong, you come and find me. Don't worry. Derek will show you what to do."

Jock got up and left me to my thoughts. They tumbled through me, creating all kinds of fucked-up images of what the hell he had been talking about. A horrible thought, about some kind of gay sex circle, ran through my mind. Unless the whole rig was going to explode, I would not leave the control office to find Jock and maybe run into the psychological effects of shift work, and discover how the team handled off-shore boredom. No fucking way!

~ ~ ~ ~

Christmas Eve afternoon. Anticipation hummed throughout the rig; drill teams, rescue teams, engineers, cooks, all grinning and winking. The conversation with Jock left me nervous. The twinkle in people's eyes brought a disjointed jumble of Jock's words to my mind: caring for each other; people need distractions, psychological effects; some things will happen; they happen all the time; accept what happens and join in if you want. Drugs, prostitution, gay sex or all the above; what the fuck was going to happen? I kept my head down and waited until Derek came to get me at 7:45 p.m. for my 8 p.m., sixteen hour shift.

Derek took me to the drill master/team leader's control room, or Jock's room. A square room, windows on all sides, located on the south side of the platform, had a good view of the entire rig. Derek pointed to various dials, indicators, and screens and explained what each did. Too much information. Derek recognised my confusion and potential panic.

"Don't worry, Alan. You only watch two instruments: the pressure and flow indicators. Both indicators are electro-pneumatic. They express information with numbers, and either blue, green, yellow or red colours. If either of them moves out of green, into any other colour, pick up the phone and call the mess. If no one answers the phone, use the two-way radio. Still no answer, then 'run like fuck' and find Jock, or one of the others. Do you understand?"

For sixteen hours, I had to monitor the indicators. I wanted to ask under what circumstances no one would answer the phone or radio, but I didn't get the chance. Derek gave me a wink and said, "Don't worry, kid. It's your turn on New Year's Eve!" Derek closed the door and left me bathed in the light of the two glowing green indicators. I didn't know if he had meant anything, but saying, "It's your turn on New Year's Eve" scared me more than the pressure and flow indicators.

~ ~ ~ ~

Quiet. Only the low hum of electro-pneumatic sensors, com-puter equipment, and cooling fans. Sixty-three dials, gages, and digital displays occupied the room. I counted them. I observed and listened, baffled by the array of information and ignorant of their meaning. Half of one wall held five CCTV screens; three different close-ups of the drilling platform; a wider angle view of the same thing; and a clear image of the helipad.

At 8 p.m., when I entered the control room, CCTV screens showed Paddy, Sven, and the captain, illuminated by the fifty thousand watt lights that bathed the rig twenty-four seven, working the drill. Shortly after 8:30, I watched them disengage the drill from the bore hole and engage the recirculation and venting system. The recirculation system was normally deployed to allow critical maintenance work to be done, or if there was a serious problem with the drill, or other part of the system. Once deployed, oil extraction was essentially "in neutral" with systems on standby until the problem had been fixed, and the actual drill/pump system reengaged.

The moment the recirculation and venting system engaged in the majority of the sixty-three dials, gages, and display systems in the control room changed from "numbers" to "pause" or "hold" or "stopped," I panicked. I was poised to call for help until I checked the pressure and flow indicators: both green.

My anxiety subsided. I sought reassurance from the CCTV screen. The drill platform was deserted. No one. I was alone. Encapsulated in a soundproof room on an oil rig, in the North Sea, on Christmas Eve, with who knew what going on in the mess. Not only that, but I had an overwhelming weight of responsibility; if anything happened to the rig it would be my fault. I wanted a drink. Or better still, a drink and a joint. Instead, my mother came to visit.

Jock's control room was hot. My attention shifted between the screens, the dials, the rig, and the ocean white caps. The paranoia of what might be going on, and the weight of the responsibility, battled for attention in my head until a vision of my mother pushed thoughts of the rig aside:

My mother's fingerless hands grappled with the tiller of a small yacht. Ominous black-green waves lapped at the ship's hull. Fred, my murdered friend from Vanuatu, and Julie, my dead sister, sat hand-in-hand on the ship's bow, repeatedly asking each other why I had let them both die. Off the boat's stern, behind my mother, an angry wave reared up and hovered above the vulnerable yacht; faces of the victims who had survived Bill's plastic room in Vanuatu, and Big Mac's basement in Glasgow, floated in the wave screaming at my mother, demanding she stop me torturing them.

Movement on one of the screens ripped me from my guilt. I blinked. Was the image on the screen real, or a bizarre continuation of my confused thoughts? A dozen or more men stood on the helipad, crowding another man. Beside the man stood a red cylindrical bag, propped up at a forty-five degree angle by two black tubes that splayed out from the bag: a golf bag. The man exaggeratedly studied the helipad before holding up a finger to test the wind. Informed, he selected a driver from the bag. He flexed himself and the club. The crowd parted and cheered. A bright orange golf ball sat teed up on one of those green mats used at driving ranges. The man readied himself, stepped forward, swung the club and hit the ball.

I followed the flight of the ball. About one hundred and seventy-five feet from the golf tee, suspended from one of the rigs cranes, hung a fifty foot tall Santa Claus. Santa had three different sized holes in his torso: smallest at the crotch, medium at the navel, and the largest hole forming a toothless mouth. I turned up the volume and pushed my face up against the screen in disbelief. Well hit, the ball flew from its tee toward Santa where, to raised hands and loud cheers, the ball entered Santa's crotch.

Shocked by the spectacle, I sat back and rubbed my eyes some more. More shock followed. Focused on the golf player, I hadn't noticed the cans and bottles in the hands of the spectators. Everyone seemed to be drinking as enthusiastically as the golf club swung. Alcohol! Alcohol on the rig. No fucking way. An immediate dismissal with no chance of getting a rig job ever again. Had they gone mad? Then I laughed. Santa being pounded by golf balls and people drinking was way less threatening than my fear of a drug induced orgy. Christ, I was such a jerk.

~ ~ ~ ~

Irreverent helipad golf was weird enough for me, but the festivities had only just begun. Kite flying followed. I thought flying kites a bit lame after the fun with Santa, until the crossbows came out. I shit you not, man. Fucking crossbows. A man with a crossbow shot arrows at a large fluorescent kite as it swirled over the ocean off the end of the helipad. More kites and crossbows appeared. Money changed hands as bets were made and lost. Drink flowed.

The kites became tangles, and Santa became the target. The arrows punched through Santa, leaving jagged holes for the wind to stretch, reducing Santa to unrecognisable fabric. Santa's remains were cut loose. He disappeared in a dramatic flourish as the wind picked him up and tossed him contemptuously to the ocean. More empty cans and bottles followed Santa. Midnight approached. I thought for sure they must be done and would go inside before anyone got hurt. I was wrong. The best, or at least the most dangerous, entertainment had been saved for last.

Moisture deserted my mouth. Sven, and another guy I didn't recognise, striped down to running shorts, tee shirt, and shoes. What the fuck were they doing? Exposed, the platform would be freezing. The men shook hands, put on gloves, and strutted to the base of the main rig crane. Each took a position on one side. A whistle sounded, men cheered, and Sven and the other man stepped onto the bottom rung of the main support column. They began to climb.

Disbelief. Madness. Crazy. Riveted, I followed the men's progress up the first three rungs of the crane. Between the third and fourth rungs, their height exceeded the range of the CCTV camera, and they passed up and out of sight. I couldn't see them, but I could watch and hear the gesticulations and cheers of the crowd at the base of the crane. The cheering reached a high note, and I guessed someone had made it to the top. Tense, I flicked my attention from crowd to CCTV. Four legs descended into the top of my screen. I peeled my dry lips from my teeth and slumped back in my chair: "Holy fuck!"

Blankets quickly draped Sven and the other climber. Satiated, the crowd dissipated like mist into different doorways. Down into the bowls and safety of the rig. After the unexpected excitement of the crew's festive excesses, silence crushed me. I stared at the pressure and flow indicators, frightened by the thought of the chaos that would occur if an alcohol and drug soaked crew had to confront a crisis.

Overwhelmed and over stimulated, I wasn't sure if I was awake or not between 2 a.m. and 10 a.m. when movement on the drill platform drew me to the CCTV screens. Jock was touching and prodding equipment. He turned to the camera and gave me a wave. Relieved, I waved back and smiled: the rig and the men had survived the Christmas Eve revellry.

Derek arrived early. Blurred eyes and puffy cheeks betrayed his consumption. "Hi, Alan, how did it go last night? Any problems?" Caught off guard by his casualness, I nodded and replied, "No problems. A bit quiet, though." Derek chuckled and said, "You did good, kid. Now go get some rest."

Curiosity made me walk quickly to the mess. I expected to find the place trashed. Instead, everything was clean and tidy, but with a faint odour that reminded me of the morning openings at The Garage in Glasgow. Impressed at their ability to party, and their discipline to remove all evidence, I skipped eating and went directly to my room and bed.

On New Year's Eve, inflatable sex dolls replaced Santa. Golf driver and orange ball gave way to cricket bat and tennis balls. Sling shots usurped crossbows. It was my turn to party and Roger sat in Jock's control room. I remember singing Auld Lang Syne around midnight on the helipad after leading a conga line from the mess, but nothing else.

A few days into January, Derek said I had become upset around 3 a.m. on New Year's Eve when someone loaded violent porn movies, depicting unwilling girls being forced to accept indiscriminate sex with faceless men, in to the movie projector. I had left shouting something about it not being my fault. Derek told me this with an inquiring eyebrow, but I provided no explanation.

~ ~ ~ ~

Christmas, and New Year's Eve, 1999, made and unmade me. I was made by being accepted by the team: welcomed into their family, and trusted with the knowledge of alcohol and drug use, I became a fully complicit member of our small drill team, and an established member of the broader platform crew.

I was unmade because my brief hiatus from drugs and alcohol ended. My affection and reliance on them returned and grew until, like the others, I mastered a perfect and almost symbiotic balance between consumption and work. Like the others, I was never really drunk or too drugged up while on the drill platform. Sure, we all had hangovers, and some sluggishness sometimes, but we seemed to compensate, or auto-adjust, for each other.

Once I had passed the festive initiations, and proved my trustworthiness, I received my indoctrination into the culture of TFA and stock urine samples.

An official unofficial policy, TFA, Touch Fuck All, crudely described the imperative to keep production going at all costs, and not compromise output for frivolous repairs. Or put another way, patch, jimmy, by-pass, or do whatever, to keep oil production going and don't bother with compliance, or adherence to critical maintenance requirements, etc. In extreme cases, this also included falsification of maintenance and safety records.

Stock urine samples enabled rig worker to drink and smoke on the rig. Rig workers would either pro-duce a year's worth, or more, of urine samples during a planned dry, or drug free period. The samples would be refrigerated and used for the scheduled alcohol and drug tests. Alternatively, some workers had friends, or relatives, provide the urine for storage.

When I expressed scepticism, Jock told me testing followed a predictable and regular schedule. The screening tested for alcohol and basic drugs only. No effort to cross reference with gender, age, ethnicity, or any other indicators to provide assurance the urine belonged to the person who handed in the sample. Also, the test was either pass or fail. No records of previous samples, which could have been used for trending analysis or continuity.

"You see," said Jock, "it's all about appearing to do the right thing. Rules say regular urine tests are to be conducted, but the rules don't say anything about how the tests are performed. This way everyone wins."

Everybody didn't win, though. Especially Jock.

~ ~ ~ ~

Acceptance, and enthusiastic participation for "all things according to Jock," led to friendships with all of the drill team, particularly Derek, Sven, and the captain:

Derek, my initial mentor, was an easy friend. Undemanding, non-judgmental, and cheerful we soon developed a jocular, even paced relationship. Sven and I shared common ground: single, early twenties, raised in cold climates, enjoyed hunting and ice hockey. We had lots to share. The captain, older than Derek and Sven, seemed to like me for some reason. In some loose, undefined way, he became a kind of cool fatherly figure who provided life advice based on a liberal and contextual interpretation of the *British Army's Code of Conduct* book.

With a veritable "drip feed" of alcohol and marijuana, my off-shift time focused on video games and music; activities which complemented drinking and smoking. Games of choice included StarCraft and Turok 2. StarCraft allowed me be a master strategist, playing one alien, or sub-human race, off against another. In Turok 2 I blasted the shit out of everything and anything that moved. StarCraft with marijuana, Turok 2 with alcohol; my alter egos competed for dominance.

Music. Loud and continuous, edged out the monotonous game sounds. The Eurhythmics, Pet Shop Boys, and David Bowie supported StarCraft. On Derek's advice, The Stranglers, The Clash, and The Jam provided the required pulsating, screaming, and frenzied background for the indiscriminate, first-person killing machine I became in Turok 2.

Finally, like the others, my shore-time became drink and drug binges enabled by plentiful supply, and more than adequate money. Jock's friend, Gregor McTavish, was more involved, and connected, than I imagined. After he heard about my Christmas shift and my participation in the New Year's Eve activities, he readily provided me with all the alcohol and marijuana I wanted. Jock informed me that McTavish played a large role in the supply of alcohol and drugs to off-shore platforms. This explained how he made a living from a small pub, in a small town, in the inhospitable backwater of Scotland's northeastern shore.

Compromised by booze and drugs, my nightmares seized their opportunity. My mother, Julie, Fred, and the victims of my "Handy Man" work, became distorted characters in the video games I played. Helpless scapegoats in StarCraft, recurring prey in Turok 2. Even though I understood the connection between my nightmares, the stimulants, and violent games, I was unable to stop playing: trapped in twisted self-flagellation.

Punctuated with bi-monthly helicopter rides, ten day binges, and festive antics, this was my life, until, in late January 2003, death came to the rig.

~ ~ ~ ~

Death's first touch was indirect. Roger, forty-two, unmarried, and the quietest member of our drill team, spent every two-week leave with his mother in Blackpool, on England's northwest coast. His father, a tram driver, died of a heart attack before Roger's third birthday. No siblings followed. For thirty-five years his mother worked three low paying, unskilled jobs to provide for herself and Roger. Retired in 1998, and toughened by work and stress, Roger's mother maintained robust health and a lively social life in the seaside resort town. With no money for luxuries, she relied, like many other working class women, on faux stage jewellery for self-adornment. After forty years, an extensive collection cluttered her bedroom; she wore different pieces every day. Roger offered to buy her real jewellery, but she always declined. Roger, proud, protective, and devoted to his mother, provided for her, as she had provided for him.

Roger waited until the third day of our off-shore rotation to tell Jock the reason for his lackluster mood: his mother had passed away the previous week. Roger gave no details. Her death had been unexpected, and he didn't want to talk about it. We all knew of Roger's devotion to his mother, and respecting his privacy, we didn't pry. Actually, I think we were relieved Roger hadn't wanted to talk about his mother's death, especially me. I dreaded the prospect of a conversation about mothers, and perhaps family. I responded with generalisations when asked about my own family background, and in keeping with "rig tradition," no one pressed me. Roger was family, and we sympathised with him, but we paid a fatal price for respecting his privacy so well. Had we asked, or even took a little initiative to gain some knowledge, about how, and why, Roger's mother died, subsequent events, and more deaths, might have been avoided. But we did neither, and by the time we did discover the details, death gorged, and more people died.

Death's subsequent call was direct and brutal. Wind gusts, up to one hundred and thirty knots, and driving rain had halted production. For three hours, Nick Porter had maintained his helicopter on standby hoping for a break in the erratic wind and rain that pummelled the rig. 6 Kilometers to the south of our rig, a small exploration rig needed immediate assistance to address a critical safety problem which could no longer be left to the TFA policy. All eight members of our own rig maintenance crew sat waiting on the helicopter. At the last minute Paddy, our own welder, had been asked to assist, and he too hopped into the helicopter.

Everyone knew and respected Nick; a great helicopter pilot, and an integral member of the illicit North Sea drug and alcohol trade. Nerves tightened as people waited. Pressured by word from the exploration rig that their situation grew desperate, Nick, against advice, took off.

Nick lifted the Super Puma helicopter off the helipad deck without incident. The helicopter nose dipped as Nick altered pitch to enable forward motion. Between dip and pitch, wind assaulted the rig. Instead of moving forward, the helicopter tilted abruptly right, and rig side. The rotors, accelerating for movement, struck the deck, emitting a grimacing metal on metal screech. The wind, its force spent, "back-drafted" and sucked the helicopter to the very edge of the ocean side of the helipad.

Had Nick realised this he might have altered his corrective action and averted disaster. Instead, Nick instinctively hauled the helicopter back to centre. With the helicopter directly adjacent to the edge of the helipad, and the back-draft continuing, Nick's actions caused the helicopter to roll to its centre so violently, it continued past centre and rolled off the helipad and plunged sideways into the ocean.

The helicopter twisted, its rotors snapped off by the rig's steel structure. We hung off safety lines at the edge of the helipad. Nothing. No helicopter, no crew, no passengers. Eleven men gone in ten seconds. Paddy had been one of our team. Nick had been a friend to all, and as pilot, he had reliably held our lives in his hands many times. One had been the "Crazy Dane": the one who always challenged Sven to the crane climb at Christmas and on New Year's Eve.

If we had been superstitious, like the mariners of the early eighteenth century, we might have made a link between the death of Roger's mother, the deaths of our friends on the helicopter, and the proverb "Bad things come in threes." We might have been more careful. Instead, we carried on as usual; TFA, alcohol, and marijuana. Complacent, fate punished us accordingly.

~ ~ ~ ~

No one from the drill team would normally have been asked to do the job, but since the loss of the maintenance crew in the helicopter accident, experienced rig workers were expected to help. Until a new maintenance crew was in place, Jock and Davey, the most experienced workers on our team, had to assist with the few critical maintenance issues the TFA "policy" could not accommodate.

Thus, a week after the accident, and two days before a new maintenance crew arrived, Jock and Davey were sent to assess a temporary repair patch on a safety-critical pipeline in the south leg of the platform. The temporary patch had been applied for more than eight months. It was one of more than thirty other temporary repairs of which less than half had been approved by industry engineers and regulators. Operating a rig with tens of unapproved temporary patches, or fixes, was common practise, and a basic tenet of the TFA policy.

No first-hand account of what happened existed. Jock and Davey were already dead when the emergency response team found them. Almost two hours passed before anyone thought to check on their progress. Another twenty minutes elapsed before their lack of reply to radio calls prompted action by the rig emergency response team.

Jock and Davey were found slumped against each other at the foot of a set of stairs about ten feet from the temporary patch on the pipe. The patch had burst and the gas responsible for their deaths still vented through the hole in the pipe. An enquiry would later determine gross negligence on the part of the rig owners for deploying untrained workers to an area for which standard procedure, for those who had been trained, required the wearing of breathing apparatus.

In the long-term, the owners were fined nine hundred thousand pounds and an out of court settlement was reached with the families. Over the short-term, we mourned them in our own way, and while we continued to work, the deaths of Paddy, Jock, and Davey ripped the heart out of our team and our "family." It wasn't long before those of us left began to talk about leaving the North Sea.

~ ~ ~ ~

Our departure from the North Sea was abrupt and impulsive. Three weeks after Jock and Davey's death, we sat in the mess morbidly analysing the event: what could, or should have been done, and wondering when we might have an accident of our own. The captain, who had assumed the leadership role, called for quiet and stated bluntly, "We all need a change. We should either shit, or get off the pot. We should all go to Africa. It's warm and we can earn a shitload of money."

The captain spoke what we all thought. Not Africa of course, but away from the North Sea. Taking advantage of our gaping mouths, the captain explained he had done some research. We could go together as a drill team. Some of us might need to have an artificial "promotion" to the next level, but nevertheless we had the experience to run a shift on one of the smaller on-shore rigs. He also revealed he had a contact in Africa that needed a drill team urgently, and would help us get started.

Motivated by our interest, the captain provided details about where, when, how, and how much money we might make. Individually, between shifts, we conducted web searches and read magazines. Even *Offshore*, which I hadn't consulted since Glasgow, contained articles about African rig work opportunities. A week after the captain's pitch, we were ready to put Africa to a vote.

Derek conceded, and boasted, he had exhausted the Soho brothels in London. Since his fiancée had left him at the altar ten years ago, he had pretty much given up on relationships and, "Yeah, sure, I'm up for some hot weather and more money."

Sven, ever the adventurer, had never been to Africa and was keen to "drill some oil and go on safari."

The captain said he had been in Africa a few times before and while it wasn't all roses, he thought making a dramatic break from the North Sea would be good for him.

Roger's only comment was to ask rhetorically, "Will there be lots of blacks?" Roger's comment wasn't the first racist remark on the rig, given rig crews were like a mini United Nations, but while surprised by how overt Roger had been, we didn't give it much thought at the time.

The loss of Jock, the nightmares, and the general depressive atmosphere of the rig, had gotten to me. I also sensed it was only a matter of time before the team broke up, one person at a time, so the idea of staying with the team, or family as they had become to me, was the most important thing for me. So I said, "Count me in."

Except for the captain, we were all naïve about Africa and particularly our destination, Nigeria. We had been selective about the web searches, and being more interested in climate and money, we had consciously glossed over many of the harsh realities that accompanied the Nigerian oil industry.

On March 2, 2003, based on weak and selective research, and buoyed by optimistic predictions of money and lifestyle, the surviving members of Jock's drill team lifted off from the platform helipad for the last time. So began a seven thousand kilometre journey that took us from the frigid desolation of the North Sea, to the frantic and stifling humidity of Nigeria's Murtala Muhammed International Airport in Lagos, Nigeria.

Another journey also began. An unwanted journey that would bring me closer than ever to my adopted "family" before I witnessed the brutal, savage deaths of each of them.

~ ~ ~ ~

Involuntary, brown-red spit accompanied Mr. Grey's mumbled acknowledgment of Alan's story, and the tragic loss of his friends. A nurse appeared, and adjusted the tube and bag supplying Mr. Grey narcotics. She regarded Alan solemnly and appeared to be about to tell him to leave. Instead, she whispered, "He doesn't have long."

CHAPTER 10

Nigeria

Bit about Mr Grey

A white man met us at the arrivals' lounge. He escorted us to air conditioned Chevy Suburbans parked curbside. Black men drove. A reckless drive, to the new four-star Lagos Ikeja Hotel, located ten minutes from the Murtala Muhammed International Airport, was enough to show me Nigeria had problems. I didn't understand these problems, but as we drove in the archetypal symbol of westernization from one modern edifice to another, I could see, hear, and with the window open, smell dysfunction and inequality.

Our stay at the hotel was brief and functional. An opportunity to shower, sleep, and eat before long-wheel based Land Rovers, which had replaced the Suburbans, collected us for the journey into Nigeria's hinterland, and the waiting oil platform. Lagos was like an untidy crowded elevator; I couldn't wait to leave.

The on-shore platform was near the oil town of town Warri in Nigeria's Delta State. A fifteen hour drive from Lagos. Through the Land Rover windows, I watched a raw kaleidoscopic of Nigeria's recent history blur by: images of poverty, unfulfilled potential, and hopelessness, juxtaposed opulence, indifference, and exploitation. Later, during week-long leave periods from the rig, the contradictions underpinning the fastest growing and wealthiest city in Africa became stark. Lagos gasped under a tyranny of inequality, corruption, and violence, fed by irresponsible foreign investment, domestic greed, and ethnic and cultural intolerance. Fueled by oil revenues, the city existed in an endless frenzy as seven million people tried to squeeze decades of development into weeks, and months.

The oil platform shocked me in a different way. The rig had the usual configuration: a vertical derrick structure, pumps, engines, cat walks, hose pipes, racks and the expected assortment of support buildings. I didn't expect guards armed with machine guns and machetes. The compound, surrounded by a narrow "sand moat," enclosed by barbed wire, and guarded by coal-black men in military uniforms, resembled a fortress, not an oil rig.

Behind the barbed wire, left of the rig, worn pre-fabricated metal and wood structures squatted in the dust. An off-kilter sign, on a rusted chain-link gate, announced the collection of shabby buildings as "Camp Facilities." The place we would spend our non-work time. On the top of derrick structure another sign, its faint black on white letters struggling through the grime, proclaimed the T-48B 1325-DE Rig had been constructed in 1977. A twenty-six year old rig! Past the rig, on the far side of the barbed wire, another shock waited. Pollution. Black substance surrounded the compound like cancer around a bone.

Open mouthed scepticism and concern spread across our faces. Except for the captain, who seemed nonplussed by the dilapidated air of the facility, and the ominous presence of armed guards. Then we heard the silence. The rig was not operating. There were no workers, only armed guards. No one else. Where was the plant manager, shift supervisor, drill team? We all turned to the captain, who now showed concern.

Our anxiousness increased as the Land Rovers noisily departed. Collective panic was imminent, until a door from the nearest prefabricated building opened. A man, the universal white hard hat of management on his head, strode out to meet us. Relieved, and not for the last time, to find a white man, we rushed toward him.

~ ~ ~ ~

Ben, or "Big Ben," as the workers called him, was the platform manager. After Ben and the captain exchanged familiar greetings, we learned Big Ben had been captain's Nigerian contact. Big Ben explained the other drill teams had gone to Lagos on leave for four days. They had operates the rig around the clock on their own for sixteen days. They needed a break.

Silently we exchanged disbelief that two drill teams would operate a rig for twenty-four seven for sixteen days. For all the shenanigans on the North Sea, no one had ever operated round the clock with only two teams. But Nigeria, and land rigs, was different. Ben explained that operating a land rig with two-thirds of the required crew was not uncommon in Africa: in the Nigerian Delta Region, short-shifted was more often the reality than the exception. On the plus side, the two crews did the work of three and split the third crew's pay between them. Of course, two crews doing the work of three was unsustainable over a long period, but could be maintained for several weeks if needed. Two, instead of three, (two-four-three) was among the many special arrangements that existed on smaller "less regulated" rigs.

Other arrangements included the off-shift crew doubling as the emergency response team. In another arrangement, the platform manager would be responsible for adhering to, reporting on compliance to, and enforcement of all local, regional, national and international environmental regulations. One look around the facility revealed the effectiveness of that arrangement.

Lastly, I had thought the TFA - Touch Fuck All - official/unofficial policy on the North Sea rigs flirted with danger, but Nigeria had gone further. In Nigeria, TFA had become NTFA which, depending on your view-point, meant either "Never Touch Fuck All," or "Nigeria - Touch Fuck All."

The first twenty-four hours were about shock management: the condition of the rig and camp facilities; armed security guards and barbed wire fences; wanton pollution, which shimmered and off-gassed in the heat of the day, and the heat and humidity. Reassured by Big Ben, and cajoled by the captain, we settled into the base camp, familiarised ourselves with the compound layout, and poked around the rig.

Mid-way through the second day the other drill teams returned from their four-day leave in Lagos. Hal led one team. Joe, the other. Both had drilled in Nigeria for five years. When we asked them about the security and pollution, they didn't understand our concerns: "This is Nigeria," said Hal.

"Don't worry, this is normal. You'll see. In a couple of weeks you won't even notice the guards and pollution. Anyway, think about the money," added Joe.

Big Ben allowed an hour or so for drill team members to exchange names, experience, team roles and superficial personal details. Then Big Ben got down to business; time to start drilling and pumping oil. The rig ran twenty-four seven. Three eight hour shifts: 6 a.m. to

2 p.m., 2 p.m. to 10 p.m., 10 p.m. to 6 a.m. Hal's team would start the rig and run it until morning when Joe's team would take over. We would shadow Joe for three or four hours to get used to the rig layout, the equipment, and the peculiarities all machinery possess. At two in the afternoon, we would run the rig ourselves.

We soon settled into the routine of on-shore drilling: work, eat, sleep, recreational activities, repeat. Three weeks on, then seven days off to go to Lagos to drink, fuck, and eat imported food to satisfy food cravings accumulated during three weeks at the rig. With one team in Lagos, the other two teams worked twelve hour shifts. A tough schedule.

On-site recreation mirrored a North Sea rig: alcohol, drugs, video games, cards and music. Two differences stood out. First, no Internet service, and only one telephone; we were more isolated on land than at sea. Second, we could hunt and shoot. Sven, who had wanted to go on safari, was excited at the prospect of hunting wild African game. Maybe a little hunting would be good for me.

We needed guns to hunt. "Not a problem," said Tim, a roughhouse on Hal's drill team. He gave me a catalog and said, "pick what you want and I'll find out how much and how long." I selected three guns. An automatic handgun, a semi-automatic rifle, and a single shot, long range, hunting rifle. Part of me didn't actually believe the guns would arrive, but the handgun and semi-automatic rifle arrived in three days, the hunting rifle a week later. I asked Tim I where to shoot. He waved his arm in a general ark in the direction of the surrounding bush and grass land and said, "Anywhere you want as long as you shoot away from the platform!"

The sight and touch of the hunting rifle brought back memories of hunting trips with my father in the back country of Northern Ontario. Especially the first time Dad let me use his rifle. I was thirteen. Until then I had hunted with a Remington 700 youth synthetic, which was a short, light rifle with low recoil and a 243 cartridge. My dad used a .30-30 Winchester. Compared to my Remington 700, the .30-30 was heavy, long and had a strong recoil. The rifle had belonged to my grandfather and my dad said that one day he would give it to me. Fourteen years had passed since my father's death. My dad hadn't featured in my nightmares, and I only thought of him sporadically. I think I blocked him out of my thoughts so he wouldn't know what I had done. The rifle provided a positive link with my father, and enabled me to think of him separately from the unwanted thoughts of Julie and the vile crime I had committed against her.

Sven ordered three different calibre hunting rifles in anticipation of going on safari. He never did go on a safari, though; the rig location and the shift system didn't allow quite enough time for him to go to the regions where on safari would have actually meant something. Instead he had to be content to shoot targets, birds, and the occasional antelope that roamed the area. Neither I nor Sven realised the lack of wild animals to shoot was because local people were hunting for food, and of course, they were much better hunters. We weren't the only ones to get guns.

The captain purchased a half dozen guns. He said they reminded him of his military days. He would disassemble, clean, and reassemble them for hours. Derek bought a gun because I had. He wasn't much interested in guns, and only came out to shoot when I or Sven pestered him for company. Derek spent most of his off-shift time immersed in pornographic publications and the pursuit of ever more innovative and depraved ways to obtain sexual satisfaction; ways he would act out by paying large sums of money to desperate women during his visits to Lagos.

Only Roger didn't buy a gun. He did not like guns. This didn't surprise anyone due to his quiet, reserved manner. However, what did raise eyebrows was Roger's interest in the machete. Every Nigerian man, and some women, carried a machete. The machete, according to Big Ben, was an essential multipurpose tool used by Nigerians to cut, chop, scrape or dig anything and everything. Of course, it could also be used as a lethal and cruel weapon. Roger's interest in the machete turned out to be more than just curiosity, though. He had the guards teach him how to use one both as a tool and a weapon. We used to joke about not wanting to run into Roger on a dark night.

Work, recreation, monthly trips to Lagos, and excellent pay lulled us into a sense of order and relative comfort. For a year, we worked and played, insulated from the harsh realities of events, not just in Nigeria and Africa, but also those occurring in our back yard: unfortunately, our contented complacency came with a price.

~ ~ ~ ~

The barbed wire, armed guards, and the armed escort that accompanied our monthly rides to Lagos still bothered me. The captain told me the guards were needed to dissuade local bandits and small criminal gangs who sometimes targeted oil drill rigs because they rightly assumed money and goods were available for the taking. In Lagos, I heard about foreign workers being kidnapped for ransom, but Big Ben assured me kidnappings occurred more in the main delta regions, rather than in our quiet backwater. Besides, Big Ben said, "The company pays local criminals to stay away from the rig. They understand that they make more money with less risk by leaving us alone. Don't worry; there is plenty of money to go around." I asked why there were so many Nigerians malnourished and living in squalor. Big Ben responded with a shrug and said, "It's Nigeria. Not our problem."

My awareness of the poverty and desperate conditions, which for the majority of Nigerians characterised their short lives, was shallow and fleeting. Images and impressions of Nigeria outside our compound only happened during our road trips to Lagos, and then only briefly through clear minds: alcohol and drug binges began the moment we climbed aboard the Land Rovers at the rig. They continued unabated until we crawled into the Land Rovers to sleep it off on the way back.

We also paid scant attention to local or national politics and had no knowledge, and no real interest, in political events or in the growing popular discontent, and the violence the discontent generated. We were also unaware of the direct connection between the growing discontentment and the oil industry.

Later, I reflected on our ignorance. I acknowledged our lack of interest, and the absence of an Internet or any outside news, but I also recognised the cynical self-interest of the oil companies. I believe that had a conscious policy to keep foreign rig workers uninformed about the oil industries' "non-drilling" activities, and the repercussions such activities caused. For example, we should have been informed about the four hundred attacks, or acts of destruction, made on oil facilities between 1998 and 2003. More importantly, we should have known more about the seven hundred and fifty plus hostage takings.

Had we know, or made any efforts to find out about these events during the fifteen months since our arrival in March, 2003, we might have been more prepared for what happened. Instead, we wallowed, content in our relative safety, our wealth, and our hedonistic pilgrimages to Lagos. The consequences of our willful blindness soon caught up with us. First, platform policies combined to make fresh water sources completely unusable. Second, a murderous ghost stalked the local population!

~ ~ ~ ~

Big Ben, the platform manager, managed all things environmental. Pressured to meet production quotas, and hungry for profit, Big Ben allocated minimum time and resources to combat and manage the environmental impact of oil extraction. The absence of local and regional regulatory enforcement added to Big Ben's indifference. Consequently, toxic drilling by-products were either pumped into natural surface depressions around the platform, or driven and dumped out of sight in the brush.

Sven and I had seen these dumping areas on our first venture out of the compound to hunt. We shook our heads, dismayed at the sludge covered ground and the abundance of dead birds and animals; dead after ingestion, or through gummed up wings, eyes, and mouths. Again we asked Big Ben about the pollution. "Was it really okay to dump the stuff in the bush?"

"Yes," said Big Ben, "all the local authorities knew and approved."

Big Ben's answer satisfied our lackluster con-science. Placated, we became so used to the sight and smell of polluted bushland we didn't notice how each time we went to shoot or hunt, we had to travel a little farther away from the platform to find unpolluted land. We also hadn't appreciated Big Ben's true meaning when he had said, "All the local authorities knew and approved"; Ben had meant "all the local authorities had been bribed and no awkward questions or concerns would be heard." Enough money to go around.

The "dump anywhere" policy was bad enough. Allowed enough time, it would have caused water problems anyway, but the NTFA policy accelerated and compounded the problem due to an automatic float sensor that had stopped working, but had not been replaced, or repaired: NTFA.

The float sensor had a simple function: sound an alert when the liquid in a storage unit, in this case a surface depression about two and a half kilometres south of the rig, reached four-fifths full. This would allow time for hoses to be laid to the next storage area. The liquid, an oily by-product of the drilling process, contained a variety of toxic pollutants. When left untreated in highly visible locations, people stayed away and human health consequences were prevented. But when left untreated and allowed to mix with water, water for human, animal, or agricultural purposes, serious health problems occurred.

By our estimates, an incredible five weeks had elapsed since the alert should have sounded. Unchecked, the liquid breached the natural rim of the open depression and meandered several kilometres farther south until it reached a tributary of the Warri River. The tributary provided fresh water for the local village and surrounding community.

Classic strategies of denial, blame, avoidance, as well as tribal and ethnic issues that typified Nigerian governance structures, and slowed any immediate action, or response, added to the problem. When the local authorities finally agreed to act, they came to confront Big Ben. Incredibly, from my perspective, they accepted cash from Ben and his assurances he would fix the "minor problem."

Ben sent Joe and one of his crew upstream to assess the situation. Unfortunately, Joe was the least qualified, and least interested, in the problems of the "jungle bunnies" as he called the native population. He reported, "No way the dirty water could be anything we had done."

Our own fresh water arrived by truck every two weeks from Lagos and was stored in two tanks in the compound. Again, we were insulated from the issue, and indifferent to the problem.

Ignoring the problem didn't work. A week later the local authorities returned. This time a tough, intelligent individual accompanied them. He listened patiently to Ben's repeated assurances that we had not contaminated the river. Then the man forcefully put several aerial photographs in Ben's hands. The photographs clearly showed a three or four kilometre trail of black liquid originating from one of our surface storage pits and ending at the banks of the river.

To Ben's credit, he didn't try to pay them off, or continue to deny the problem might be connected to the drilling operations. Instead, he immediately offered to go with them and survey the site himself. Ben was gone for almost five hours. The captain had been pacing impatiently the entire time. Ben returned, shaken. Ben, the captain, Hal and Joe shut themselves in Ben's office for half an hour before they emerged and issued orders to stop drilling.

Ben organise us into three work teams. First, one team would go to the storage pit and lay hose and pipe to a new storage area to allow drilling to restart; production and profit remained the priority. The second team would load the pickup trucks with whatever cleaning agents we had in stock and dump them into the river upstream from where the liquid entered the river. The last team gathered shovels and plastic sheeting to build a dam of some kind to prevent more liquid seepage into the river. I joined the team responsible for getting the cleaning agents to treat the river. Ben impressed me with his efficient response. Maybe Ben and the oil companies did care about the environment.

They didn't. I was wrong and the situation got worse, not better. First, the cleaning agents dispersed, not cleaned. The agents broke up pollutants into smaller and smaller particles until nature and time could work on actually "clean." Worse, the dispersal agents were designed for use in open water conditions where the vastness of an ocean, or large lake, agitated the water to enable a natural cleaning process. In a contained, low-flow river, the dispersal agents would do little other than provide an illusion of cleanliness and treatment. Lastly, we only had three fifty-five gallon drums of the agent in the storage shed. The drums were rusted and bore a manufacturing date of 1992, making them more than ten years old. I didn't know much about dispersal agents and how long they lasted, but three rusty drums of ten year-old chemicals did not seem like as much of an effective response as I had first thought.

While we made much of loading and transporting the "cleaning agents," the dam builders had gathered their materials: about ten rolls of thick plastic sheeting and a bunch of shovels and rakes. Thinking of our intended "chemical response," I thought even less of the planned dam building response. This was confirmed when we got to the river and discovered the seepage area for the oil entering the river stretched for a least a kilometre along the river bank. Heavy backhoes and bulldozers were needed, not a bunch of guys with shovels and plastic bags. Dams built with plastic and shovels would not have any measurable effect on the flow of oil into the river. The seepage would only stop when the liquid stopped flowing.

Had I been less naïve, I would have understood the plan was always to appear to do something corrective and preventative while Ben, and the platform owners, found out who, and how much to pay, for the problem to go away. Hal, who led the cleaning agent team, said, "whatever the dollar figure, it would be a lot less than a real clean up and compensation costs and lost profits."

Two days later, pipe to a new natural depression had been laid, ineffective plastic sheets lay along the river bank, and the oil slick on the river had been "cleaned"; only small particles remained. The local population and officials received and accepted assurances the particles would disappear in the near future. We would add cleaning agents every day until the river became completely clean again. Meanwhile, undisclosed sums of money passed into the hands of the appropriate officials, and drilling resumed.

After the flurry of activity, Ben called us together. "Everything has been taken care of. No need to worry about it. Just keep on drilling." As Ben wound up his pep talk, I asked him who had been the guy with the aerial photographs. He shrugged and said dismissively, "Some fucker with a group who wants emancipation or something."

We found out sooner, rather than later, the "fucker" belonged to the Movement for the Emancipation of the Nigerian Delta (MEND), which aside from criminal activities, maintained and supported an armed force that advocated the nationalisation of Nigeria's natural resources, especially oil.

Polluted water wasn't the only problem the local people faced. Unbeknown to us, blood also flowed. Lots of it.

~ ~ ~ ~

Murder and maiming were common in Nigeria. A surge in the number of deaths during an election period, apparently underway as we polluted the local river, was not unusual. The unusual part was how the local people attributed the murders, fifteen so far, to a "machete wielding, white ghost, dressed in billowing robes, wearing a wide brimmed hat adorned with colourful flowers and ribbons." According to witnesses, the "ghost" held out a string of pearls to lure the man. When the man reached for the pearls, a machete "appeared out of nowhere" and sliced off the man's hand. The ghost would then methodically dismember the body until only the torso remained. The torso was propped up on its bloody leg stumps with the man's head placed, with its mouth between the stumps, facing the man's own genitalia: a gruesome self-fellatio.

We had heard stories about the cruelty Nigerians inflicted upon one other, but even by their standards, the "ghost's" actions were disturbingly cruel and sadistic. While horrified by the description, we harboured scepticism at the idea of a ghost murdering people. Partly because of our scepticism, and partly due to our ethnocentric view that all ghosts were white, or at least transparent, we failed to catch the significance of the ghost being described as "white." Of course, what the locals meant by white was "white man," and we were the only white men in the area. This fact was brought to our attention on the third day of resumed drilling after the river pollution incident and animosity toward foreign white workers ran high.

A crowd of almost fifty machete and club toting men and women gathered outside the main gate. They chanted for justice and called for us to turn over the "white ghost killer." The leader of the group was none other than the "fucker with the aerial photographs."

We thought it a joke until a guard fired his AK 47 in the air. A machete sliced his thigh in response. A moment of stillness followed before the crowd began to move into the rig compound. They shouted more about the white ghost, and banged their machetes and clubs, leaving little doubt about their willingness and ability to use them.

Big Ben emerged from his office flanked by the captain and Hal. Each carried an AK 47. The captain sprayed a line of bullets into the ground a few feet in front of the advancing crowd. The crowd fell back several metres, but continued to shout and call for justice. Ben stepped forward to the centre of the "no man's land" between the crowd and the rest of us who stood behind the captain, Hal, and the two remaining guards.

Ben's approach to the middle ground agitated the crowd. They bounced and edged forward. Ben stopped and tried to speak. The crowd grew louder. The captain tensed. He stepped left to provide a shooting angle that would pass Ben. I expected the crowd to rush Ben. Spontaneously, or as I later thought, choreographed, "aerial photo man" held up his hand. The crowd quieted and stilled.

"We have come for the white ghost," said the man, serious and firm.

Ben coughed to stifle what may have been a chuckle of disbelief.

"Ghosts do not exist. What the hell do you really want?"

"You will give us the ghost, or we will search the compound and find him ourselves."

Ben wiped his brow in thought. The man continued.

"The ghost killed again last night near here. Some men saw the ghost and chased it here. The ghost flew over the fence into this compound. Two of the men stayed and kept watch all night. The ghost has not left and must still be here. Let us search for the ghost and we shall destroy it."

Ben asked photo man to wait while he consulted with the captain and Hal. I listened as they concluded the mob must not be allowed into the compound, the rig, offices and living quarters. Ben said, "Once the mob gets in, they will loot and wreck everything and it will be impossible to move out." He told the captain and Hal he had already called the regional Minister and had been told government troops would be here in a few hours. They needed to stall for time.

The captain said they didn't look like they could be stalled for long. He suggested Ben invite the leader into the office to discuss the best way to conduct the search. Then offer him money to keep things quiet until the troops arrived. Ben agreed and returned to the middle ground, but as he provided details to photo man the mob screamed, "The ghost has come"!

~ ~ ~ ~

I had never seen a ghost. I didn't believe anyone had. Ghosts aren't real. People use ghosts to explain the unexplainable, or things they don't understand. But, in the backwaters of Nigeria, confronted by a machete wielding mob, I admit the grotesque figure that appeared without warning, about thirty feet to the left of the chanting mob, looked like a ghost.

The villager had been right. The ghost wore a billowing white robe and a wide brimmed hat full of colourful flowers and ribbons. Silhouetted against the sun, the ghost appeared to sway and shimmer above the ground. I squinted and scrutinised the ghost. The robe hung more like a woman's dress, the kind elderly ladies wear with lots of pleats and ruffles. Similarly, the hat was old fashioned, as though it belonged to a mature woman who might wear it out to church or to a garden party on a hot Sunday in summer.

Contradicting the image of an elderly lady, a chalk white, wrinkle-free face stared out from under the hat. Thin, red lips stretched wide. Off-white teeth ground out a malevolent smile. Above the lips, dark mascara adorned eyes, grossly emphasised by heavy, white foundation cream that covered its face, neck, and upper chest down to the dress neck line, projected rage and hatred.

Poking out from beneath the dress hem, white, stocking clad legs ran down to pale blue, low heeled, flat shoes; the kind I remember my mom calling "sensible shoes" for old women. The back of the shoes had been flattened down and the ghost's foot protruded a couple of inches out the back.

I wasn't sure about anyone else, but for a moment, caught between horror and humour, I might have gone either way. Then, dark brown and bright red blotches, splattered all over the white dress, came into focus. My experiences with fingers in Vanuatu and Glasgow told me about the stains: past and recent blood.

Satisfied with its entrance, the ghost held out its left arm, its hand gently caressed a long string of off-white pearls. They swayed tantalisingly back and forth, like a magician's hypnotic trick. While the swaying pearls held everyone's eyes, the ghost's right arm manoeuvred out from behind its back. A hand clasped a bright, polished machete, its tip embedded in the base of a human head. The ghost held the machete high and thrust it at the stunned and paralysed mob. The head flew off the machete, and rolled threateningly toward the mob like some gruesome video game character trying to gobble up all before it.

When the head rolled, the ghost charged the mob. The ghost bellowed racist slurs and wielded the machete in horizontal and vertical slashes. Surprised, two men received fatal blows to their neck and head. Several others got deep cuts and wounds on arms and torsos. The crack of a gunshot punched the air. The ghost arched forward as the impact of the bullet entering its back brought its deadly charge to an abrupt end.

Unlike ghost stories, the bullet did not pass through the ghost. It met flesh and bone. A widening pool of blood attested to the bullet's deadly purpose. When the ghost collapsed, the mob, confidence regained, surrounded the prostrate figure and rained machete and club blows upon it in a frenzy of fear and hatred. Blood, bone, flesh and clothing flew in all directions until the rage was exhausted and the demon exorcised. Satiated by slaying the ghost, the mob fell silent and departed. Only photo man lingered to stare, full of deceit and hate at Ben and the rest of us.

Immobile. We stared at the mangled pile of meat as hungry flies descended to reap the harvest. Ben turned away and looked toward us. I could see his mind doing mental calculations; he quietly asked, "Where's Roger?"

Reluctant, assuming the worst, we searched for Roger. In his room we found white dresses, shoes, hats and pearls, an assortment of rotting ears, fingers, one complete hand and two polished machetes. A shrine had been assembled around the photograph of an elderly lady dressed in the same style as "the ghost." We assumed the lady was his mother.

Two bowls of pearls sat below the photograph; one three quarters full of off-white pearls, the other a quarter full of blood red pearls. Ben tipped out the red ones and counted out sixteen: one for each person hacked to death by "the ghost." The captain reached around Ben and pulled a clear, plastic folder from underneath the two bowls of beads.

Roger's mother stared out through the plastic, her features distorted by the poor quality of the photograph and the faded, black ink of the newspaper print. The captain took out the photograph and unfolded the newspaper cutting. The headline shouted, "Harmless Pensioner Bludgeoned to Death for Fake Pearls" and a sub-heading informed readers, "Illegal African Immigrant Wanted Pearls to Buy Drugs."

All the signs had been there. The sudden unexplained death of Roger's mother. The out of character racist comments, the machete obsession, going out at night. We had been too self-absorbed to notice.

We burned Roger's belongings. Ben released a story saying Roger had returned home to England to care for his sick mother. No one believed the story, but on the other hand, argued Ben, no one outside of the rig ever said Roger had been the "white ghost." No official inquiry or investigation occurred, and like many things in Nigeria, life, good and bad, moved on.

~ ~ ~ ~

Work resumed the next day in a sombre, disconnected environment. We moved slowly, as though time had stretched and it took longer to do things. Late in the afternoon Ben gathered us together. "We need to take a few precautions," he said.

First, Ben warned us not to go out of the compound alone. Better still, not to leave the compound at all unless in the Land Rovers for the trip to Lagos. Second, Ben had discovered photo man was actually Asari Okah, a senior member of the Movement for the Emancipation of the Nigerian Delta (MEND).

When we asked what that meant for us, Ben explained MEND was a powerful local militia group which obtained money by "bunkering" or stealing oil from rigs. MEND had the support and complicity of many middle and high ranking military officers, politicians, and organise crime leaders. MEND also engaged in prostitution, smuggling, and most ominously, kidnap for ransom.

Mouths gaped. Simultaneously we talked about leaving. "We didn't sign on for all this shit," said Joe. Ben raised his hand and told us yes, the current situation might be a bit volatile, but he and the rig owners had things under control. The right people would be paid soon enough. A couple of days or a week at the most. Meanwhile, we need to be careful, and avoid incidents or confrontations. He added everyone would get a big bonus for sticking it out until things calmed down.

After Ben's talk the mood quickly changed from sombre to nervous. The mood wasn't helped much by the captain, who began to carry a handgun and a small backpack everywhere he went. In addition, Ben had contracted additional guards. Four more showed up the following day, which only added to the anxious and jumpy atmosphere.

I didn't know what the fuck to do. Stunned by the whole Roger thing, I couldn't purge the image of Roger/the ghost charging the crowd and being shot, hacked, and chopped to death. I had liked Roger. He had been the most normal of us all. A quiet guy, who looked after his mom, didn't drink too much, or say anything bad about anyone. Just got on with his work. Always polite and helpful. The archetypal nice guy next door. *Shit,* I thought, *what the fuck goes on in a person's mind?*

Five quiet days followed. Ben's assessment and predictions held. Hal and his team had departed for a week's leave in Lagos and no angry mobs had called. Rig routine kept us focused and fed our subconscious denial of any real problem; if we just worked hard, everything would return to normal. Perhaps this deluded sense of security led Sven and Derek to leave the compound to shoot for a few hours.

~ ~ ~ ~

Rifle fire sounded the alert. We all tensed at the first shot. The captain immediately drew his handgun and climbed part way up the crane stack to get a better view. Big Ben ran from his office, his AK 47 tucked under his arm, demanding an explanation. The captain called down that Sven and Derek had left the compound to shoot at the target range we had set up about seven hundred and fifty metres from the compound gate.

The captain fired off a couple of rounds to get their attention. Sven and Derek turned and the captain vigorously signalled for them to come back. They misunderstood his signal: Sven and Derek let off a few shots of acknowledgment and returned to shoot at the targets.

Meanwhile, Ben stood at the main gate. Indecisive, he hopped from foot to foot. He turned to one of the newer guards. "Go get Sven and Derek." The guard set off at a trot. About a hundred metres from Sven and Derek, he stopped to call out to them. He never made the call. Bullets, an automatic on full burst, hammered into and through the guard's chest and legs. The body contorted, danced, and crumpled into the dirt out of sight.

Sven and Derek turned as the guard danced. They stood, rooted and vulnerable, as heavily armed jeeps sped toward them from the tree line. The jeeps slid to a stop in front of Sven and Derek, obscuring my view. Later the captain, who had taken binoculars from his now ever present backpack, reported Sven and Derek had been clubbed with the butt end of rifles and thrown into the jeeps. He also told us he had seen Asari Okah, the MEND member, give the orders from the seat of the lead jeep. The kidnappers whooped, hollered, and wasted bullets in celebration. The jeeps disappeared into the tree line. Sven and Derek were gone.

Ben ran back from the compound gates. The captain descended the crane and collected Joe and his crew, which had stopped operating the rig when the gun shots began. Frightened, we clustered in the centre of the compound, shouting and arguing, panic imminent until Ben raised his hand like a Scout Troop leader. We calmed, eager for leadership. Ben paused to replenish empty lungs. Behind Ben, the gate swung open: guards, three new and three original, weapons and personal belongings in hand, ran off down the dusty road.

When the guards ran, Ben abandoned his effort to settle our fears. He screamed, "Get your fucking guns and take cover." He had to shout it three times before we moved. We ran without knowing what the fuck we should do. Chaos ensued for twenty minutes as we gathered guns and knives, and whatever we could use as a weapon. Inexperienced, we returned to the centre of the compound, rather than take cover. Scared shitless, we turned to Ben for direction, but fear had paralysed him. We were oil rig workers, not soldiers.

The captain took charge, telling us with assurance to check our weapons and make sure the safety was on. We didn't want to accidentally shoot one another or worse, shoot something on the rig that might explode. He directed each person to various spots around the compound so we wouldn't shoot each other in a crossfire. He told Joe to send one of his crew up the crane as a lookout, and told Ben to get on the fucking phone and get some help. The captain told me to stay with him. With these preparat-ions in place, we did the only thing we could do. We waited.

Our wait ended an hour later. Three jeeps emerged from the tree line and raced toward the compound. They skidded to a stop inside the gate. Two of the jeeps manoeuvred to flank the third jeep. Muscular black men in camouflage fatigues swept the compound with tripod mounted heavy machine guns. Others jumped out and covered us with AK 47s. We were out gunned and outnumbered. From the centre jeep "aerial photo man," Asari Okah, of the Movement Emancipation of the Nigerian Delta (MEND), stepped arrogantly down.

With a loud, mocking voice he demanded Big Ben to "come out wherever you are."

Ben had recovered his nerve. He strode out to face the militia leader and in a brave display of bluster said to leader, "What the fuck was he doing in his compound?" Okah whipped Ben across the face with the short stick he held in his hand. Ben fell to his knees, and blood oozed from his split cheek. Okah circled Ben and delivered an obviously prepared speech loud enough for us, and his men, to hear:

"I know you have called your political and military supporters in Lagos and they will soon send government troops. This does not concern me. Here is what I want, and what will happen. You, Big Ben, and whoever you work for, will provide me with fifty thousand dollars in return for your two workers. If you do not, I will cut them up and deliver them to you in pieces. The government troops will be here in forty-eight hours. We will not. They will search for us, but will not find us. They will steal, rape, and maybe even kill the local people. Then they will leave. You have brought pollution to the local river. You brought the white ghost. You will be held responsible for bringing the government troops here. There is no sympathy, or support, for you in this area. When the government troops leave, we will return for our money. I know one of your crews is in Lagos. They are due to return in a few days. Make sure the fifty thousand dollars comes with them and we will return your workers."

Speech over, Okah turned to leave. He stopped and tossed a small cloth package on the ground in front of Ben and said, "I almost forgot. Here is a little something to keep you focused." Okah climbed in his jeep. Men got back in the left and right jeeps. Rear wheels spat dirt and dust into the air as they conducted movie-like skids and turns on their way out of the compound. Okah's jeep swerved childishly to knock one of the gate posts down.

Ben had not moved. "He's in shock," said the captain, as he helped Ben to his feet. For some reason I picked up the cloth package. I wish I hadn't. When I unfolded the cloth, two blood-stained fingers stared back at me. Both white. I dropped the fingers as memories of my own "Handy Man" work tore into my mind.

~ ~ ~ ~

Predicting the future was a pastime in Nigeria. Even the most humble tribal elder, midwife, or herbalist, would lay claim to possessing foresight, but I had to be impressed at the future telling abilities of Asari Okah: government troops arrived within forty-eight hours. As predicted, they searched without success for Okah and his men. They also tortured, raped, and stole anything useful or valuable from the local people. Dispensing more misery, they burned a few huts and humiliated the local tribal leader.

Satiated, the government troops approached our compound. They waited outside the gate while the major in command entered and spoke to Ben. He demanded we pay him several thousand dollars for their services. Ben became apoplectic. I thought we were as likely to be killed by the government troops as we were by Okah's militia. Only the intervention of the captain, who assured the major that calls to Lagos would be made to ensure his excellent work would be rewarded, saved us from disaster. Placated, the major and his soldiers left. We didn't feel any safer.

After the major departed, Ben said he had a call from Lagos to say Hal and his crew would be delayed a few days, but not to worry as the "package," the fifty thousand dollars, would be with them. Unfortunately, Asari Okah was not a patient man.

Dust from the departing government troops still lingered when Okah and his menacing jeeps reappeared. Like before, his caravan swept into the compound and Okah called for Big Ben. Ben went out to meet him, flanked by Joe, and two of Joe's crew. Each held an AK 47. I stood with the captain, near the sleeping quarters, and out of sight of two of the three jeeps. Okah, thuggish, demanded his money. Ben explained the crew in Lagos had been delayed for a few days, but they had the money and would be here soon.

Okah smiled, and uncharacteristically commiserated with Ben. He lamented how the inefficiencies of Lagos were well known to him and delays were indeed the rule rather than the exception. Relieved, I thought things would be all right. The captain read Okah differently. He tensed and reached into his backpack, which seemed a lot bulkier than it had been earlier in the day.

Ben, like me, relaxed. A lot of tension left the air until Okah said, "I will need a token of your goodwill. I cannot leave here empty-handed." Apprehension and tension returned.

"What do you want?" asked Ben.

"I will need another of your workers," replied Okah with a twisted smile.

"No fucking way you jungle bunnies are getting another one of us," shouted Joe stabbing his AK 47 at Okah. Amused by Joe's outburst, Okah held up his arms in mock surrender. "Very well," said Okah, "perhaps I was being unreasonable." As Okah spoke, the captain grabbed my arm and pulled me behind the shelter of the wall. Gunfire erupted from the jeep-mounted machine guns and dissected the bodies of Ben, Joe, and Joe's crew members.

Okah stepped toward Ben. He withdrew a pistol and pointed it at Ben's head. Between blood and bile, Ben whimpered, "Why did you shoot? The money is coming." Okah smiled wide and said, "Yes, Ben. Thank you for confirming the money is on the way. We will meet the Land Rovers and take the money. We don't need you anymore." Boom. Ben's head exploded as the bullet tore into and out of his skull.

The scream that had lodged in my throat broke free and echoed around the compound until it drew the attention of Okah and his men. He motioned his thugs to get me. The captain slapped my face and calmed me with a fixed stare. He opened his backpack and withdrew four hand grenades.

The militia men sauntered. Cocky, sure of their superiority and ability to take a few rig workers. The captain pulled the pins from two grenades. He mouthed numbers five and six. On seven, he stepped around the corner and rolled the two grenades toward the advancing group of about eight men. We didn't wait for the explosions. The captain pushed me along the side of the building until we stopped at its southeast corner, about thirty feet from the jeeps.

I peeked around the corner of the building. Debris and body parts lay everywhere. Dust swirled and mounted machine guns fired wildly into the general area where we had been. Okah, uninjured, but covered in dirt, signalled for the guns to stop firing. In the chaos the captain stepped out from behind me and threw the remaining two grenades at the nearest jeep. One rolled and stopped between the two jeeps. The second landed on the gun platform of the nearest jeep.

Eyes met. Okah stared at the captain and immediately understood the danger. He sprinted away from the jeeps. The men in the jeeps looked at me, the grenade, and back to me, wasting precious seconds which may have saved their lives. The first grenade exploded, showering dirt but doing little harm except for the driver who had gotten back into the jeep thinking it would protect him.

He wasn't protected. The force of the blast smashed his head against the jeep's metal frame, forming it around the frame like child's play-dough. The second grenade, nestled up against the machine gun and ammunition, and whatever other munitions were in the jeep, exploded with vengeance. The jeep soared twenty feet off the ground. Metal, bullets, bones and flesh flew. Flames licked, air sucked, and men screamed. The captain, grim faced, sprayed automatic fire across the compound. Then he grabbed my arm and pulled me away.

We exited the compound through a gap in the chain link fence. The captain told me he had cut the hole a few days earlier, just in case. Five hours later I sat huddled and shaking in an inflatable canoe fitted with a small 1/2 HP gasoline motor. We moved up stream at about four kilometres per hour. Like the fence, the captain had stashed the canoe and motor as part of his contingency planning: something I was to learn the captain was good at. The captain told me to hold to the centre of the river and concentrate on keeping the bow into the current, as the canoe wasn't meant for two and would not stand up to a side swell. While I steered, the captain made calls on a satellite phone he pulled from his backpack.

CHAPTER 11

Saving Sven and Derek

I held the centre of the river for six hours. For the first four hours, children, bellies swollen, and women, weighed down with water containers, waved from the river bank. Since then, dense brush and steep banks had crowded the river; no more people waved. Two hours earlier the captain had switched to the reserve fuel tank. I nudged the container. Near empty, it moved easily. The captain told me to steer to the left bank. He leaned forward, searching. "There, Alan. Steer for the green tape."

A branch stretched out into the river. Ragged, green tape trailed from branch to water. "Go around the branch, Alan." I angled the canoe around and a man-made inlet, about four feet wide, opened up. "Straight in and cut the engine," said the captain.

The canoe drifted into shallow water, about twenty feet long and five feet wide. At the far end, a narrow swath of brush had been hacked back. The captain paddled-pushed us to shore. Fear filled me. I didn't want to be hacked to death like Roger, or have my stomach ripped open by a burst of machine gunfire like Ben and Joe. I didn't want to be taken by Okah.

The captain stepped out and pulled the canoe up. I didn't move. I wanted to stay in the canoe, out of reach in the middle of the river. The captain waited. He didn't shout, or command, or cajole. I edged out of the canoe and sat on the shore. The captain pulled the canoe out of the water and covered it with brush. He scanned the brush, his confidence appearing to wane a fraction. He held a finger to his lips, indicating I should be quiet. I grimaced, telepathically pleading for assurance our landing place was safe and we would live. Moments passed. Gears shifted, an engine whined, and tires slipped. Grass and undergrowth flattened as a camouflaged 4x4 Toyota pickup truck burst through the brush and skidded to a stop twenty feet in front of us.

If I'd had a gun, instead of a paddle, I would have emptied the magazine. I turned and ran into the river and sank as the soft, muddy silt sucked my booted feet and clothed body. The captain threw me the line I had used to tie off the canoe. He helped me back to shore, a wide smile stretched across his face.

A man stood by the captain. He too smiled in amusement. I spluttered water and mud from my mouth as the man said to the captain, "I doubt your friend would be able to out swim the crocodiles." He was right. In my panic, I had forgotten crocodiles inhabited the river and I scampered away from the water. The man and the captain joined in a friendly embrace. Without further dialog, the captain gathered his gear, and told me to get in the pickup truck.

~ ~ ~ ~

Two hours later we jerked to a stop in front of an army issue, green square tent. Four other tents and three more Toyota trucks, two of which held truck mounted, heavy machine guns, stood nearby. Ten men surrounded our 4x4. Each levelled a weapon in our direction. When the captain and the other man stepped out, guns lowered and a chorus of shouts and exclamations greeted the two men. Handshakes were extended to the captain. I was observed, but not engaged.

A uniformed man gave me worn but clean military clothing. He led me to a fire and handed me canned ration food and a bottle of fresh water. The captain had disappeared into the largest of the five tents that made up the camp. No conversation or explanation accompanied the clothes or food. One thing was undeniable, though: these were white men, and after the events at the rig, their presence made me feel safe.

I ate and drank. The captain joined me by the fire. He brought two cups of black coffee with him. For a moment I imagined he was my dad and we were resting beside one of our end-of-day campfires ready to discuss the day's hunting and make plans for the following day. I had a million questions for the captain, but I sat, sipping coffee, lost in the embers. Sensing my need to know and recognising my incapacitated "in shock" condition, the captain explained the situation and my options.

"The man who picked us up at the river is an ex-SAS officer. We served together for fifteen years in the British Army."

I didn't know what SAS meant but the captain said it with such respect and reverence I nodded comprehension anyway.

"His name is Colonel Peters. He is currently employed by an American oil company to protect their interests in Nigeria. The other ten men are also ex-military. They are all British except for one who is an American ex-Green Beret."

Green Berets I had heard of.

"I have been in contact with Peters for the last few days, and I contacted him with the sat phone to arrange our pickup from the river. Over the last hour, I have contracted with Peters for him and his outfit to help me find and rescue Derek and Sven from Okah and his gang."

"Are you crazy? They're already dead. Probably hacked to pieces and fed to the fucking crocodiles."

"Perhaps," said the captain, "but there is a good chance they are alive. No one pays a ransom for a dead captive. I think they are alive, but won't be for long. Maybe two to three weeks until they either get tired of hauling them around, or they don't see any way of making money with them. I have about seventy-five thousand dollars in bank accounts, and I am going to use the money to pay for Peters and his men to help me find and rescue Derek and Sven. I don't know what you want to do. For about three thousand dollars Peters can find a reliable local to take you to Lagos. From there you can get out of Nigeria. You're not a soldier. No one will blame you for getting out while you can."

I wanted to get out. I wanted to run. I could give Peters the fifty thousand dollars I had saved up to help pay for his men. Then I thought about Fred in Vanuatu and how I had let him down. I thought of Jock, Davey, and Roger. I thought about Julie and what I had done. I thought about all the people I had hurt in small, dark rooms. Derek and Sven were my friends, my family, and this was a chance to do something right. I had lived with a lot of guilt for a long time. I had done a lot of bad things and had run away and blamed others many times over. I would not be able to live with the guilt of leaving Derek and Sven to Okah. I had to try. Staring into the dying fire, I told the captain I wasn't a soldier, but I had fifty thousand dollars and I could shoot. The captain smiled grimly and clapped me on my back.

For the next three days I fired different weapons. I couldn't control the buck and speed of the sub-machine guns. I was better with the handguns, but I couldn't hit anything unless I was within twenty feet. "You'll be dead before you get that close," said the captain. The truck-mounted machine guns and RPGs were too dangerous: too much chance of friendly fire casualties. I had always been a good shot. My father had taught me to be patient and wait for exactly the right moment before pulling the trigger. Based on my hunting claims, the captain and Peters decided to test my long shot talents. I was given a rifle and the ex-Green Beret set up targets at fifty, seventy-five, one hundred, one fifty, two hundred, and three hundred metres. I hit up to two hundred metres with one shot. Three hundred metres took three shots to nick the target. Not bad, without a scope and with no practise.

Peters and the captain decided my most useful, and safest role, would be as a sniper. To help me with my new role, they gave me a British Army issue L115A1 sniper rifle. "This is currently being used by British military in Afghanistan and Iraq," said the captain with pride.

The L115A1 used an 8.59 caliber cartridge. "A decent shooter could hit the target at six hundred metres. A good shooter could hit the target at up to one thousand metres." The rifle had a five cartridge detachable box magazine as well as bi-pod stand and day and night scopes. Not only did I fire it, but under the captain's instructions, I followed the military mantra of learning how to disassemble, clean, and reassemble as quickly as possible. I never learned to do it with my eyes closed, or without dropping anything, like they do in the movies, but by the end of day three I knew what

I was doing. I began to believe I just might have something to offer.

The Green Beret was tasked to teach me a few tactical basics. He gave me a crash course on how to assess rooms or buildings section by section, for booby traps or hidden compartments. He also showed me how to make smoke bombs, man traps and weapons, such as bow and arrow or sling shots, from everyday things and natural materials. I don't think he expected me to actually do any of these things; more a way for him to pass time. The lessons were interesting, and much later in life, after I had left Africa, they proved unexpectedly useful.

When I wasn't shooting, cleaning the rifle, or receiving instructions from "Mr. Green," as the other ex-soldiers called him, he told me stories of past conflicts he and other had been involved in. He described the tactics they had used to find people, how to encourage captured opponents to reveal information, and most importantly, lots of tips on how to stay alive: the most important ones being, never engage a superior enemy, use appropriate force, and run when you have to. I might have been on some kind of extreme survival vacation show, preparing for the inevitable climax, only there was no exit door or time-out option. Reality arrived on the morning of day four. The captain, who increasingly used military terminology, told me "actionable intelligence indicates the target is sixty kilometres north of our location. We leave in thirty minutes."

~ ~ ~ ~

On a paved highway, sixty kilometres would have been a short drive, but paved roads did not reach into Nigeria's hinterlands. Four hours later Peters called a halt. He consulted a map, the captain, and another solider before he dispatched three men to make a "forward reconnaissance" by foot. The men reported back after three hours:

"There was evidence of a camp at the target coordinates. Signs indicate the camp was abandoned within the last six hours. We found tracks of eight or ten vehicles. They followed standard military dispersal and evasive procedure; three different tracks led away from the camp: north, east, and west. Not south, which would have led them to us."

We played cat-and-mouse for the next four days. Information would come via sat phone of a possible location for Okah. We would head for the location as quickly as possible to find the camp hastily vacated with no clear indication of which track to follow. My nerves wound a little tighter each time and I became jumpy and edgy. In the evening of day four, the captain sat by the fire. Without comment, he placed a small reefer of marijuana in my hand. The timing of the captain's reefer was prophetical. The next day time to use the L115A1 sniper rifle arrived. I needed to be calm.

~ ~ ~ ~

Luck, rather than intelligence, led to our first encounter with Okah. We had made camp about 3 Kilometers from a small village and Peters had dispatched two men to scout the village to make a friend or foe determination. The men returned to report the village was occupied by government troops, committing the usual brutalities.

The mention of government troops and usual brutalities reminded me of the major who had come from Lagos to the drill rig to supposedly help combat Okah and his men. Rather than helping us with Okah, they committed atrocities on their own people and demanded payment from Ben! The captain had similar thoughts and he left with the scouts to look for himself. The captain determined that the same major who had come to the rig was in charge of the government troops in the village. I didn't know the captain had suspected some sort of collusion between Okah and the major. Based on this suspicion, the captain and Peters decided to check the feasibility of having a little chat with the major.

Four hours later I lay crouched behind some bushes three hundred metres from the village, staring at the mud and grass huts through the daytime scope of my L1151A rifle. A scruffy, wild eyed, government soldier beat an elderly man enthusiastically with a baton. Women and children sat in silence until the soldier, exasperated with whatever the elderly man had or had not done, slashed the man across the head with a machete. An old woman charged the soldier with flailing arms and shrill screams until the butt of the soldier's rifle smacked into the woman's head and she fell into the dirt to join the man.

I had the soldier in the scope's cross hairs. Despite a caution from the captain that killing another human being was different than killing a deer, I held no reservation about shooting this man. I hadn't told the captain about Max and Bill in Vanuatu. I didn't shoot him, though. The captain ordered me not to shoot until two of our Land Rovers had taken up position at either end of the village and the major was in sight. Peters and the captain had a plan.

The major would be alerted of the Land Rovers' arrival and would come out to investigate. When he showed himself, I was to shoot the soldier standing nearest the major. One shot only. I hoped it would be the soldier who had beaten the man and women. He deserved to die. The expectation was the major would realise his vulnerability and agree to talk. I would then keep the major in the cross hairs. Peters and the captain wanted to avoid a full on battle with the major as many villagers would be killed.

The Land Rovers stopped noisily at the edge of the village. Startled soldiers called for their major. He came out of a hut, uniform disheveled, and smoking a cigarette. I shot the nearest uniformed man next to him. Peters emerged from behind one of the Land Rovers and signalled for the major to meet him halfway. The major looked at the dead soldier at his feet, motioned to another, spoke a few words and then walked slowly toward Peters… While the two advanced toward one another, soldiers emerged from various huts hastily pulling on clothing and zippering up pants, leaving no doubt about what they had been doing. By the time the major reached Peters, more than thirty soldiers had emerged and had positioned themselves defensively around the village.

The conversation was short. I never found out the content of the discussion, or how Peters got the major to talk, but whatever the exchange, Peters returned to the Land Rover and left for the rendezvous point. As instructed, I fired a shot into the ground about three feet from the major and waited until the third Land Rover arrived to pick me up. Ten minutes later Peters advised us the major had told him Okah was less than twelve kilometres south of our current position. If we hurried, we could be close enough to enable a night time reconnaissance.

We hurried. As dusk fell we stopped about two kilometres from the camp location. Peters called us together and outlined his plan. Scouts would establish "target presence" and determine numbers and firepower as well as defensive positioning, escape routes, and more importantly, signs of Derek and Sven. Depending on the reconnaissance information, and if possible, we would attempt an early morning extraction to avoid a full-on confrontation.

Peters was giving final instructions to the reconnaissance team of four when the gunfire sent everyone diving for cover. The gunfire came from the direction of Okah's camp and was interspersed with faint shouts, cries, and general commotion. After a momentary lull, a searing scream shredded the night air and my stomach knotted.

Engine sounds filled the night air and mortar shells fell about four hundred metres to our left. The engines roared and headlights flashed erratically as a convoy of about ten vehicles began heading away from the area. I thought we would follow. I ran to the Land Rover in expectation of a pursuit.

The captain and Peters walked calmly to each other and conferred for several moments. I shouted they were getting away and we should get going, but the captain held up his hand for quiet. He explained that charging off into the night after an enemy skilled in guerrilla warfare would get us all killed. They had either known we were here, or had guessed someone was nearby. Either way, a trap might easily have been set, and chasing after them in darkness would make us very vulnerable. Peters directed his men to maintain lookout and wait until morning to investigate. The night dragged. I was impatient for the morning. Hopeful and desperate to find some trace of Derek and Sven. We did.

~ ~ ~ ~

No booby traps or hidden gunmen awaited us in the deserted camp: only empty alcohol bottles, pornographic magazines, cigarette packages, food containers, human excrement, spent cartridges, blankets, sleeping bags and Derek. He was hard to miss.

Secured to a stubby tree by a split car tire around his torso above his navel, Derek's naked and half charred body hung several feet above the ground, his arms splayed wide above his head and anchored to the trunk by nails through his hands.

Black acrid smoke curled up his torso as the hard rubber compound of the tire smouldered. Through the swirling smoke his blackened skin appeared "shrink wrapped" to his rib cage; teeth and jaws pushed through the skin; his eyes moisture-less depressions; his mouth fixed unnaturally wide as though his jaws had locked in a last spasm of agony. Below the tire Derek's legs hung unharmed and motionless against the tree, patiently waiting for the brain's synoptic signal to move.

I cried. We cut him down. We buried him. On his grave I swore I would kill Okah.

We all asked the same question; had it been a coincidence Okah had decided to kill Derek and abandon his camp at exactly the same time as we arrived, or had Okah known about our arrival? Both Peters and the captain agreed the major had played us and had contacted Okah to alert him of our arrival. Okah had decided to kill Derek as a message to leave him alone otherwise Sven would meet the same fate. They also agreed the major had contributed to Derek's death: he would be held accountable.

With only three or four days left before the money to pay for Peters and his men ran out, I became anxious. I was also pissed that Peters and his men would stop searching when the money ran out. "Why?" I asked the captain.

"Don't forget," he told me, "these guys are already working for an American oil company. They should be doing other things right now. Peters is taking a big risk by helping us. Also, the money is not just to pay them. We needed equipment, food, gas and the information we have to buy."

~ ~ ~ ~

Overwhelmed by Derek's death, I hadn't paid much attention to our location. When we pulled away from Derek's grave, the captain told me the drill rig was only about forty kilometres away. I responded bitterly that I never wanted to go near the rig again. Okah and the major could have the rig for all I cared. The captain signalled for a halt. He and Peters stepped out of their Toyotas and began to study a map one of Peters' men had spread on the hood of the car.

Twenty minutes later the captain came to me and said, "Brilliant, Alan." Responding to my puzzled look, the captain said he realised Okah had really wanted the rig. Derek and Sven's abduction had been part of their plan to provoke a situation, and if need be, draw any of us who remained away from the rig.

By taking Derek and Sven, Okah would have a better chance of getting the rig intact and also be able to force them to help him operate it. A working rig would provide much more money than a kidnap and ransom. The captain didn't think Okah had wanted to kill Derek until our presence forced his hand. Derek's death had made Sven more valuable to Okah. Sven, who would be needed to help operate the rig, might still be alive.

The captain's logic made sense. I began to understand Okah might be operating from, or close to, the rig. Based on this reasoning, we decided to head to the rig and see if Okah was there, or if we might pick up his trail.

I was excited at the prospect of having something concrete to do. Action we had thought of ourselves rather than based on intelligence via the sat phone. With our own intelligence, Okah might not be fore-warned of our next step. My excitement faded when the captain told me we would need a day to get to the rig and, whatever happened, it would be the last time Peters would be available to help us. In other words, this was our last chance.

~ ~ ~ ~

Our route to the rig followed the still polluted riv-er; signs of our ineffective clean-up visible. Black streaked, plastic sheets flapped in the breeze on the river bank. Empty, fifty-five gallon drums, already rusted, lay discarded in the dirt. I wondered if the original storage unit overflow was really the result of the NTFA policy, or had it been a deliberate act by Okah to stir things up in the area and provide him with an initial pretense for action? If it had been deliberate, Okah must have been ecstatic when Roger's nocturnal activities surfaced.

Late the next day, twelve days since we had first contracted Peters and his men to help, we stopped about a kilometre north of the river, three kilometres south of the rig. The captain and I knew the area well and provided Peters with first-hand knowledge of the shallow ravines and gullys that would enable us to get within four hundred or five hundred metres of the compound without being seen.

Through my daytime scope, the twisted and charred wreck of the Land Rover the captain's grenade had landed in lay askew on the ground inside the compound gate. Bullet holes riddled the walls of the buildings, plastic sheets replaced blown out glass, and personal belongings of rig workers littered the ground.

Off to the far side of the compound near the fence, a bare foot protruded from a rough mound of dirt about four feet high. Pieces of soiled and ripped clothing lay mingled in the dirt and small animals, birds, and insects scurried about to feed on the rotting flesh of the mounds' occupants. Bile and anger rose inside me as I recalled the deaths of Ben, Joe, and Joe's crew who had stood with them. Horrible as their deaths had been, I thought of Derek; at least their deaths had been quick.

Six pickup trucks of various makes and vintages stood haphazardly inside the compound. Armed men draped in, on, and across the vehicles. Others lounged around the compound on chairs and boxes that had been brought out of the buildings. One group had dragged four single beds outside. On three of them, men drank and smoked while they watched the fourth bed sag as a man rutted a women. When the man finished, another took his place.

The rig was operating, although it didn't sound quite right to me. Even though I was about four hundred metres away, the rig sounded strained. I recognised the sound. It usually happened when there was a blockage in the line and the pump struggled to overcome the resistance.

When this happened, the pump would be stopped and high pressure air would be injected to dislodge whatever had caused the blockage. On the drill plat-form several men were talking and gesticulating in what appeared to be a discussion about the sound. I could not hear the words, but the raised hands and jutting heads indicated disagreement. Two men held another. A third slapped and punched him: Sven!

The captain, crouched beside me with his own binoculars, must have seen Sven at the same time because we turned to each other with hope, rage, and determination. Sven was alive. When we turned back to the rig, Sven had disappeared. Frantic we scanned the rig and compound for Sven.

Mr. Green, who had taken up position thirty metres to our left and had a different view of the rig, crawled over and reported he had seen a white guy of Sven's description taken off the main drill platform and hung by his hands from the hook of the rig crane.

Moving to Mr. Green's vantage point confirmed it was Sven and not some other kidnap victim. Sven's body was bloodied and soiled. With his hands tied above his head and looped over the crane's hook, Sven hung limply on his knees, bare feet poking out from tattered trousers, his ankles tethered to the deck by a length of heavy chain.

Sven's chin rested on his chest, allowing only brief glimpses of his haggard face. Blood stains, new and old, mixed with dirt and sweat on his hands, arms, and shirt told a story of repeated coercion. I wanted to run to him, cut him down, and kill all those fuckers in the compound. I raised my rifle and began scouring for a target, my cross hairs resting on everyone insight hoping Okah or the major would be one of them. There was no sign of either of them. "Not yet, Alan," whispered the captain in my ear, "not yet."

~ ~ ~ ~

We made a simple plan: diversions to keep the armed men occupied while Mr. Green and three others breached the fence and rescued Sven. The most important part of the diversionary tactics would be to destroy, or disable, as many of the six vehicles as possible to prevent an immediate pursuit. The captain, who would lead the diversionary task, explained he and three others would make a pre-dawn entry into the compound and attach remotely triggered explosive charges on each of the vehicles.

When the captain had set the explosives, he and his men, along with Peters and me, would take up position around the exterior of the compound to provide cover to Mr. Green and prevent intervention. When Mr. Green signalled, via flare, he had Sven and was out of the compound area, we would fire shots into the compound for a few moments to create as much confusion as possible before we withdrew to the Toyotas.

I balked at the thought of not staying and killing everyone, but the captain told me the objective was to free Sven and get all of us away alive. We did not have enough fire power to combat Okah's force when they got organised. Besides, four or more other vehicles remained unaccounted for. There was also the possibility the major and his government soldiers were in the vicinity. If they were, and they combined forces with Okah's men, we would be greatly outnumbered. Reluctant I agreed, but I thought to myself I would wait until the last possible moment in case Okah or the major came into my cross hairs.

Ten minutes was all it took. Ten minutes for everything to go completely wrong. The captain and his team had successfully placed explosives on four of the six vehicles. They were crawling toward the last two when the roar of engines shattered the pre-dawn calm. About ten jeeps and pickup trucks sped up the dirt road toward the compound gates. Headlights blazing and horns honking, they skidded to erratic stops, sending dust and sand into the air. Men, thirty or forty of them, began pouring out and started shouting for everyone to get up and get their weapons.

The captain and his team were underneath the last two trucks and would soon be discovered. Escape options dwindled as more than fifty armed men filled the compound, all becoming increasingly alert and agitated as the major, who had stepped out from the last jeep, strode to the centre of the compound and began issuing orders.

I stole a quick glance at Peters, who was staring fixedly at the place where the captain was. He turned quickly toward me and said, "Shoot the major now!" Five seconds later the major's shouted instructions ended with a gurgle and he clutched his throat in a reflex response to my bullet tearing into his neck.

In the same instant, the captain blew the explosives he had already set. Four of the original six vehicles simultaneously defied gravity and contorted into the air, sending metal fragments whining and flying through the compound, cutting into upright bodies like buckshot into ducks, puckering flesh indiscriminately. Smoke, fire, and smaller explosions followed. The captain and his men came out from under the trucks firing as they tried to make their way to the gap in the fence. They didn't make it. One of the recently arrived pickup trucks opened fire with its heavy machine gun. Bullets cut into their backs before they had gone ten steps.

I swung my rifle to the machine gunner and emptied the remaining four bullets into him and the truck. This was a bad idea. My shots gave away our position and before I could load another magazine, a second heavy machine gun fired toward us. Peters pulled me down as the shots went high and wide as the gunner, uncertain of our exact location, swung his gun left and right. We crawled quickly toward the area where Mr. Green intended to enter the compound. We found him and his team hiding by the fence. They had cut the fence, but had retreated when the other trucks had arrived. They deferred to Peters who told them to abort. I grabbed Peter's arm and shouted we had to get Sven. Instead of replying, his eyes stared past me. I turned to follow his stare.

Sven still hung by his wrists from the crane's hook, but his knees no longer rested on the platform. His body now stretched below his writs as the heavy metal chain that secured his ankle tightened as the crane lifted him slowly into the air. Helpless, I clenched my gun as the chain ran out of slack and became taut. The crane stopped and quiet descended all around the compound.

A voice called out from somewhere on the rig, "I know you are out there. Know what happens to those who come to our country to steal our oil." The crane motor hummed. The crane ratcheted upward a notch and Sven screamed. And screamed. "You will all end up this way," shouted the voice I identified as belonging to Okah.

I raised my rifle and searched desperately for Okah. I couldn't locate him. The crane motor hummed again and one of Sven's writs detached from its arm. His body spasmed and writhed in agony sending him spinning like some grotesque pirouetting Cirque du Soleil dancer. Sven's spinning body came to a stop and my cross hairs centred on Sven's petrified face. His ravaged eyes pleaded for mercy. I pulled the trigger.

Half carried by Peters and Mr. Green, I made it to the waiting Toyota. Defeated, we fled. A safe distance away, and sure we had no pursuers, Peters turned to me and said he was sorry for what had happened. He promised he would find Okah someday and kill him.

In a few days he would arrange for my passage to Lagos so I could get out of Nigeria. I held onto Peters and told him that I was going nowhere. I had promised on Derek's grave I would kill Okah and I wanted to stay with him until it was done. Peters was silent for a while, and then he nodded and said the captain had been right about me.

~ ~ ~ ~

I stayed with Peters and Mr. Green for almost two years. I never found out what the captain had been right about, and I never found or killed Okah. I learned a lot about survival and killing, about honour and death. I witnessed more inhumanity than I ever thought possible. I became cold, hard, and ruthless.

Stimulated by violence and death, memories of Julie hurtled back with a vengeance. I began to believe all that had happened to me, and anyone I came into contact with, was punishment for my original crime.

In early 2006, Mr. Green drove me to the Port of Lagos and put me on a rust coloured freighter to begin a fifteen thousand kilometre circuitous journey home to Canada.

The endless passage wound through the Mediterranean, back down past East Africa, across and around the South Pacific and down past Chile, up past Argentina and through the Caribbean and the U.S. East Coast until we docked in Halifax, Nova Scotia, in the winter of 2007.

I disembarked unceremoniously in early morning shadow. Four other men of Middle Eastern decent, whom I had not seen during the voyage, also disembarked in the shadows. Other Middle Eastern men in expensive cars greeted them and they drove away together. I shuffled away, intent on solitude, wanting nobody, needing nobody, trusting nobody. I hated the world and everyone in it. The whole world could just fuck off and leave me alone.

~ ~ ~ ~

Alan lifted his head, eager to hear what Mr. Grey would say about the last part of his story. All he got was the low hum of his shallow breathing as he rested, secure in his narcotic induced sleep. Alan regarded him for the last time, momentarily envious of the contented and peaceful expression on his face. Before leaving, Alan pulled a blanket around Mr. Grey and returned to his own room.

Alan passed his psychological examination without any problem. His lawyer, John Gardener, made the required arrangements and Alan exited Serenity Rehab Centre on July 15, 2012, ten weeks after his original arrest.

Sobriety and telling his story to Mr. Grey had forced two things to Alan's mind. First, sobriety made him realise he had been a complete asshole when recognition of Alex and the others at the Royal York hotel had driven him to beat and rob the homeless to feed his compulsion for vodka and oblivion. He didn't recall everything he had done. He wasn't sure he wanted to. What he did know was he had hurt a lot of helpless people and he owed them.

Second, telling his story to Mr. Grey had allowed long suppressed memories back into his consciousness in a way that enabled him to consider them more objectively, almost rationally, for the first time. Most of the memories horrified him. Especially the knowledge of what he had done and was capable of. Others though, especially the ones about the day in the forest and the death of his sister, provided him with a sense of purpose that had been missing from his life for twenty years. He now knew it was time to stop running. It was time to bring those people really responsible for his tormented existence and the death of his sister to account. It was something he should have done a long time ago.

First, he would atone to those in the city's railway and sewer tunnels. Then he would find Alex, Corey, Brett and Dale; and he would punish them.

CHAPTER 12

Atonement

Cautious and suspicious eyes peered from the tunnel. The confident strides of the clean shaven, well-dressed man contradicted their experience. Prosperous men feared the tunnel. More unusual, their own kind followed the man. Perhaps they were chasing him into the tunnel? No, not chasing, definitely following. The followers carried packages and pushed shopping carts filled with boxes, bags, and bottles.

The man halted at the edge of the shadow cast by the tunnel roof. Directed by the man, his followers unloaded the carts and divided the goods into fifty or more individual piles. The followers backed away and the man stood alone, waiting. A voice called from the darkness.

"What do you want? You had better fuck off before we kill you."

"I want to give you these," said the man pointing to the piles of goods.

"We don't want your fucking charity. We take what we want."

"It's not charity. It's what I owe you," whispered the man.

News of the well-dressed man spread throughout the underground homeless network. Eight more times the man appeared unannounced to give food and supplies to the homeless. During the ninth, a TV crew appeared, and the man never returned.

Alan's actions were nominal. A few clothes, medicine, cigarettes and food would not solve their problems. He knew he gave them as much, or maybe even more, to appease himself rather than them. No matter how token his effort, he felt better. Proof to himself perhaps that some measure of humanity remained in him.

CHAPTER 13

Where Are You Now?

Finding an apartment was easy. Deposit money, three months advance rent, no kids, no pets, and a letter of guarantee from a lawyer, opened doors. Alan settled on a furnished, fifteenth floor, two bedroom apartment located on the corner of Queen and Yonge. The view from the compact balcony included Lake Ontario, the CN Tower, Union Station, the Gardener Expressway, and in the distance, a glimpse of Grange Park. About five hundred metres to the right stood the buildings between which Alan had made his hovel; a reminder of life's fickleness.

Alan sat on the lumpy sofa and inventoried his purchases: laptop, modem, router, printer, TV, digital camera, cell phone, iPad. They contradicted the mature furniture of his furnished apartment. Not that it mattered. He didn't plan to stay long.

Alan completed the unpacking and began to study the instruction manuals. Thoughts of his tormentors, Alex, Corey, Dale and Brett, interrupted his concentration. Where were they now? What were they doing? Had they become cruel adults? Did they still find pleasure in wrecking people's lives? Alan's anger multiplied. How many others were taken into the forest? Who else had been tricked into committing some despicable crime? How many more Julies?

What, thought Alan, *if they had changed? Become husbands and fathers. Respectable citizens, contributing to society, and doing good to mask the harm.* Alan pushed this double edged thought away. Even a thoroughly virtuous life would not redeem them. They caused his sister's suicide, broke his mother's heart, and condemned Alan to twenty years of torment. No. Whatever they had become, they deserved to be punished.

~ ~ ~ ~

Alex wanted to be found. His father had been a dentist, and like his father, Alex was in the dental business, kind of. Alex did non-dental work for dentists. His slick website, Dental Services for Dentists, promised to let dentists use the skills that had taken many years, and lots of money, to obtain, "focused on the clients' needs" rather than on "completing forms and ordering supplies." "Hiring staff" and "keeping track of costs," while vital to success, should be left to experts rather than squeezed in between "fee paying clients."

"For a modest fee," proclaimed the website, "Alex and his team of dedicated professionals will effectively and efficiently manage all non-dental aspects of a busy, modern dental office." All the "professional and highly qualified" dentist need do was "come to the office and make people smile."

If electronic sales mediums could be believed, Alex had changed little in the past twenty years. His six feet, blue eyes, blond hair, and perfect white teeth, leaped from the screen to project confidence, respect, and trust.

Other photographs depicted lesser mortals who worked for Alex, as well as the required short and superficial summary of his family life with his wife, two children, dog, cat, etc. All crafted to present Alex as a caring family man, and thought Alan, to conceal the vain and manipulative bastard inside. Indeed, it was Alex's vanity, in the form of an "attached biography," that provided Alan with the first seed of how Alex's successful career would come to an abrupt end.

Included in the self-adorning biography was mention of how Alex, and his three life-long friends, enjoyed fishing and relaxing at his cottage, especially in September when they took an extended Labour Day weekend break. Consistent with Alex's personality, the cottage was located on a private island on an exclusive, fly-in only lake in Northern Ontario. Perhaps not surprising, given Alex's confident and invincible self-image, the website provided a link to a professional photograph of Alex at his cottage: in a short sleeved white shirt, white trousers, and barefoot, he sat content, and gazed with paternal pride at "his" pristine lake.

The photograph left no doubt of Alex's success. The message to the would-be dentist client blatant: let my success become your success. But, for the right pair of eyes, the photo contained another and unintended message. In the bottom left corner of the photograph, a series of blurred letters and number blended into the foreground. With a few mouse points and clicks, the letters and numbers became visible. Alan smiled to himself as he took careful note of the exact longitude and latitude of Alex's cottage. Whoever took the photograph had used a geotagged enabled camera. A few more mouse clicks to satisfy his curiosity revealed that many smartphones and GPS enabled cameras often recorded the exact longitude and latitude where the picture had been taken. A potentially fatal gimmick.

~ ~ ~ ~

A search of Alex's website revealed Brett. He was listed as the Services Manager for Alex's Dental Services for Dentists. In school, in town, and on the hockey rink, Brett had been Alex's muscle. Brooding, violent, and unpredictable, Brett was slavish to Alex's commands. Curiously, the website listed no specific duties or responsibilities for the Service Manager position. His curiosity compounded when Alan dug a little deeper into Brett's past.

While Alex had sort of followed in his father's footsteps with his "Services for Dentists," Brett had become a client of lawyers, rather than a purveyor of legal services like his father. Brett's unpredictable violence had become more frequent, and he became less attractive to the world of hockey as it evolved away from the overt, body-checking, "goon" era, to a less overtly violent and more skill-based game. Unlike hockey, Brett had been unable to change.

With court reports, and the back pages of the Powassan's local paper, available on-line for a modest subscription, Alan followed Brett's petty criminal life: an ignominious seventeen years of sporadic but legitimate employment as doorman, security guard, and "chauffeur" interrupted by periods of incarceration at tax-payers' expense for assault, fraud, petty theft, possession, DUI and other unsavoury activities.

Three years ago, according to a small "People on the Move" article in the local paper, Brett had at last turned his life around to become the Services Manager for Dental Services for Dentists. *What,* mused Alan, *could Alex and his dental service possibly need his former enforcer for?* No doubt Brett was happy being told what to do by someone he liked and trusted, but what was he being told to do? Something didn't sit right, thought Alan. Anyway, Alan now knew where they both worked, and a little observation would lead him to their homes. Then he would consider his options.

~ ~ ~ ~

Brett led to Dale, and Dale led to Corey. Dale had become a prominent figure in Powassan. The on-line back editions of the Powassan local paper contained hundreds of editorials and articles attesting to Dale's civic mindedness. Not that Dale needed editorial or news exposure: advertisements for Dale's businesses adorned large sections of the newspaper.

In 2007, Dale's father had provided unsatisfactory service to a disgruntled automotive customer. Upon telling the complainant to "fuck off," he was struck on the head with a tire iron and died of internal hemorrhaging on the floor of his own show room. Dale took over the business, and learning a lesson from his father's death, managed to convert his crass, acrid, and deceitful personality into the charming, humorous, and truthful person he had always thought himself to be. This make-over also seemed to include a strong affection for white wine which, according to some editorials, was instrumental in Dale opening the first, and only, specialty wine shoppe in Powassan.

That was the image reported by the paper in the numerous articles detailing Dale's community spirit, contributions, and participation in the town council. Then again, judging by the number of his advertisements in the paper, editorial freedom might not be so free.

One thing had not been made-over: Dale and Corey had remained symbiotic. Corey, the town bully, and son of the then town doctor, appeared with Dale in several of the paper's photographs, which listed Corey as an employee of Dale's. Disturbingly, the only photographs of Corey with Dale were when Dale was donating or doing something related to children. Also, Corey always stood close to the children. An ugly memory of Corey, a fudge bar, and a kid called Crawley slid in and out of Alan's mind.

Alan reviewed his notes. Two of his tormentors, Alex and Brett, were in Toronto and two, Dale and Corey, still lived in Powassan. According to Alex's website, they remained friends and relaxed together at an isolated cottage in Northern Ontario. Alan mulled this over, and a plan took root.

They all liked to fish at Alex's island cottage located on a fly-in only lake in Northern Ontario. This seemed a bit tame according to Alan's recollection of these four bastards, and Alan wondered if fishing was the only thing they did at the remote cottage.

With the coordinates from the geotagged photo of Alex, Google Map, and topography maps, Alan studied the location of the island, noting the inflowing and outflowing rivers at either end of the lake and the roads, trails, and water access points to those rivers. He had acquired many skills during the last twenty years, but flying wasn't one of them. And besides, he didn't plan on advertising his presence. The prospect of confronting those responsible for his sister's death made Alan feel purposeful and calm. Feelings he had not had for a very long time.

Alan needed equipment to visit Alex's remote cottage. Toronto had plenty of outdoor supply stores. Mountain Equipment COOP provided him with the kayak, camping gear, binoculars, clothing, boots and even prepackaged food. Even hunting Okah in Nigeria with Peters, he didn't think he had been so well provisioned. Budget Car Rental provided the 4x4. Prepared and provisioned in two days, Alan drove seven hundred kilometres north up HYW 400 and HYW 11, on route to the nearest access point on the Mattagami River, which would place him approximately ten kilometres south of Alex's cottage.

CHAPTER 14

Reconnaissance

Based on the maps, Alan gave himself six days to conduct a reconnaissance of Alex's remote northern cottage: two days in, two days out, one day for assessment and one contingency day. The cottage had been built on Sand Top Island on Lake Proulx. No navigable river flowed in, or out, of Lake Proulx, and the only viable, non-flight access point would be from the adjacent Lake Gunette. At one point, a narrow strip of land separated the two lakes, and that was Alan's destination. The Mattagami River flowed into Lake Gunette.

He would enter the Mattagami River from the closest accessible dirt road. To avoid detection, and the possibility of being caught in someone's memory, or someone's scenic photographic efforts, Alan decided to enter the river four kilometres upstream from the nearby Provincial Park dock. City dwellers used the dock as a jump-off point for weekend wilderness canoe trips. They left their vehicles up against the dense bush, and hoped they would not be broken into, or stolen, while they were gone.

Alan followed highway 11's meandering and barren route north for seven hundred kilometres, and turned off onto Rural Route #3. Twenty kilometres farther,

Alan turned left on to a marked dirt road that led to the Provincial Park dock. The Mattagami River ran parallel to the dirt road about one hundred and fifty metres east. He edged along, searching for a break in the trees and bushes pressing up against the road. After selecting, cutting, and clearing a space in the bush to hide his 4x4, Alan hauled his kayak and supplies to the river. Alan made a rough camp at the base of a tall pine tree, ate two power bars and drank a half litre of water, and lay back for a few hours of sleep before his planned midnight departure.

~ ~ ~ ~

The vibration of his watch alarm woke Alan at 11:45 p.m. A bright moon helped him check his supplies, and at 11:55 p.m. he pulled his dark green kayak to the river bank and slid into the calm river. The best available light weight camping equipment, together with highly nutritious dehydrated food, a hand pumped water purifier, a very expensive GPS, and quick-dry clothing ensured the kayak rode high in the water and presented no manoeuvrability issues. Besides, the first six or eight hours would be easy going as he would be paddling with the river's natural flow. The river meandered into Lake Gunette, which, according to his maps, was at its narrowest, less than a one kilometre portage to Lake Proulx, the location of Alex's cottage, and his actual destination.

The maps indicated no official portages, and none had been mentioned on any of the website postings of self-promoting wilderness backpackers. Alan hoped at least one enterprising individual had previously succumbed to the explorer's fetish, and traversed the intervening land between Lake Gunette and Lake Proulx, to satisfy their curiosity. Either way, he intended to head for the narrowest and lowest strip of land between the two lakes. He would either find remnants of a previous portage route, or make one himself.

The river flowed faster than he had estimated and he spat out into Gunette Lake in a little less than four hours. The faster time was a bonus coming in, but would mean a harder paddle on the way out. Something he would have to plan for. Alan followed the murky outline of the western shore, and paddled his way toward the lowest and narrowest piece of land between the two lakes. After another two hours, and several checks on his GPS, he arrived at the desired location. The early morning light provided just enough to find a landing spot and drag his kayak into the forest undergrowth.

After a cold meal of re-hydrated oatmeal and raisins, Alan raised his binoculars and scanned the horizon and shore line. Predictably, at 5 a.m., no one could be seen on the lake, but soon others would come out of the Mattagami River, intent on traversing the lake in one day. The shore line was lifeless, human or otherwise. Alan probed every indent, rocky outcrop, and unnatural looking formation on the shore. After an hour he accepted that Lake Proulx had not been exotic enough to attract any intrepid explorers and he would have to make his own portage.

Alan reached into the kayak and retrieved a machete. He stood contemplating the forest and a place to begin. A weak flicker from the sun striking a reflective surface about fifteen metres to his left drew Alan's attention. Guided by the sporadic light, he moved cautiously toward the reflection. A rusted biscuit tin lid lay up against the side of a tree. Moss and undergrowth had tried with some success to integrate the metal into the forest, and Alan guessed the lid had been there for several years.

More exploration revealed vague remnants of a path heading toward Lake Proulx. Encouraged by the discovery, Alan followed the rough track. Fallen trees hampered progress, but in general, the track was passable with modest effort. An hour later Alan stood on the shore of Lake Proulx. Sand Top Island, and Alex's cottage only a short paddle away.

Two more hours and Alan had brought his kayak and supplies from Lake Gunette to Lake Proulx. Impatient to begin, Alan settled down with his Nikon 10 x 42 binoculars to survey Proulx Lake and Sand Top Island. Alex's cottage stood on a wide southern peninsula, positioned to gain both morning and evening sun. With a cold smile, Alan reflected how the peninsula would make a decent trap.

Alan studied the island and cottage until he was certain there were no visitors. He also confirmed that Alex's cottage had exclusive rights to the lake. He hadn't expected other cottages, but experience in Africa had taught him to check every assumption. He paddled his kayak confidently toward the island and then circumvented its approximate four hundred thousand square metre mass. According to his GPS, and his estimate, the distance from the island to his camp on the shore was six hundred metres. Not a huge swim, but far enough to make an average swimmer reluctant to try. By kayak, about six minutes. He paddled there and back twice to be sure.

After circumventing the island, Alan paddled directly to a small floating dock, which had been well placed to benefit from the shelter of a large rock outcrop. To the left of the dock, about thirty feet from the shore line, a rudimentary lean-to stood braced between, and against, several pine trees. Later examination of the lean-to yielded a fifteen foot aluminum boat, assorted fishing equipment, and a well-used 20 HP outboard engine. Alan secured his kayak and climbed on the dock. He stood and listened. Satisfied with the silence, he walked cautiously up a rough path from the dock to the cottage, taking note of the layout and features.

A veranda, with sections jutting out over the water, encircled the single story cottage. Three fire pits had been built on the north, west, and eastern points of the cottage. Another path led to the outhouse, a good two hundred feet in the bush.

Alan followed the veranda around the cottage and peered through the windows at the basic cottage layout: a large open space served as kitchen, eating, and lounge area. A fireplace occupied one end, and the main entrance the other. A rifle rack hung empty over the fireplace. The cottage had four bedrooms. Two on the east and two on the west. Each of the two bedrooms was separated by a sliding glass door that opened onto the veranda. A generous number of skylights compensated for the low ceiling, and worn but expensive looking furniture provided a sense of comfort. The kitchen housed a fridge and stove powered by gas supplied by twenty pound tanks, which could be connected from the outside via a valve on the outside wall. Alan later found thirty or more empty gas tanks strewn behind the outhouse.

Alan stood back from the cottage and searched the area around the front door until his eyes settled on an old cast iron skillet hanging between front door and window. Behind the skillet was a key to the cottage. Before opening the cottage Alan made an imprint of the key in some putty he pulled from his pocket. Alan went through the cottage, making a thorough mental and paper sketch of the layout. He did the same for the immediate area around the cottage, the dock, and the island in general. Activating his cell phone, and seeing a weak but definite signal, Alan completed his last check.

With his reconnaissance complete, he sat on the dock and made a preliminary list of the things he would need to bring with him on his next, and final, visit: animal trap, smoke bomb, piano wire, eye drops, syringe, handgun, bow string, solder and torch kit, two-way radios, electronic signal jammer, an inflatable sex doll and an old sack.

Toward mid-afternoon, as Alan paddled away from Sand Top Island, he stopped his kayak and looked back at the idyllic scene with a regretful but determined expression.

CHAPTER 15

Memories

Noon, August 10th, 2012: the fifth straight day of thirty-four plus degrees Celsius. The city's asphalt was viscous, and the apartment's air conditioning hadn't cycled off since early morning. Sipping a light beer on the uneven sofa of his rented, furnished apartment, Alan stared vacantly at the Toronto Harbour print that occupied centre stage on the wall, its faded colours embarrassed by the wall's bright new paint. The print pulled Alan in: intermittent glimpses of the elevated Gardiner Expressway showed evasively between the modern high-rise apartments that hugged the lake shore.

Jolted by the scene, Alan reflected how only twelve weeks ago he had frequented the no-man's land between the support pillars of the expressway: a homeless drunk, driven by guilt and fear, drifting through life, wanting escape but unable to end it himself. Now, he was mostly sober, had a roof over his head, money in the bank and most important, his guilt and fear had been transformed into a clear purpose.

Hot, damp air and light beer combined, and Alan recalled his principle tormentor, Alex Fodor.

Alex was used to things being done his way. At school, he had always been the leader of something until ultimately, he became captain of the town's hockey team. He knew professional hockey would not be in his future, but he didn't care because being the captain of the town's hockey team in the "here and now" got him everything he wanted and valued: respect, admiration, favours, girls and the opportunity to do just about anything. His excellent grade point average also helped. In addition, the hockey team won more than it lost, and Alex's dad was the best dentist in town. Or at least his dad's clients were the "best" in town. At an even six feet, one hundred and eighty pounds, with crisp blue eyes and short blond hair, and of course perfect teeth, thanks to his father, Alex was, in his own mind, and in those of many others, the most popular and handsome seventeen year old in Powassan.

At seventeen, Alex didn't understand the word vanity. Even if he had, he wouldn't have believed it applied to him. Constantly consulting every reflective surface to ensure he "looked good" was just natural when you looked as good as he did. Anyway, if other people used mirrors more often, there would be a lot less bad hair, dandruff, yellow teeth and bad breath, nose hair, busy eyebrows, and all the other assorted and distasteful blemishes that seemed to feature on everyone except himself. Even the best looking girls always had something wrong with them.

In many cases a combination of athletic and academic abilities, coupled with handsome features and an affluent background, would provide a solid foundation on which a person's character could develop and mature. In this respect, Alex was no different than others, except Alex's character developed in a more antithetical way. Leadership characteristics manifested themselves in manipulative actions; physical abilities became reference points for other people's deficiencies; affluence bred selfishness; respect and admiration enabled deceit and entitlement. All of which combined to conceal ever growing narcissistic and sadistic tendencies; fresh on the outside, rotten on the inside.

~ ~ ~ ~

The discomfort caused by the humpbacked sofa brought Alan back to the present, and he stretched to remove the knot in his back. Alan discarded his empty beer bottle and reviewed the list he had made on the dock of Sand Top Island four days ago: animal traps, smoke bomb, piano wire, poison, latex gloves, syringe, handgun, bow string, solder and torch kit, two-way radios, signal jammer, inflatable sex doll and an old sack. To his preliminary list he added: fireworks, six four foot x one half inch pieces of dowel, two disposable butane lighters, drill and bits for metal, a grey sponge, six inch nails, night vision goggles, and a remote controlled detonator.

Next to each item Alan noted how or where he would get it. Then he listed them into two sub-tasks: those he would make himself, and those he would buy from major stores. The smoke bomb he would make himself here in his apartment, along with the arrows for the bow, and the modifications to the animal trap. The remaining items would come from stores such as Home Hardware, Home Depot, Radio Shack, erotica stores and Princess Auto. The handgun could neither be made nor purchased without a lot of paperwork, information, and time, none of which he wanted to do. He would return to the streets for the gun.

~ ~ ~ ~

Toronto's centre for sporting and outdoor goods stores occupied a good portion of Front Street east of the CN Tower. Alan first stopped at Bayside Hunting and Outfitters. After selecting a couple of bow strings, a spotty faced clerk provided an enthusiastic explanation of how the latest XK 7.7 Predator Trap would be exactly what Alan needed. He also described how the XK 7.7 was ready to go "out of the box!" with cushioned, non-hardened, rubber pads with ten inch inside jaw spread, and a thirteen inch outside jaw spread.

Alan considered the trap and calculated what it would take to modify it for his purposes. Misinterpreting Alan's thoughts, the clerk assured Alan the trap would not cause any significant injuries to beavers, coyotes, or wolves, and that "catch and release" would not be a problem. Alan smiled at the clerk's naïveté and said cheerfully, "All right, I'll take four."

At the Shopper Drug Mart across the street, in air conditioned comfort, Alan picked up several bottles of eye drops, three disposable lighters, a box of latex gloves, two syringes and some personal hygiene products. Another innocent and benign everyday cash purchase no one would remember. From the drug store, Alan took an East bound tram for Eglington Street West and the Canadian Tire store to purchase the solder kit and two-way radios.

Satisfied with his purchases, and succumbing to the afternoon's heat, Alan treated himself to a taxi ride back to his apartment, with a brief stop to pick up a six-pack.

~ ~ ~ ~

After the bags hit the living room floor, five of the six-pack of beers were left to cool in the fridge. Beer in hand, Alan bypassed the sofa and seated himself on one of the two white, plastic patio chairs that competed for space with the dirty, white table on the tiny balcony.

He looked out and down on the sprawling city fifteen stories below. An electronic billboard flashed repeated promises of rippling abdominals and bulging biceps in just six weeks by joining Global Gyms. While Alan wondered what the small print might say about this promise, the unpredictable world of subconscious synoptic connections turned the billboard's image of the sculptured body into memories of Brett and Corey. Both had physical attributes like the man on the billboard, but with different personalities:

The thud of a dumbbell hitting the floor echoed through the gym, broke Brett's concentration, and dragged his mind away from its looped image of him brutally and unnecessarily crushing another hockey player into the boards. Brett completed his second one hundred and seventy-five pound bench press rep and strode with purpose toward the muscular kid who had dropped the dumbbell to the floor after an unsuccessful arm curl attempt.

Afraid, the kid backed away from the approaching defence man and his well-earned reputation for unpredictable violence. Brett effortlessly picked up the offending dumbbell and returned it to the weight rack while transfixing the retreating kid with his brooding, brown eyes. In the absence of any direct instruction to "teach the kid a lesson" or "show him who's boss," Brett returned to his weight bench and his workout. Relieved, the kid quickly exited the gymnasium.

With his daily morning workout complete, Brett methodically unwrapped his fourth piece of gum and inserted it into his mouth, chewing deliberately to ensure a slow and even release of the flavour. He hated being rushed. A lemon-like taste flowed over his taste buds as he once again wondered how his friend Corey always had different types and flavours of gum for him.

Behind his back, Brett's six feet, four inches, two hundred pound, muscle laden frame prompted people to refer to him unimaginatively as the proverbial "brick shithouse." To his friends, Alex, Corey, and Dale, he was their "friendly giant, " ever ready to assist with any enforcement duties, either on or off the ice. As Dale often joked, all you have to do with Brett is "point and shoot." This suited Brett just fine. He didn't like making decisions. Brett liked it best when people he liked and trusted told him what to do. He was not so happy if anyone else told him what to do, though. His Frankenstein-like personality was a huge disappointment to Brett's father who, as one of

Powassan's two lawyers, was much more disposed to being the one doing the telling than the one being told. A disposition he had expected his son to have inherited.

The more Alan thought about Brett, the more he wondered what Alex, and his Dental Services for Dentists, would need a man of Brett's talents and temperament for. Concluding again something was not quite right with the Alex-Brett situation thrust memories of Corey into Alan's mind. *Corey,* thought Alan, *had been one fucked up kid:*

"Hand them over, you little fucks". "If I find you are holding some back, I'll shove them up your arse." With broken nose, chipped teeth, and six feet of well-developed muscle, the Powassan's leading defence-man towered over his first victims of the day. The fourth and fifth graders hastily emptied their pockets of candy bars, gum, and money.

They knew from experience Corey meant what he said. He had actually done it with a fudge bar last term to the Crawley kid. Corey had laughed himself into a frenzy, calling Crawley a fudge packer the entire time. The purple birthmark on Corey's neck pulsated as he glared impatiently at the treats and money being placed on the picnic table in front of him, and he toyed with the thought of sticking all the candy bars up all of the little fuckers' butts.

The kids scurried away while Corey focused on his haul: twelve chocolate bars, four packs of gum, red licorice, a cupcake and an apple. He should have paid attention to which one of the little fags had the cupcake and apple, he thought malevolently. He flattened out the crumpled bills and stacked the coins: six dollars and forty-three cents. "Hardly worth all this hard work," he said to himself. At the school entrance, Corey stopped to pocket the money and gum, and toss the candy bars in the garbage.

Corey didn't really need the money, or the gum either, but money was money and giving different kinds of gum to Brett made him very happy which, given Brett's personality, was good policy even for Corey. Corey's dad was the town doctor and while Corey had just about anything that money could buy, it couldn't buy the hopeless, frightened look in the eyes of the little fags he took things from. He didn't need stuff. He just liked taking it; the strong took from the weak.

Corey saw himself as strong and manly. The best defence-man on Powassan's hockey team and the kind of guy everyone should be afraid of. The kind of guy people should want to have for protection. Unfortunately, Corey's self-awareness did not consider the possibility it was guys like him people would want protection from. Neither did his self-awareness register that his hockey prowess, and his father's stature in the community, were what allowed him to continue as the tolerated town bully.

Alan thought back to the newspaper reports and shuddered at the recollection of Corey always being present whenever Dale was doing something with children. Dale, reflected Alan, had been a real trouble-maker.

Most times Dale made more trouble than he was worth. No doubt about it. But he was funny, and he was the fastest winger in the hockey league. Because of Dale, Powassan's hockey team won more than it lost. Not only did he never stop talking, but he also mimicked other people's voices. But his greatest skills, outside of the hockey arena, were an ability to contort his face and alter his gait, which enabled him to physically impersonate just about anybody. In addition, Dale had a knack of saying the most hurtful thing possible in any situation.

Dale reserved most of his impersonating efforts for three priv-ileged groups: anyone in a lower grade; anyone smaller than him, and anyone who didn't play hockey. All of which gave him a huge and endless pool of victims. Everyone was vulnerable to a verbal assault, with the caveat he was accompanied by one or more of Alex, Brett, or Corey, because at five foot, six inches and one hundred and forty-five pounds, he wasn't quite a runt, but he wasn't the biggest either.

Many people had been taken in by Dale's soft blue eyes, blond hair, and girlish features, which at first impression prompted people to open up to him. They soon learned their error as Dale exploited confidences for the sake of cheap, hurtful laughs. Often adding to, or stretching, the "truth" for entertainment purposes.

As with his friends Alex, Brett, and Corey, much was tolerated for the sake of a successful hockey season, and as long as he kept scoring on the ice, it seemed most people managed Dale by avoiding him as often as possible.

For his part, Dale was secure in his own mind that his crass impersonations, acrid wit, and distortion of confidences were viewed by others as charming, humourous truths. Besides, anyone who didn't like it could just "fuck off"! A sentiment also popular with Dale's father, who owned Powassan's only Ford dealership, two gas stations, and marina. He also provided the bulk of the sponsorship for the town's hockey team.

Alan smirked as he recalled reading in the back issues of the Powassan's daily paper how Dale's dad had been bludgeoned to death in his Ford showroom by a customer who he had told to "fuck off."

~ ~ ~ ~

Five-thirty a.m. Sheets clung to his body like shrink wrap, trapping his sweat and stymieing his body's natural cooling abilities. He didn't remember coming to bed, or understand why he had wrapped himself so tightly in the sheets. Alan peeled the sheets from his naked body and walked to the window. Through the horizontal metal blinds, a combination of early morning light and smog softened the edges of the buildings and blurred the lights, momentarily reminding him of how they had used smoke bombs to drive insurgents from their hiding places into the waiting bullets.

The smoke bombs they had used had been made with potassium chlorate, sugar or sucrose for fuel, sodium bicarbonate and a powdered organic dye to colour the smoke. They had come in convenient little cans with pull rings! Compact, easy to throw, and effective. Unfortunately, their supplies were often delayed, or "lost," and sporadic availability meant they had often needed to improvise and make their own.

It would be convenient to pick some up from somewhere, but they weren't an everyday, over the counter purchase. On the other hand, the ingredients were. Alan grabbed a pencil and paper and refreshed himself on how to make a smoke bomb: sugar, saltpeter, skillet and aluminum foil. Pour about three parts saltpeter to two parts sugar into the skillet on low heat and stir the mixture slowly. When liquefied, remove from heat and pour onto a piece of foil. Let it cool and peel off the foil. Add a candle wick, light, and presto - smoke. He would also add fireworks which, when ignited by the burning smoke bomb, created a sense of panic. Mr. Green, the ex-Green Beret, had shown them how to do that in Nigeria. It was an effective modification.

Today he would complete his over the counter shopping. Then he would get a gun.

~ ~ ~ ~

Alan was surprised how difficult it was to find suitable clothes. The Salvation Army and thrift shop clothes were too good and too clean. The Shepherds of Good Hope Mission for men also had too good clothes. Tired of his pursuit, Alan spotted a homeless man of similar build and offered him one hundred dollars for the clothes off his back. The homeless man refused and shuffled away. Alan stood incredulous until he recalled the only possessions a homeless person has are the clothes on their backs and what they can carry.

Alan returned to the thrift shop and purchased an assortment of men's pants, sweaters, and shirts, as well as jackets and hats. He then approached another homeless man and suggested a swap and ten dollars. The homeless man took the clothes down an ally and returned to exchange his rags for the ten dollars. Alan placed the pungent and soiled clothes in a black garbage bag and shuddered at the thought of putting the clothes on later.

Two thirty a.m. Relentless heat, adhesive humidity, and the black garbage bag had not improved the stench of the homeless man's clothes. Alan retched several times while changing. Suitably dressed, Alan stepped out from behind the dumpster and headed for the homeless district and the Express Way arches where anything could be brought or sold. Alan hoped his own clothes would still be behind the dumpster when he returned.

Impenetrable darkness sucked the city's light into the arches. Alan approached the arches. He sensed movement and tasted animosity. He faltered, staggered, and held onto a wall for support. He was afraid. The unofficial gatekeepers mistook the faltering steps for the normal impaired walk of the homeless and let Alan pass into the arches proper.

Gulping air to calm his nerves, Alan reached into an inner pocket and withdrew a brown, paper-wrapped bottle and tipped it hurriedly to his lips. As the water flowed, he cursed himself for not bringing something stronger. Earlier he had consumed a few shots of his old Prussian Soldier friend, but had thrown the rest away and replaced the vodka with water. That hadn't been easy, but he needed to be sober: nobody sold a gun to a drunken person, especially in a place as lawless as the arches.

After about an hour of quiet inquires, and being passed from one person to another, rough hands grabbed Alan's arms and a weak flashlight scanned his body and rested on his face.

"What you want with a gun, eh? You gonna hurt somebody?"

"Yes. I am gonna kill some fucker who fucked with me."

"Wait."

Alan thought the instruction strange considering his arms remained held. Doing anything except waiting was impossible.

"How much you got?"

"Seventy-five dollars."

"What the fuck? Seventy-five dollars. What the fuck. Kick his arse and throw him out."

"Wait, I have watches and rings too. In my pocket. Let me get them."

Alan had collected seventy-five dollars in small bills and had bought some watches and rings from a pawn shop a few days earlier. Better not to have too much money with him in the arches. Also, a drunk with seventy-five and some "stolen" jewellery would not stand out.

After more waiting, a heavy cloth package was placed in his hands.

"You had better be a good shot. Now get the fuck out."

Alan's arms were released. He left the arches, returned to the dumpster, and shed the homeless man's clothes, but not the stench, before heading to his apartment.

Showered and naked except for deodorant, Alan sat on an old humpback, opened a second beer, and unwrapped the package. A battered and dirty revolver lay innocently on a grimy cloth. Alan picked it up and felt the gun's weight. A short leather hoop hung from the bottom of the butt. He smiled to himself as he recognised a WWII era Webly Revolver that had been standard issue for officers in Her Majesty's Army. Alan snapped open the chamber. One bullet. He smiled as he thought of the seller's parting jibe that he had better be a good shot. *Not a problem*, thought Alan.

CHAPTER 16

Ready, Set, Go

Tempered by the first cool touches of an approaching fall, the city's asphalt returned to a normal consistency, no longer sounding as though car tires rode over double-sided tape. The Labour Day weekend was only five days away as Alan headed north on HYW 400 toward Thunder Bay. In three hundred and ninety-seven kilometres, HYW 400 would change to HYW 11, and towns and gas stations would become less frequent. Tomorrow was Tuesday. His tormentors would arrive at Sand Top Island on either Thursday or Friday, depending on which four days their long weekend encompassed.

Driving within the speed limits, Alan reflected on the previous week's preparations and thought how well everything had gone. While satisfied with his preparations, Alan wrestled with his plans and the prospect of confronting the people who had destroyed his life.

Sure he had killed before. Lots of times: once for pleasure, once for mercy, and once in self-defence, but mostly for survival, never for a just cause like this. Except maybe the time he participated in the execution of twenty or so government troops in Nigeria. For several weeks they had raped and killed the civilians they should have protected and while no real code of justice existed among the mercenaries, a kind of spontaneous and unspoken understanding that enough was enough occurred. They caught the troops unprepared, herded them together, and opened up with everything they had. When the firing stopped they did not shout, or whoop, or take photographs. They shouldered their weapons and carried on with the day's assignments. Some people deserved to die.

Through the distortion of time and distance, as well as the opium of purpose, Alan's thoughts of his time in Africa and Vanuatu became almost whimsical. Even reflections about the North Sea oil rig seemed pleasant and somehow with purpose. Perhaps because many of the things he had learned in those places would be so useful to his current objective.

After an overnight stay at a Stephen King-like motel on HYW 11, Alan arrived at the dirt road which led to the Provincial Park wilderness dock. Alan set his odometer at zero and drove three point eight kilometres until he saw the tree he had used to mark the spot where he had hidden the 4x4 on his reconnaissance visit.

Alan stepped into the bush and tied some rope around a swath of brush the same width as the 4x4. Then he gently pulled the brush over and drove the 4x4 into the space behind. A little camouflage netting from the sporting store, some brush gathered from farther into the woods, and the 4x4 would not be seen by passing cars. Certainly not by weekend wilderness types, who arrived on one frantic schedule to get to the jump-off point for their back country adventure, and departed on another to get back to the city to tell everyone how awesome their trip had been.

Like his first trip, Alan rested and waited until midnight before he entered the Mattagami River. Unlike before, his latest and greatest light-weight camping equipment, dehydrated food, and other basics had to share space with his other supplies.

The kayak rode a little lower in the water, but Alan didn't mind the extra weight.

~ ~ ~ ~

The overnight trip down the Mattagami through Lake Gunette, and the short portage to Lake Proulx, was uneventful. After a cold breakfast and brief nap, Alan was ready to begin. Alan reclined against a tree trunk and observed Sand Top Island through his binoculars. Nothing had changed since his reconnaissance trip in August: peaceful, beautiful, inspiring.

Back at his camp, hidden fifty feet from shore in dense bush, Alan collected the WWII revolver and the four animal traps and paddled leisurely toward the island. After circling the island, Alan tied up at the dock as though he owned the place.

With the key made from the imprint taken during his reconnaissance, Alan entered the cottage and stood in the centre of the open concept room. After a few moments Alan walked to the dining table. He moved two of the four chairs away, and then knelt down to look at the underside. Pleased with the three inch lip, Alan taped the WWII revolver to the underside of the table with that essential piece of camping equipment: duct tape. Satisfied the gun was secure and out of sight of any of the sofas or lounge chairs, Alan exited the cottage and locked the door behind him.

Alan followed the well-worn path to the outhouse, stopping many times to examine the ground as well as the undergrowth and bushes that lined either side of the path. After three attempts to sink a trowel into the ground, he found a suitable location about forty feet from the outhouse. Alan dug and scraped a shallow rectangular depression in the centre of the path and placed one of the animal traps, with jaws open, in the depression and covered the trap with twigs and leaves.

Alan poked the centre of the depression with a thick tree branch and was satisfied to hear and feel the snap of the jaws closing on the branch. He was even more pleased when he tried to withdraw the branch; the six inch nails he had soldered to the jaws had penetrated deep.

Alan removed the trap and refilled the depression with its own excavated soil and loose stones. Two steps farther on, another shallow depression was scraped out and refilled; with the holes prepared, the traps could be quickly inserted. Alan didn't want anyone to stumble into the traps until he was ready for them to.

With this done Alan opened two of the four traps and placed them off the path in the adjacent under-growth: one on each side of the place where the first trap would be on the path.

With two traps set in place out of sight in the un-dergrowth, and satisfied he could easily find the two pre-dug depressions by moonlight, Alan took the remaining two traps with him and headed back to his kayak and paddled confidently to his camp.

After an early supper, Alan settled down in his bivouac to catch up on the lost sleep from the previous night's paddle. Bathed in the twilight of the setting sun, Alan drifted into a calm and undisturbed sleep. Mean-while, four long-time friends completed their respective last minute preparations for an early morning departure to their long anticipated annual weekend away.

CHAPTER 17

Justice

Engine sound drifted across the lake. A twin engine float plane turned to make its landing on the early morning calm waters of Lake Proulx. Eight thirty a.m.: earlier than expected. The plane taxied to the small dock, the door thrust open, and a large, red canvas bag hit the dock's wooden boards followed by a tall, blond haired man with perfect teeth who turned to catch another bag tossed from the plane's interior by unseen hands. With the plane's engine gurgling in neutral, more men, bags, boxes, bottles, gas tanks, coolers, fishing rods and a rifle case spewed onto the dock. Without comment or signal, the pilot pushed the throttle, and the engine spat, and the plane taxied directly to flight.

Invisible in the lake side foliage, Alan watched through binoculars as the men shuttled their supplies from dock to cottage. After fifteen minutes of familiar team work, the four men returned to the dock, addictions in hand. Alex, Brett, and Corey held brown or clear glass bottles in one hand and cigarettes in the other. Dale preferred wine and a cigar. Voices rose and fell in sequence, accompanied by gesticulations for emphasis. Fishing and drinking predictions were made, challenged, doubled and remade. Contentment and satisfaction oozed across the lake to unknowingly mingle with a very different sense of contentment. Alan lowered his binoculars in anticipation.

~ ~ ~ ~

Muffled sound caused Alan to move from his camp back to the water's edge. Fishing rods glinted in the morning sun, accompanied by the clink of bottles and vacation banter as the men walked from cottage to dock. Dale and Corey pulled and pushed the aluminum boat into the water, while Brett hefted the 20 HP outboard-motor.

Alex watched, directed, and waited. With gas tank and motor connected, Brett pulled the starter rope repeatedly until the engine submitted and signalled its awakening with grinds and blue smoke. With rods, alcohol, and nicotine, the occupants departed the dock and headed away from the cottage to the middle of the lake: far enough for the peninsula to allow Alan to paddle to the island without risk of being seen.

Alan sat in the kayak and launched himself into the lake from the slip he had made with drift wood and forest brush. Six minutes later, one minute faster than he had done during his reconnaissance, Alan reached the nearside of the peninsula and secured his kayak fifty feet from the dock. Backpack in latex-gloved hand, Alan scurried up the low bank toward the outhouse path and down the path to the cottage.

Alan stopped to raise his binoculars and verify the location of the fishermen before he entered the un-locked cottage. From his backpack, he withdrew a plastic package containing, as promised by the tattooed sales clerk, one fourteen pound inflatable, flesh col-oured, silicone, semi-solid love doll. Next he withdrew a micro cylinder of compressed air used by cyclists for rapid tire inflation, an old peanut sack, and a professional, cordless, butane soldering iron complete with push-button Piezo ignition. Last, Alan brought out a syringe with an ultrafine 0.11mm needle.

Alan inflated the doll. Irreverently prostrate with legs spread toward the cottage door, the computer generated and machine-made replica of female genitalia was at odds with the sack covered head - a misplaced modesty. The prostrate form shook Alan and transported him back twenty years to the musty, damp shack in the forest. Nauseated, Alan held the door frame for support, until anger refocused his mind.

With the doll in place, Alan reached for the rifle on the rack above the fireplace and took it outside the cottage. With the soldering kit, Alan dripped several drops of solder in the barrel of the gun. Alan waited a few moments for the drops to solidify, and then added several more. Satisfied the gun barrel was blocked, Alan re-entered the cottage and replaced the rifle on the gun rack.

After another quick check on the fishermen, Alan opened the fridge and found what he had expected: bottles of white wine all lined up on one side of the fridge. Ignoring the vintages, Alan selected the third and fourth bottles, and placing them on the floor between his legs, uncapped the syringe and eased the needle through the foil into the corks and on into the wine. A few innocent bubbles indicated that fluid had left one vessel for another. Alan withdrew the syringe and replaced the bottles in the fridge.

Alan walked to the south-facing patio window and scanned the lake for the boat. The boat bobbed gently, and in the absence of any natural markers, appeared to be in the same place it had been ten short minutes ago. A fish was caught and released. Just like they were caught, thought Alan, but would he release them?

Alan collected his equipment, left the island, returned to his lookout point and settled down to wait.

~ ~ ~ ~

Judging by the weave of the boat, the volume of the dialog and the beaming smiles, two things had happened during the four hour fishing trip: fish had gained a significant majority in the cooler over brown or clear glassed bottles, and previous bets and challenges had been successfully resolved.

Drunk and happy, the four men climbed out of the boat on the dock. Alex lit a cigarette and sauntered toward the cottage. Dale headed for the outhouse. Brett and Corey carried the cooler. Rods were left in the boat. Empties couldn't swim and hadn't made it back.

Alex opened the cottage door but did not enter. Through his binoculars, Alan observed the back of Alex's body snap straight, as a hand jolted up to push sunglasses from his eyes. Alex turned sharply and ran, his mouth open wide, dirty words tumbling out past clean teeth. Brett and Corey neared the cottage as Alex approached them: more dirty words accompanied by flapping arms and hands. The cooler hit the ground as Brett and Corey rushed to the cottage door. Together they looked inside. Then the three of them exchanged expletives, gestures, and accusations.

Dissatisfied with each other's responses, they sought Dale who approached from the outhouse - one against three. Startled by the accusations, Dale made for the cottage door. Four loud voices echoed around the lake. All denied knowledge of the silicone lady until Alex quietened and drew them together in a conspiratorial huddle.

Directed by Alex, Brett dragged the doll out of the cottage and stamped it flat. Corey picked up the flattened doll and stuffed it into a black garbage bag. Meanwhile, Alex had gone into the cottage and returned with the rifle. Alex spoke to the others and each set off in different directions. Dale took the boat and drove twice around the island·while Brett and Corey divided up to search the cottage, and any accessible points along and around the path to the outhouse. Alex walked around the cottage veranda with the rifle in hand like a spooked sentry on the ramparts of a vulnerable, imperial outpost. Alex tried his cell phone several times without success. The signal jammer affixed to the underside of the veranda was working perfectly.

~ ~ ~ ~

Alan switched to night vision binoculars. He watched as each of the men took half-hour turns to walk the cottage veranda in the hope that whatever their imaginations had conjured up to fear would itself be frightened by the sight of a rifle carrying guard. Another precaution was curtailment of outhouse trips in favour of pissing off the veranda into the lake. Alan wondered if this had more to do with the risk of being shot by an alcohol-buoyed guard, rather than falling victim to what, or whomever, might be out there.

Alan had no doubt they had made the connection between the doll and what they had done to him, his sister Julie, and probably many others, too. He wished he had thought to place a short-wave transmitter in the cottage to hear what they said.

By 4:30 a.m. guard duties had petered to an end as fatigue and alcohol took their toll. Alan paddled gently toward the dock and stopped behind the stern of the aluminum boat. Alan reached over the stern and located the fuel line. He pierced the fuel line several times with a fine needle point, providing an opening for fuel to seep out at a tear drop rate. Next, the connector securing the fuel line to the engine was loosened to within a half turn of coming off. Then, below the loosened connector, Alan used double sided tape to attach a matchbox sized plastic box containing a remote controlled spark generator.

With this done, Alan sat back and looked toward the cottage for signs of movement. Nothing. Alan placed a hand-operated carpenter drill and carbide bit up against the stern of the boat, about one inch above the water line. A squirt of lubricant muffled the sound as the bit made short work of the thin, aluminum skin. Within ten minutes, seven half-inch diametre holes were spread port to starboard across the boat's stern. Into each of the holes, Alan fitted a small piece of pre-cut grey sponge and smoothed them out until flush with the interior hull.

It would not stand up to serious inspection, but Alan was not worried about inspections. Besides, the sponges would only last for about thirty seconds before becoming water-logged and flushed out. *Long enough*, thought Alan.

By 5:15 a.m. the boat was ready. Alan struck the boat with his paddle several times. The unnatural sound reverberated up to the cottage. In response, flashlight light bounced frantically around the cottage interior in step with competing voices hushing, questioning, and urging for quiet. In the silence, Alan struck the boat again and made several noisy paddle strokes without moving. Shouts and bodies erupted simultaneously from the cottage door as the men, fear forgotten, competed to be the first to reach the dock.

Corey, ever the quickest and most nimble, led the pack shouting some fucker was trying to steal the boat. Alan let them draw close, then dug his paddle in and headed straight out into the lake. Sensing an advantage, Corey and Brett leapt into the boat, their combined weight plunging the sponges below the water line.

While Corey united the mooring line, Brett viciously pulled the starting cord and the engine spluttered to life. With the throttle wide, the little boat lunged in pursuit and began to close the one hundred and fifty or so feet with ease. Brett sneered in anticipation as he drove the boat forward, intent on ramming the fleeing kayak.

With less than thirty feet to go, Alan pressed the button on the remote control. Yellow-blue flame streaked from the engine and fuel line and wrapped itself around Brett's legs and lower torso. His hand released the throttle, and the sound of the dying engine was replaced by the screams of a man whose flesh and clothing were being seared into one indistinguishable fabric.

In desperation, Brett threw himself into the lake while Corey stood staring transfixed at the water flowing in through the now sponge-less holes, dousing the fire, and flooding the boat. Brett, pain numbed by the lake, hung on the side of the boat while voices from the shore roared at Corey to get the life jackets.

In the panic and morning half-light, Alan paddled back to his base.

~ ~ ~ ~

With the noon sun at his back, Alan's kayak bobbed on the undulating water. Kayak and body a perfect silhouette against the sun's yellow hue.

Maintaining the kayak at a constant right angle to cottage, Alan paddled with feigned caution about seventy-five metres from the cottage veranda. He knew from earlier observations that the cottage occupants had maintained a constant vigil on the lake since the early morning incident with the boat.

Alan watched the watchers from his kayak. Figures scurried across the large patio windows until the patio door jerked open and Alex, Corey, and Dale hustled onto the veranda. Brett, using the door frame for support, lurched behind them, his face contorted with pain as the in-elasticity of burned skin on his legs struggled to accommodate movement of muscles and joints.

Alan ignored the profane-laced tirade, and noted with satisfaction how Alex took charge as usual, imparting instructions that resulted in an increase in the volume and voracity of their threats and taunts. Alan presumed it was an attempt to distract him from Alex, who had stepped into the cottage.

Moments later the curtain on the window of the bedroom adjacent to the patio door rippled as it was drawn sideways in unison with the cautious opening of the sliding window. A rifle barrel inched out, resting on the sill as the barrel's trajectory was aligned with the target, perfectly back-lit by the midday sun. Alan kept his body large and as still as possible, assuring the shooter of an easy shot.

The boom of a bullet leaving a rifle at three hundred feet per second did not disturb any of the island's natural inhabitants, nor did it reach Alan's ears. Instead, a small wisp of white smoke drifted out the bedroom window as the curtain detached from its rail and dropped out of sight below the sill. A bellow of pain and rage followed, escaping the confines of the cottage walls to race out off the veranda and over the water.

Alex staggered onto the veranda, blood seeping past ineffectual fingers as his hand pressed to the right side of his face to hold the flap of flesh that had been his cheek in place. Caged by the veranda rail, Alex uttered incomprehensible sounds, his whole body vibrating with anger and shock. His cheek flesh flapped and sprayed blood and sent Dale into a spasm of dry retching while Corey's mouth worked overtime as he held out a towel in an ineffective gesture of assistance. Brett waited for instructions.

Through his binoculars, at only seventy-five metres, Alan savoured his front row view of the physical and emotional drama unfolding on the veranda. He smiled to himself at the thought of how Alex's slick website, Dental Services for Dentists, and its image of Alex projecting confidence, respect, and trust contrasted with the disfigured, insult-hurling madman on the veranda. Pleased at the success of his plan, Alan broke water and headed back to his camp.

~ ~ ~ ~

Twilight masked Alan's early evening return to the island. Three of his tormentors would be incapacitated to some degree by their injuries: Brett might not be able to walk at all by now, Alex's head must be painful, and Dale would have opened and consumed at least one of the poisoned bottles of wine. With three down, Alan was not concerned if Corey ventured from the cottage and discovered him on the path to the outhouse. *In fact,* thought Alan, *in another five minutes it might be worth encouraging the most able bodied of the four to leave the cottage alone.*

Alan had already paced out the forty steps from the outhouse to the first shallow hole on the path he had dug earlier. After prying open the jaws of a trap and setting the spring-loaded mechanism, Alan placed it in the hole, and covered the trap with ferns and nature's debris from the surrounding bush, careful not to trigger the other two traps already set and placed on either side of the path. He repeated the process with the second shallow hole and within the expected five minutes, the traps sat waiting for prey.

With the jaws stripped of their factory supplied, soft rubber and replaced with four six-inch nails, these traps would not be conforming to the spotty faced clerk's assurance, "the trap would not cause any significant injuries," and "catch and release" would not be a problem.

Originally, Alan had planned the traps as a passive instrument of torture, letting fate determine which of the four would venture up the path to the outhouse. But, Africa had taught him the reality of the need, and the potential benefits, of occasional "in-situ" plan changes.

Hidden in the shadow of a tall pine, just off the outhouse path about thirty feet from the cottage, Alan checked on the occupants in the brightly lit cottage. *I guess they don't expect to be shot at*, thought Alan. Dismayed at their lack of caution, Alan recalled a situation in the Nigerian Delta State when a supposed rebel leader had stood with equal naiveté in a flood-lit room until his brain matter created abstract art on the white washed wall behind him after a soft-nosed bullet fragmented inside his skull.

Through the windows, Alan surveyed the scene: Brett lay on the floor with wet towels on his legs and lower abdomen. Alex sat at the table, trying without success to secure gauze to the ragged gash on his cheek without impeding his ability to talk. Dale, slumped dejectedly on one of the two sofas, a glass of wine in one hand and a half-full bottle in the other, appeared either drunk or unwell. Corey paced and talked. Alan wasn't sure if Corey was talking to himself, but the lack of animation in the others seemed to indicate a one-way conversation.

Come get me, Corey, said Alan to himself as he threw several weighty rocks at the cottage. The third rock breached a window with ease, sending broken glass into the room and jolting everyone inside to involuntary action. Dale, reactions dulled by alcohol, spilled a large amount of his wine, but held onto his glass as he burrowed into the sofa in attempted concealment. Alex turned toward the window causing the poorly applied bandage and gauze to peel away from the wound, resulting in voluminous expletives.

Unfortunately, Brett's chosen convalescence place was on the floor within landing distance of the rocks and debris. He emitted exotic-like screams as glass and rock rained on his first-degree burns. Corey's erratic pacing turned into a starter's sprint as he lunged toward the cottage door, passing through before it was half open.

Caught off guard by Corey's explosive movement, Alan turned and ran up the outhouse path thinking how "in-situ" plan changes might not have been such a bright idea. Focused on seeing the beam of light across the path provided by the miniature flashlight, placed there as part of his change in plans, Alan was unaware Corey had gained to within arm's length of his back.

Alerted by the light beam, Alan surged forward to ensure a clean jump over the waiting traps as Corey lunged desperately to grab Alan's back. With nothing to grasp, Corey flailed, stumbling forward and downward onto his knees. His left knee hit the dirt and received a minor scrape and bruising. His right knee landed full on the spring of the animal trap, triggering the nail studded jaws to clamp closed in zero point one two seconds. Bombarded with pain signals from the nerves embedded in the complex knee region, Corey's body spasmed up and sideways to the left, propelling him in a left-side roll into the adjacent bush. The involuntary roll onto his back sent Corey's left elbow down onto a second trap, with less meat and bone to cut through the nails clamped metallically against each other.

Vanuatu and Glasgow had inured Alan to vocal expressions of human pain and suffering. In Nigeria, all factions had used modern and ancient techniques to torture, maim, and kill opponents in calculated efforts to influence a course of events. Perhaps the context of being on a remote island in "nothing ever happens" Canada, far removed from the *Apocalypse Now* or *Platoon* like theatre of African mercenary realities, allowed Corey's anguished crescendo to slip fleetingly into Alan's consciousness and ignite a brief spark of sympathy. Perhaps it hadn't been quite so personal before.

Alan recovered his micro light from the path and without a backward glance walked unhurriedly to his kayak. Alan paddled away from the island as nosily as possible and used his micro light to ensure the remaining occupants of the cottage would see him leave. He wasn't certain his noisy paddling could be heard over Corey's screams, and he wanted Corey taken back to the cottage, and not left to die in the shadow of the shit-house - however appropriate it might have been.

~ ~ ~ ~

Predawn assaults on targets were always effective in Nigeria. Fatigue, hunger, dissent, uncertainty, injury, fear, or overconfidence and complacency, all combined to favour the attacker.

Guerrilla style on his stomach, Alan crawled around the cottage veranda placing a short stick at the base of each of the three patio doors between the back of the sliding screens and the window jam. From the outside, it wasn't possible to prevent the actual door from being opened, but the stick would prevent the screen from opening. *Not perfect*, thought Alan, *but the odds were good enough*, and experience had taught him that when faced with an impeded exit during a time of panic, the next exit alternative should be sought before trying to remove the obstacle.

After placing the third stick, Alan dropped off the veranda and crawled around to the front of the cottage, pausing several times to confirm the lack of movement inside. At the front door, Alan withdrew a tailor's tape from his pocket. The tape was cut off at sixty-four inches: six foot four, or seventy-six inches, less twelve inches for the head. Alan held the tape up against the first overhang support post on the right of the cottage door and looped the piano wire around the post and through the pre-made slip knot. Alan pulled the wire taut to the left side and wrapped it multiple times around the post. The wire cut deep into the wood, reassuring Alan that even if the wire did not connect onto the small target area, serious damage would be done.

With the wire secured in place, Alan retreated from the cottage and settled behind the cover of a small rock outcrop where, using night vision goggles, he checked the smoke bomb to ensure that the fuse was dry and upright. Satisfied with the fuse, Alan removed his night vision goggles and risked a test of the disposable lighter which sparked into flame without hesitation. Alan retraced his steps back to the cottage and trod lightly up the steps onto the veranda. He pressed himself flat against the cottage wall next to the window he had broken earlier with rocks.

Aiming for the back of the cottage, Alan threw the lit smoke bomb through the window and watched it land and roll to the base of the rear patio door. The thump of the cylinder hitting the floor caused Alex and Brett to stir and force open tired eyes. When pale white smoke began flowing, Alan counted backward from twenty, anticipating the explosion of the firecrackers designed to heighten panic in the targets. Alex and Brett's other senses began to come on-line as the sight and smell of the smoke entered their consciousness and signalled the primeval danger of fire. As they attempted to rouse Corey and Dale, the firecrackers exploded with deafening effect in the closed area, sending Alex scrambling for the south patio door and forcing Corey into frightened wakefulness.

Frustrated by the jammed screen door, Alex screamed at Brett to open the fucking front door and get out. Stimulated by fear, and fuelled by pain induced adrenalin, Brett unlocked the front door, throwing it open as Alex stumbled across the room careening into Brett's mid-back and propelling him out onto the veranda.

Like a cheap hockey shot, Alex's unintended impact caused Brett's back to arch inward, snapping his head backward and bringing his chin up to align his exposed throat with the waiting piano wire. Skin, muscle, and sinew were cut effortlessly as Brett's two hundred and forty pound frame and forward momentum met the slender wire. Only the automatic spreading of his arms catching on the two posts prevented full decapitation, leaving his body hanging precariously by neck vertebrae.

Alex's momentum had carried him on through and under Brett, and he lay sprawled on the ground, unaware of the red rain of blood gushing from Brett's neck and showering down on him. Alex turned to look for Brett as the vertebrae succumbed and Brett's body slumped to the ground. Unable to process the horror, Alex fainted and fell onto Brett's headless torso. Corey had managed to drag himself to the doorway, gulping for air and intermittently calling to Alex and Brett for help, unaware from his vantage point that neither of them could answer. There was no sign of Dale.

Avoiding the pooled blood, Alan reached down to the unconscious Alex and attached a two-way radio via belt clip to Alex's trousers. Before turning to take up position away from but in sight of the cottage, Alan caught Corey's pleading eyes and looked back with indifference.

~ ~ ~ ~

Unconsciousness provided only a temporary escape from the shock, and Alex choked out unintelligible sounds as he pushed himself off Brett's still warm corpse and scrambled backward and crab-like away from the cottage steps. Alex's movement and sound roused Corey, whose pleas for help had steadily diminished in frequency and forcefulness while Alex's mind had shut out the horror.

Corey's cries forced Alex back up the cottage steps onto the veranda. Alex grasped Corey under his arms and pulled him into the cottage. The door thudded closed against the contorted and mutilated scene outside.

Alex struggled to drag Corey toward a bedroom, and he called Dale for help. Dale did not respond. With Corey propped unconscious against the wall, Alex staggered toward Dale who was lying face down on the sofa. The neck of a wine bottle was wedged between Dale's body and the sofa's back. An empty wine glass discarded and toppled on the floor. "Brett is fucking dead, you fuck. This is no fucking time to be drunk, you arsehole. Get up and help me with Corey!" Alex grasped Dale's shoulder and pulled him around ready to slap him into wakefulness and sobriety. Alex's arm stopped at the height of his back swing as Dale's head, responding to Alex's pull, rolled unnaturally to face him.

Dale's entire face sagged. Off white foam trailed from his mouth to his chest, evidence that the Tetrahydrozoline, contained in the eye drops Alan had inserted into Dale's wine bottles, had caused the expected seizures and breathing problems. Alex followed his nose to Dale's cream coloured khaki shorts; dark stains of piss and shit were a testament to Dale's ignominious end.

Repulsed, Alex dropped Dale and stumbled into a chair at the table. Alex forced his head from his hands. Brett was dead. Dale was dead. Corey was, or soon would be, dead. Alex sobbed.

Alone and defenceless, his tears mixed with the blood of his friends Brett, Corey, and Dale which had stained his clothes and hands. "Why, why? What did we do?" he mumbled to himself. Physically exhausted and emotionally decimated, Alex's arms fell to his side in surrender to whatever awaited. His hand struck something hard on his hip; a two-way radio was attached to his belt.

With a hope only the desperate can imagine, he reached for the radio. Clinging to his misguided hope, red stained hands held the radio with reverence, as though its presence would bring imminent rescue.

From his vantage point outside the cottage, Alan watched Alex's decent into hopelessness, waiting patiently for the right moment to offer him a way out.

When Alex held the radio up, and Alan saw the spark of hope in Alex's eyes, he pressed the transmit button and spoke to his tormentor for the first time in almost twenty years.

~ ~ ~ ~

"How do you want to die, Alex?"

The dispassionate words cruelly extinguished Alex's spark of hope. The radio slipped from his blood smeared hands and lay on the table, transformed by the question from an instrument of rescue to a conduit to death.

"Pick up the radio, Alex."

Alex realised he was being watched, and his head swiveled to seek the demon.

"Pick it up!"

Alex vibrated with fear and needed both hands to hold the radio. He squeezed the button.

"I don't want to die. I don't deserve to die. Don't kill me. Please. I'll give you whatever you want. Money. Anything. Just don't kill me."

"I only want your death."

"Wait, wait. Who are you? Why the fuck are you doing this?"

Alan wanted to lock eyes with Alex and tell him who he was and why he was doing it. But he had already waited twenty years. He could wait a little longer.

"You can die quickly in the cottage with your friends, or you can come outside and face me. Which way, Alex? Come on, Alex. You've always been the one to lead and make decisions. This should be easy for you. How do you want to die?"

"No. No. I don't want to die. I don't want to die," screamed Alex into the radio.

"I'll make the decision easy for you," said Alan. "Look under the table."

Confused, Alex bent down under the table. The WWII revolver stared back. The gun gave Alex another spark of hope. He grasped the gun and shouted into the radio.

"Ha, you fucking jerk. You fuck. Come get me now and I'll blow your fucking head off."

"Well, I hope you're a good shot Alex because the gun has only one bullet. Yes, you can take a chance you will get me with one shot, but look around, Alex. Do you think you have a chance? Or you can use the bullet on yourself. That's more like you, Alex. Take the easy way out."

Alex opened the chamber. One bullet. Cursing he threw the gun on the table and ranted and raved at the world and its injustices. How he didn't deserve this. He was an important man with a business and family. This wasn't fair.

Resigned, Alex picked up the gun and held the barrel to his temple. With his other hand, he held the radio. "Fuck you!" said Alex as he pulled the trigger.

The gunpowder exploded with an impressive flash. A blast of air and gas blew fragments of blank cartridge paper into Alex's temple, ear, and eye knocking him off his chair and onto the floor. Disoriented and dizzy from the blast, Alex scowled in disbelief at the gun. He pulled the trigger several more times only to hear the click of the empty chamber.

"I couldn't let you off that easy, Alex," mocked Alan.

Incensed, Alex screamed in rage and forced himself from the floor. He hurled himself at the cottage door and wrenched it open to slip on half-congealed blood and trip on and over Brett's prostate body. On the edge of madness, and driven by a raw need for escape, Alex crawled through the dirt toward the dock.

~ ~ ~ ~

Alan had watched Alex's attempted suicide with satisfaction. Pleased the blank prop cartridge had worked so well, and relieved Alex had not stuck the gun in his mouth, which might have killed him.

After mocking Alex via the radio, Alan walked toward the dock and calmly notched a home-made arrow onto his recently made bow and waited. Alex crawled through the dirt toward the dock, and stopped when he saw Alan. He pulled himself up on his knees said, "Why? Who the fuck are you?"

Unprepared for this Alan said, "You know who I am and what you did."

"What are you talking about? Tell me. This is a mistake. I don't fucking know who you are."

"You mean you've forgotten destroying my life and killing my sister? Was it so trivial to you? You're worse than I thought." Alan let go an arrow into Alex's right arm.

Alex sagged under the blow and moaned, "Why, why, why?"

"I'll tell you why. I am Alan Davies. When I was seventeen, you and your fucking friends took me into the forest, got me drunk, and made me rape my own sister. She knew it was me. She killed herself with an overdose because of what you made me do."

Alan shot another arrow into Alex's other arm.

Alex laughed. "Alan fucking loser Davies. You are still a loser, Alan. The girl wasn't your sister. She was some hooker we paid to fuck virgins like you. We had lots of kids out there. Yeah, maybe it was a bit sick, but all the other kids enjoyed their free fuck. Oh, you fucking loser, Alan. We did you a fucking favour."

"No, Alex. You are lying. I heard my sister's voice. I didn't know it at the time but later, after Julie told me in her suicide note, I remembered the voice while I was doing it." Alan's voice faltered as he notched another arrow.

Blood mixed with bile as Alex spat and said, "That wasn't your sister, you stupid fuck. It was Corey doing one of his voices for a laugh. You fucking loser shit."

Alan put an arrow into each of Alex's thighs and a final arrow into his stomach. The arrows pinned Alex to the deck of dock, reminding Alan of how, in Nigeria, mercenaries used to stake out injured rebels on the plains to attract hyenas and vultures as an inducement to provided information.

"Then why would Julie tell me she was the girl in the forest?"

~ ~ ~ ~

Alan watched sun fish swarm beneath the dock, feeding on Alex's blood as it seeped through the dock and splashed into the lake's clear water. While Alex's life drained away, Alan thought of Julie and the day he returned home from school to find police cars and ambulances parked askew in front of his house. How he had been restrained by people he did not know. How he stood by helpless, watching Julie's vacant eyes as she was bustled past him to the waiting ambulance. How his actions drove Julie to her suicide. How his actions had been orchestrated by Alex and others for their amusement, and now, how his actions had delivered justice.

Assured of the rightness of his actions, Alan left Alex to the sun fish and departed Sand Top Island for the last time. Each sweep of the paddle cleansed Alan's mind of torment and guilt as his chest, released from its long-held tightness, finally allowed his lungs to inhale and exhale to their maximum.

With the kayak pulled up high out of the water and out of sight, Alan sank into his bivouac and the comfort of his sleeping bag which had been warmed by the day's sun. Tension and its release partnered to pull Alan's eyelids closed as his mind, purged by his actions, plunged unrestricted into dreamless free fall.

~ ~ ~ ~

The sounds of early dawn creatures worked their way into Alan's mind to bring him back to reality. Through crusty eyes, Alan enjoyed the tree branch shadow play across the top and sides of his bivouac. The luminous dial of his wristwatch informed Alan it was 5 a.m. Monday. He had slept for twelve hours.

Energised by his sleep, Alan broke camp and erased as much as possible any overt signs of his brief residence. He was certain the ensuing investigation would include a search of the proximate shoreline and his camp would be discovered within forty-eight hours or so. While unconcerned he had left anything that could be traced back to him, he did not need to take any risks.

By 7:30 a.m. Alan had decamped and moved his equipment to Lake Gunette. All that remained was to portage the kayak, secure the waterproof bags fore and aft, and paddle his way out of the lake and up the river Mattagami to his egress point. An hour later, after stopping to eat and check the lake for back country adventures, Alan eased his kayak into the water.

As Alan approached the end of the lake and prepared to enter the river, he looked up as a twin engine float plane flashed across the blue sky. Alan followed its path as the plane rose slightly to cross the narrow piece of land separating Lake Gunette from Lake Proulx. He spared a sympathetic thought for the pilot and the sight awaiting him on the dock of Sand Top Island. Alan dug his paddle deep and pulled hard against the oncoming current of the river, intent on being on the road before the weekend adventurers returned to their own vehicles and their frantic race back to civilisation.

By four p.m., the 4x4 was loaded, and Alan was ready to depart. After listening to ensure no other cars were on the road, Alan took the rope he had used to tie a swath of brush and pulled the brush over and drove the 4x4 out onto the dirt road. After releasing the brush and helping it spring back, Alan brushed out the tire tracks that headed from the road into the bush. Satisfied at the unlikelihood of the tracks and the temporarily depressed brush behind the bushes ever being found, Alan gunned the engine and headed up the dirt road. Another weekender compelled to rush back to reality.

CHAPTER 18

A Letter from Mom

On the way to the cottage Alan had overnighted in a motel to ensure he was rested for the coming days' activities. On the way back, fortified with twelve hours sleep and emotionally lightened by the end of his nightmare, Alan drove non-stop to Toronto, reaching the Don Valley Parkway at 10 a.m. on Tuesday.

With morning rush hour traffic already parked in overpriced downtown lots, the Don Valley Parkway was clear and Alan exited easily onto Gerrard Street and mingled with city traffic. Alan stopped at the beer store for a two-four and at Tim Horton's for two breakfast bagels and a large coffee.

Grateful his kayak did not prevent him from using the underground parking, Alan slid into his parking space. Balancing coffee, bagel, and the two-four, as well as a bag containing valuable and potentially incriminating gear, Alan struggled toward the elevator. An exiting older woman held the doors for him, a disapproving eye resting momentarily on the two-four.

The first bagel disappeared while twenty-four beers where stacked neatly in the otherwise empty fridge, standing like ill camouflaged soldiers against a stark white landscape. The second bagel was intermittently consumed and drowned with hot coffee while Alan showered and changed clothes. Refreshed and smelling much better, Alan noticed the flashing light on his phone.

Only his self-appointed lawyer, John Gardener, had the number. Alan entered the required code and listened to his lawyer first apologise, and then explain he had discovered a letter addressed to him in the folder his father had used to keep his mother's documents in. John had no idea what the letter contained and with more apologies promised to mail the letter to Alan right away. The call log told Alan his lawyer had called the previous Tuesday while he paddled downstream to Lake Gunette.

Curious, but also tired and thirsty, the letter could wait. Besides, due to the long-weekend, the letter probably wouldn't arrive until today, so he opted to have a much needed beer before collecting the mail.

In fact, he decided to have two beers. With beers in hand, he went out onto his tiny balcony and seated himself on his usual white, plastic patio chair. The electronic billboard still proclaimed Global Gyms" abdominal promise, but Alan's mind no longer made a subconscious connection with the physical attributes of Brett and Corey. Instead, his mind only registered the advertisement as another landmark to help orientate the body to its current location. A testament perhaps to the theory that advertisements only influence those already looking for what is being advertised.

Eight beers later the weak fall sun had passed its zenith to become partially obscured by mid-height downtown buildings. Predictably, Alan's mouth felt dry despite having been moistened by the constant flow of cool amber liquid, and his stomach had long ceased to benefit from the two mid-morning bagels. Stumbling slightly, as much from dehydration as alcohol, Alan decided to venture out for sustenance and coffee.

Two blocks west from his apartment Alan found a Second Cup where he paid twice the amount he had paid at Tim Horton's for the same order: two eggs, and something bagels, and a large coffee. The bags for the bagels were more robust and sealed, and the cup and lid were prettier and a bit more functional, but honestly, thought Alan, egg is egg, bagel is bagel, and coffee is coffee!

Alan munched the first bagel and something and sipped his coffee as he entered his apartment foyer. He stared at the mail boxes and recalled his lawyer's message about a letter. True to his promise, a large manila envelope with J. Gardener, Lawyer, printed on the back side above the flap, waited in the small mailbox.

With the envelope tucked under his arm, Alan rode the elevator to his apartment. After breaking the robust packaging off the second bagel and taking a large bite, Alan ripped open the envelope. A small, slightly faded, white envelope fell out. The lawyer's business card had been paper-clipped to the envelope, an unspoken and hasty confirmation of John Gardener's commitment to send the letter as soon as possible.

~ ~ ~ ~

Large, looping handwritten letters proclaimed Alan's name in plain, black ink on the faded, white envelope. Alan didn't recognise the handwriting, but something inside told him his mother had written his name boldly and firmly, almost determinedly.

Holding the envelope, Alan began to sweat and tremble as he recalled the last letter he had received from a family member, twenty years ago:

Why, Alan? Why? How could you do that? I tried to tell you. To get you to make it stop. Why didn't you want to listen? Why did you ignore me? Why didn't you help me? Did you hate me so much? Mom doesn't understand either. Mom doesn't understand either! Why? Why? WHY?

No. He would not read the letter. He had fixed the past. He didn't need his mother's rebukes from the grave. He had suffered enough. He had punished those responsible.

"Yes, yes, I raped Julie, but I didn't know it was her," screamed Alan as he threw the unopened letter across the room and roughly grabbed two more soldier-beers from the fridge.

Unable to resist his mother's call, Alan grasped the envelope. Dread vibrated through his body as he ripped the envelope open.

Dear Alan, please forgive me. I failed you. I am sorry. I only had strength for Julie, and I didn't think about what might be going on with you.

Alan reread the opening lines. *Please forgive me. I failed you. I am sorry.* Alan had not expected a plea for forgiveness. He didn't understand how his mother had failed **HIM**.

I know how close you were to your dad and how his death must have been very hard for you.

"Yes," thought Alan, "but Dad died before I raped Julie." His mother's words made no sense.

Oh, Alan, things were much worse than you think. At the time, I couldn't bear to share the truth with you. I should have. I hope it's not too late.

"Worse! How? No, Mom, I could not have talked with you about Julie. When I discovered from Julie's letter she had told you I had raped her, I had to leave. I

233

had to run. I couldn't face you knowing that I had made Julie kill herself. I am the one who failed you and Julie."

Alan, your father did not die in an accident.

Disbelieving, Alan re-read the words.

Alan, your father did not die in an accident.

"Not true, Mom. Everyone, including the police, said Dad had an accident. He drove too fast. He couldn't make the turn and slammed head on into the tree on River Road."

Oh, the crash looked like an accident. It had to. That was the plan.

"Plan," thought Alan. "What fucking plan? What was she talking about?"

Alan, I made your dad kill himself. I didn't give him a choice.

"Fucking crazy talk. Who wrote this letter? Not my mother." For a moment, he thought Alex had somehow written the letter as one final twisted torment.

Your dad agreed. An accident was the best way out.

"Out of what? What had happened?"

Oh, I hurt so much. I don't know how to tell you, Alan. I haven't spoken to anyone else about what happened, but you deserve the truth. One day you will come back. I hope the truth is better than the lies.

"The truth," thought Alan. "God, I know the truth, Mom. I have lived with it for twenty years."

Alan, your dad raped Julie.

The words bore into Alan's head. *Your dad raped Julie. Your dad raped Julie.* "No. No. I raped Julie, Mom. Me, not Dad. This is fucked." Alan threw the letter down and paced around his apartment knocking things over. No. No. No!

Compelled, Alan picked up the letter.

The first time something happened was in the spring the year before Julie died and before you disappeared. Our marriage wasn't going well, and your dad was drunk and came home when I was out. Julie was getting ready to go out when your dad went into her bedroom, and... Oh Alan, Alan, he made Julie do things.

Julie didn't know what to do. She said she had tried to talk to you, but you avoided her and didn't want to help, or worse, she actually thought you might know already, but didn't want to accept it.

Alan sobbed. "I didn't know, Julie. I didn't."

A month later in May, your dad raped Julie again. I knew something was wrong. Julie didn't tell me until June, before school ended.

I confronted your dad. I told him the only way out was for him to kill himself. If he didn't, we would call the police. Your father didn't deny it or apologise or anything. He just nodded, got in his car, and drove into the tree.

Between horror and sadness, tears breached his eyes and dripped from his cheek, smudging the words, but not erasing their meaning.

Julie wanted to tell you what had happened. She wanted you to understand about your dad. To help her, and us, pull together as a family. But we couldn't talk to you. Oh, it was partly our fault for waiting for the right moment, or the right way, and then something happened to you.

You withdrew from everything and everyone around you. You went to school, ate, slept and didn't talk to anyone. Every time I, or Julie, tried to talk you looked away or left. We didn't exist for you. You couldn't bear to look at us!

"That's because I had raped someone, Mom. I was ashamed and guilty. And Alex and the others kept taunting me, suggesting they knew something I didn't. I had nightmares, and I kept hearing the voice from the rape. A voice I thought I knew, but never let myself face."

We didn't understand why you avoided us so much. I began to think like Julie. Somehow you knew about what your dad had done, but you blamed us.

I thought things would get better for Julie after your father's death. But Julie didn't get better. She spent long periods crying and sobbing in her room, and wouldn't go to school. I took time off to be with her, but I'm sorry, Alan, I couldn't be there all the time.

Oh, Alan, I didn't know what to do. Please forgive me. Please forgive Julie.

Alan replayed Julie's note in his mind again:

Why, Alan? Why? How could you do that? I tried to tell you. To get you to make it stop. Why didn't you want to listen? Why did you ignore me? Why didn't you help me? Did you hate me so much? Mom doesn't understand either. Why? Why? WHY?

Then he understood. Julie's letter had not accused him of rape. Her note had been about him being a self-absorbed teenager, wallowing in self-pity and loathing while his own father raped his sister: a selfish brother who shut out his sister when she needed him most. He had seen in Julie's note what he had wanted to see, what he had needed to see: an excuse to run away from his own abhorrent behaviour.

Then Alan remembered Alex's dying words:

"Alan fucking loser Davies. You are still a loser, Alan. The girl wasn't your sister. She was some hooker we paid to fuck virgins like you. We had lots of kids out there. Yeah, maybe it was a bit sick, but all the other kids enjoyed their free fuck. Oh, you fucking loser, Alan. We did you a fucking favour. That wasn't your sister, you stupid fuck. It was Corey doing one of his voices for a laugh."

Alan's face contorted, mirroring his knotted emotions, unable to come to terms with what his mother had told him. Unable to accept the sin of his father, unable to accept his mother had sent his father to his death. Unable to accept he had been a coward, and in that cowardliness, abandoned his sister and mother, to deal with their terrible burden alone.

Alan was numb. Twenty years of guilt for something he hadn't done. Of running, of hiding, of indifference to the suffering of others because no one could suffer as he had. But now he was guilty; guilty of being a coward, guilty of murder.

The phone rang. Automatically, Alan picked it up.

"Hello. Hello. Alan? It's John Gardener. Did you receive the letter?"

"Yes."

"I don't want to pry, Alan, but was there anything in the letter I need to know or do anything about?"

"No," said Alan.

"Nothing you need to know. Some people deserve to die."

"What was that?" said John Gardener to the buzz of a disconnected line.

Alan stumbled past the lumpy sofa and out onto his cramped, fifteenth floor balcony. He pressed himself against the waist high rail and leaned his upper torso out and over. He closed his eyes and swayed in the swirling warm air currents. Traffic noise spiralled up from the streets below. A voice mingled with the sound of engine, brake, and horn. An image joined the voice. Julie hovered in front of Alan, her eyes soft: her voice gentle and kind.

"I forgive you, Alan. I understand. You have suffered enough. You're not to blame. I love you, Alan."

He removed his hands from the rail and reached for his sister. Wind and gravity sucked at his body and he teetered ground-ward.

Julie thrust her hands at Alan and said, "No, Alan! Stay. It's not your time. You don't deserve to die."

Wind and gravity eased their grip, and Alan fell back against the patio door.

Alan staggered back inside and wept.

Made in the USA
Middletown, DE
31 March 2019